SECRETS
of
STONEBRIDGE

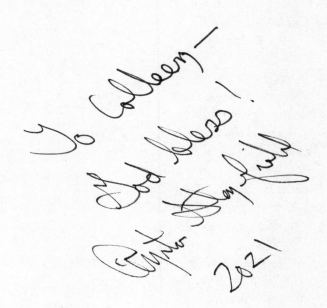

To Colleen —
God bless!
Carter Stanfield
2021

OTHER BOOKS AND AUDIOBOOKS
BY ANITA STANSFIELD

SECRETS
of
STONEBRIDGE

a regency romance by

ANITA
STANSFIELD

Covenant Communications, Inc.

Cover image © Mary Wethey / Trevillion Images
Cover Design by Michelle Fryer

Cover design copyright © 2021 by Covenant Communications, Inc.

Published by Covenant Communications, Inc.
American Fork, Utah

Printed in the United States of America
First Printing: July 2021

27 26 25 24 23 22 21   10 9 8 7 6 5 4 3 2 1

ISBN 978-1-52441-536-5

CHAPTER ONE
abandoned

Somerset, England, 1819

REGINA ELLIOTT EVERLEIGH AWAKENED TO the annoyingly loud chirping of a great many birds outside her bedroom window, and she had to fight the urge to open the window and start tossing her shoes into the trees to frighten the little nuisances just enough to encourage them to go sing their cheerful songs elsewhere. She had no desire to hurt the birds; she just didn't want to hear them, and she resented being awakened by them when sleep was her only reprieve from a life she had grown to hate. She also considered the fact that she owned a great many shoes, and she'd not once put any of them on her feet for months now. There had been no need, given that she'd not left the safety of her own rooms since the day she had come home from her husband's funeral, unable to get up the stairs quickly enough, desperate for the safety of the only place in the house where she had the right to declare her preferences and see that her personal orders were carried out.

Gina groaned and rolled over in the bed, opening her eyes only long enough to see daylight barely managing to peer through the cracks where the draperies didn't quite close. She wished the draperies could be fastened tightly and permanently and that no daylight whatsoever would ever be allowed into the room. Dwight was gone and never coming back. He'd become a bright light in her life from the moment she'd met him, and even though his behavior toward her had become less favorable following their marriage, she'd still done everything in her power to remain positive and hopeful that their relationship would improve over time. She'd invested all her hope in the idea that they would grow old together, with a passel of children and grandchildren surrounding them. But nearly two years of marriage had not yet given them a child, and then a horrible and senseless accident had taken Dwight from her, and the hope she'd been clinging to had been snuffed out. The vast mixture of her thoughts and feelings regarding the state of their marriage at the time of his death was confusing at best; she tried every day to remember only what had been good between them, and she worked very hard to push away memories that tainted her recollections of all they had shared. With Dwight gone, she felt no need for the sun to taunt her over the absence of a husband or child in her life, any more than she wanted the singing of birds attempting to convince her that there was any reason in the world to be cheerful.

Gina's personal maid and dear friend, Emerald, swept into the room like a gust of wind, as if she had some kind of strange psychic ability to know that the object of her responsibility was now awake, even though Gina had not made any noise that Emerald could have possibly heard.

"Good, you're awake," Emerald declared in a voice that was naturally loud. She was incapable of whispering or even speaking softly.

"How could I not be?" Gina muttered as Emerald dramatically pulled back one of the draperies as if she were revealing something magical hidden behind it. Sunlight burst into the room with the same kind of bravado that had ushered Emerald in only moments earlier.

"It's a beautiful day!" Emerald announced, and Gina peered over the edge of her bedcovers to get a glimpse of the young maid who was as tall as the average man and thin as a pencil, with hair that was slightly more brown than red, and barely restrained in the pins that held a bun in place more on the top of her head rather than at the back, and where the force of gravity would consign it to a messier state by the end of day. One glimpse was all Gina needed to feel assaulted by the unusually bright sunshine, and she pulled the covers over her face, muttering a grumbling sound that contained no actual words.

Gina could hear Emerald opening *all* the drapes and she could feel the room getting brighter despite keeping her face beneath the bedding. Through the open doorway she heard the approach of footsteps in the hallway and immediately recognized them as belonging to Ruby, Emerald's sister. Emerald was only a few years younger than Gina, and Ruby was younger than her sister by less than two years. Her height did not even reach the shoulder of her sister, and she was as shapely as Emerald was thin. Her hair was more red than brown, although she too wore it pinned up in a way that was identical to her sister, since they shared the problem of gravity causing havoc with their heavy and unruly curls.

"Is she awake?" Ruby asked in a voice that was half the volume of Emerald's. Gina often found it difficult to hear Ruby speak if there was any other noise nearby, whereas it was impossible not to hear Emerald, even if she was in the next room.

"She is!" Emerald said, and with those two words Gina knew that some form of a lecture was coming. In most situations, a maid would never speak so comfortably and casually to the person for whom they worked. But Emerald and Ruby had grown up with Gina, and they mutually shared an attitude of responsibility for Gina's best interests, every bit as much as they worked together to care for her daily needs. Occasionally they both shared tea or a meal with her since she'd not eaten any meals outside her rooms for months now. But she couldn't recall both being in her room together at this time of day. She sensed some kind of conspiracy and discreetly slithered deeper beneath the covers until they flew abruptly from over her face and she found herself looking up at Emerald, with the much shorter Ruby at her side. Both were scowling with determination, and Gina wished she could feign ignorance regarding what this might be about, but she knew *exactly* why they might feel the need to unite in confronting her. Nevertheless, that didn't mean she wanted to discuss the matter—even with these women she trusted completely. She only wanted to continue on as she had been doing since Dwight's passing. Life beyond her bedroom, sitting room, and personal parlor held no interest for her whatsoever. She had devoted herself to Dwight in every way, perhaps believing that her efforts could eventually create positive changes between them; but now she would never know. She'd worked hard to convince herself that there was a happy and hopeful future with him. And then he'd abandoned her. Of course, she knew he'd not intentionally met with a riding accident that rainy spring morning, but he *had* gone out riding when she had requested that he stay in due to the weather being so dreadful. He'd promised he wouldn't be gone long, insisting that he only felt the need for a brief jaunt to get some fresh air. But the drizzle had turned to a downpour, and the meadows and woods through which he frequently rode had become muddy—or at least that's what she'd been told by those who had found his body. When he'd not returned after many hours, his cousin and some of the servants had gone searching for him. It had been the unanimous opinion of all who had seen the location of the accident that the horse had apparently lost its footing on a muddy incline and Dwight had fallen from the saddle. The horse had loyally remained with its owner of many years, unharmed but very dirty. Apparently, Dwight had died instantly, according to what the local doctor had said about the way he had hit the ground. Gina found some comfort in knowing he hadn't suffered, but in the depths of her grieving she had never been able to shake the feeling that he'd abandoned her, even if he'd never meant to do so. And with his death, all hope of creating a better marriage—and becoming a mother—had shattered into far too many pieces to ever be mended.

"Dearest Gina," the soft-spoken sister said, sitting on the edge of the bed only a moment before Emerald sat beside her. They were completely in the attitude of friends now, and Gina knew they loved her and were legitimately concerned, but that didn't mean she wanted to hear what they had to say. She sat up and braced herself for what she was about to hear, keeping the covers pulled up to her neck as if they might protect her. "No one in this house," Ruby went on gently, "has been the tiniest bit critical—least of all us—over your need to grieve the loss of your dear husband. Why, Mrs. Darby has said to us a great many times that each person must grieve at their own pace and in their own way."

This was far from the first time that one of the sisters had passed on the housekeeper's wisdom regarding Gina's dramatic aversion to venturing out of her rooms since the day of Dwight's funeral. But something in their demeanor had changed, and Gina felt relatively certain that the household consensus had altered. She wasn't surprised—or even offended—to think of everyone beneath this roof talking about her, and she hadn't really cared as long as they were all willing to allow her to remain secluded. She had a feeling that was about to change, although she'd believed for quite some time that this day would come, and perhaps a part of her had even been hoping for it; perhaps she needed the insistence of those who cared about her to help her do what she couldn't find the strength to do on her own.

"However," Emerald drawled, the very volume of her voice making the impending announcement seem ominous, "even Mrs. Darby has come to believe that your hiding away like this has likely gone on too long, and that it's time you venture out if only for some fresh air and a bit of exercise."

"It can't be good for you," Ruby said even more softly, "to hardly even be walking much at all, and . . . forgive me Gina for being so bold, but . . . none of us can deny that you've taken to eating a great deal more than you once did." Gina could *not* deny it, even though she felt ashamed, and she was well aware that in a house such as this—with some people preparing food in the kitchens, and other people delivering it to her rooms, and still others taking away the trays of dishes with hardly a crumb left upon them—that her eating habits would be common knowledge. She didn't understand the reasons exactly, but it was certainly true that since she'd lost Dwight, eating the delectable foods that came from the worthy hands of Mrs. Chester, the head cook, had soothed her confused and ailing heart and had given her a strange kind of comfort. Her appetite had continued to increase over the months, and she'd become especially fond of rich, buttery sauces and the sweet cakes and biscuits that were created with such skill. She'd become embarrassed by the amount of such things she could consume every day, but not enough to discipline herself to request smaller portions or fewer sweets; in fact, it was quite the opposite. She had increasingly requested *larger* portions and *more* sweets, and food had become what felt like her dearest friend. The result had been that she'd become even more sluggish when she could feel the weight of her body increasing. And the clothes she owned no longer fit her, which only gave her additional incentive to spend her days in loose-fitting night dresses and dressing gowns that helped hide the woman she'd become since Dwight had abandoned her. Even knowing he would be disappointed in her was not incentive enough to do anything to solve the problem. But she didn't *want* to live like this indefinitely, even though she hadn't been able to gather the courage to ask her friends for help; or perhaps she simply didn't know what exactly to ask for.

Gina hung her head and tried to hold back the threat of tears as Ruby continued. "We only want what's best for you, dearest. Let us help you . . . just a little at a time . . . to take some steps that might help you get back to your old self. You've always been so vibrant, and . . ."

"Such a cheerful disposition," Emerald took over. "We understand something so traumatic as what you've been through will always be with you, and in some ways, you will never be the same. We are not at all negating your grief, dearest. Nevertheless, we cannot allow you to keep living like this . . . which is no life at all. We want you to preserve your health, and to find some hope for the future. You are still young, with so much life ahead of you."

Gina sniffled and wiped her eyes with the sheet she was holding to tightly. "I know you're right," she admitted, "but . . . I don't even know where to begin. I *do* need your help, but . . ." Gina couldn't even finish as a knot gathered in her throat, a knot so huge and tight she felt as if she might choke on it and stop breathing.

"Might we share with you a plan we've been discussing?" Ruby asked, her soft voice and gentle nature making the question more palatable.

"Of course," Gina managed to squeak past the knot, although new tears came along with the words and she kept her head down, even though she understood that they had to know she was crying.

"We believe the first step is for you to simply get out of these rooms," Emerald said, her voice startling Gina slightly. "Since you've become quite unaccustomed to any exercise, a walk in the gardens is likely too much to start with. But it's a lovely summer day, quite pleasant. And it was Garn's suggestion that we all take a carriage ride into town and briefly visit the bookshop you once loved so much." Their brother Garn's work involved caring for and driving the carriages, and Gina understood that the sisters would confide in him as much as they would enlist him in any kind of conspiracy. "A new book always used to lift your spirits," she went on. "And perhaps having something new to read might distract you from feeling the need to eat quite so much."

"We don't mean to be abrupt . . . or critical . . . about that," Ruby said as if she could soften Emerald's directness. "Nevertheless, it is a concern, and we want you to be healthy." Gina sniffled, and an awkward silence followed before Ruby added, "Tell us what *you* think, dearest."

Gina coughed as she forced her voice past that hovering knot in her throat, and more tears came. She had cried buckets of tears in the first few weeks following Dwight's death, and then it was as if they'd all dried up and she hadn't even been able to force herself to cry for months—even though she'd felt like she wanted to, even needed to. Perhaps the very fact that she was crying indicated that this loving intervention from her friends had been long overdue.

"I know you're right," Gina admitted and sniffled again just before Emerald handed her a clean handkerchief, which she put to good use. "I suppose I simply haven't had the . . . motivation, or . . . perhaps the . . . presence of mind . . . to know what to do. I feel so . . . stuck. And I cannot deny that these rooms have become terribly boring." She finally gained enough composure to look up at the concerned faces of her friends. "I can't possibly go out, however. I've not a thing to wear that will fit me. I hate to even think of all the lovely gowns and dresses in my wardrobe that I'll never be able to wear again."

"Nonsense!" Ruby said in a tone that was more like her sister's. "Your present situation is surely temporary, dearest. I daresay a gradual refining of the foods you eat, and a gradual increase of your physical exertion will get everything back to normal, and you'll be back to your old self. In the meantime . . ." she added with some kind of triumph in her voice as she stood and walked to the wardrobe, opening one of the doors with a dramatic flourish. "Emerald and I have taken the liberty of altering two of your dresses so that they should fit you nicely right now."

"Oh, my," Gina said, as surprised as she was relieved. She knew both sisters had remarkable sewing skills, which contributed to their both being excellent lady's maids, but Gina had never expected this, and certainly never would have come up with the idea herself.

Ruby continued, "We looked through your dresses to find those that might be the easiest to adjust, and we both assist you enough that we believe we've been able to estimate your current size accurately."

"We'll not know for certain until you try them on," Emerald said, standing as well, making an elaborate motion with her arm, which indicated that she expected Gina to get out of bed and do so this very moment. Gina was glad that she'd bathed the previous day, and Ruby had helped wash her hair so that it felt fresh and clean. Now knowing that the sisters had been conspiring this plan to get her out of the house, she suspected they had timed this conversation for the day following a good bath. Sometimes bathing alone took so much motivation and energy for Gina that she didn't feel like doing anything at all for the remainder of the day. But she couldn't use that as an excuse to not go out today, especially if one of the altered dresses fit her well enough that she could feel somewhat confident in leaving the house.

With a little comfortable assistance from Emerald and Ruby, Gina found herself standing in front of the long mirror in her room for the first time in weeks, maybe months. She'd avoided looking at her reflection when she'd hated what she'd been seeing. Her face—which had always been somewhat rounded in shape—was very clearly fuller than it had been before she'd lost Dwight. But the blue and lavender dress that Ruby was buttoning down her back actually made her feel somewhat pretty, and the fullness of the skirt that splayed out in gathers from the fashionably high waistline did well at hiding the weight she had gained. The stripes of alternating colors of the skirt aided in the effect of making her appear thinner than she knew herself to be. When Ruby was able to finish buttoning the lavender bodice without any difficulty, the sisters both laughed with delight and stood back to admire Gina as if she were a work of art they had helped create.

"Oh, you look lovely," Emerald declared with enthusiasm.

"Indeed you do!" Ruby added. "Now, let's do something with your hair to make it presentable, and we'll be on our way."

Gina sat down at the dressing table—a place she had also avoided for months, due to the huge mirror in front of her. Emerald left to tell Garn to ready the carriage, to get Gina some breakfast, and to let Mrs. Darby know that they would be going out. She exited the room as if she had the privilege of announcing that royalty would be descending upon their household. Ruby took her place behind Gina and began brushing through her hair, a ritual that had been taking place on the sofa in the sitting room or on the edge of the bed. But as Gina observed her friend and extremely skilled maid sliding the brush through Gina's dark golden, slightly wavy hair, she recalled fondly the countless times that Ruby had assisted her this way each and every day for years so that Gina could leave her rooms and spend her days engaged in a variety of activities, surrounded by other people. Gina had once loved brisk walks in the garden in almost any weather, as well as long rides over the surrounding countryside. She had loved receiving company or visiting others for meals or tea. And she'd also loved spending hours in the village, shopping and relaxing in her favorite tea shop. She had enjoyed remaining aware of the needs of the local people, and offering assistance by way of visiting the ill or injured, always taking baskets of abundance that was easily found in the kitchens and pantries of the grand house in which they lived.

Gina watched with deep fascination while Ruby tucked, and pinned, and styled her hair, and she felt sad to think of all she'd lost since Dwight's death— much that had nothing to do with Dwight—but she also felt a tiny glimmer of hope that she might actually be able to find that same woman again, and even if it was a slow and gradual process, she already felt as if she could no longer bear remaining stuck in such an isolated, self-pitying state. She felt more than a little afraid to venture out after being confined for so long. But her desire to feel alive again was stronger than her fear, and she felt grateful beyond words for the love and encouragement of her friends.

❧

Emerald and Ruby graciously accepted Gina's expressions of gratitude as they finished helping her get ready to go out. The two maids flanked her as if for protection as they traversed the hallway stretching from Gina's rooms to the stairs, and then down the wide staircase that led to the main foyer of the house, outside of which the carriage would be waiting. Gina felt very much out of breath once they reached the bottom of the stairs—partly because she was so out of practice in just walking any significant distance, and partly because she felt entirely overcome by the experience of such an enormous undertaking in contrast to the way she'd been living. She mentally continued to order her fears and concerns away and kept telling herself to be brave and enjoy this excursion. She concluded that she didn't even have to get out of the carriage and go into the bookshop if she didn't want to; just getting out of the house and going for a drive was a big step. She mentioned this to Emerald and Ruby after she'd taken a couple of minutes to catch her breath, and they both heartily agreed. They seemed so pleased with themselves for their accomplishment of getting Gina dressed and styled and almost out of the house that they might as well have been a couple of cats who had just enjoyed a tasty meal.

Gina drew in a deep breath before she stepped outside of Stonebridge Manor for the first time since the day of her husband's funeral. She took a few steps toward the waiting carriage, then impulsively stopped and turned to look up at the magnificent structure that had housed the Everleigh family for generations. Its architecture was unique in the way it cleverly displayed several parapets fortifying the top of the house, and the seemingly countless chimneys, as if they were there for beauty rather than practicality. Gina couldn't see anything from where she stood except the nearest rising wall, but it too was beautiful simply from the way the dark-gray stone from which it was structured was so expertly fashioned and fixed together to create a structure that would stand for centuries. Gina felt a once-familiar urge to walk the grounds so that she could admire the house from a distance as she'd once done frequently, but even if she wasn't about to set off to go into town, she doubted she would have the strength to do so right now. Being able to once again take long, brisk walks was something she would have to gradually work toward, given how many months she'd been so sedentary.

Garn drew her attention to the waiting carriage, and Gina turned to see that his sisters were already seated inside. Their brother was not a man one would consider handsome, and ironically his height was about halfway between that of his sisters. His hair too was a mixture of red and brown in what Gina considered almost equal parts. Depending on the light in which he might be standing—whether indoors or out—his hair could look either red or brown. He offered her a wide smile that always made him *more* handsome, since his teeth were almost perfectly straight, and just like his sisters, he'd always taken good care of them so that they were white and in better condition than many others of his class.

"You look lovely, m'lady," he said, holding out his hand to help her step into the carriage.

Gina resisted the urge to say aloud the self-deprecating thought that came into her mind, that she didn't feel at all lovely, knowing how much she had changed physically since Dwight's death. But she swallowed her words and smiled at Garn, simply saying, "Thank you," as she slipped her hand into his, allowing him to help her maintain her balance as she stepped carefully into the carriage, sitting down across from the sisters who still looked extremely pleased with themselves. Gina just smiled at them and felt the carriage rock slightly as Garn stepped up onto the box seat, and a moment later they were moving. Just being inside of a carriage in motion felt strange to Gina, even though she'd been traveling short and long distances in carriages since her infancy. But everything prior to Dwight's death had come to feel somehow dreamlike, and she was finding it difficult to adjust. She had a moment of wishing she had protested over the idea of this excursion, and that she was safely tucked away in her rooms instead of heading toward town in the carriage, but she distracted herself by craning her neck to view the house from a distance as the carriage reached a point far enough away for her to get a good view of its grandeur and majesty. She'd grown up in a home that was equally large and majestic, but Stonebridge had a unique beauty that she'd instantly fallen in love with the first time Dwight had brought her here. It had felt like home from that very first moment, but of course Dwight had had a great deal to do with that. Throughout their courtship and betrothal, she had believed she would have felt at home with him anywhere; it had simply been an added benefit that his home was so unique and beautiful.

When the carriage moved over the crest of a hill and into a stretch of woods where the house could no longer be seen, Gina settled comfortably into her seat, wishing she didn't feel a sudden dread at the thought of even stepping outside the carriage once they arrived at their destination.

"Are you all right thus far?" Ruby asked.

"You look a little haggard," Emerald declared with her typical vocal volume; the statement filled the carriage and seemed to bounce off every surface of the interior so that it echoed in Gina's ears.

"You should be kinder," Ruby gently scolded her sister.

"I'm simply telling the truth," Emerald declared. "She's looked pale for months now; it's a fact, for certain. Perhaps it's just more obvious now that we're not in the same environment as we have been day in and day out."

Gina did her best to absorb the comment with dignity, rather than letting it offend her. "If I look pale and haggard, then it would do well for me to attempt to get outside even for a little while every day. Perhaps that will help."

"An excellent idea," Emerald boomed.

"That should surely put some color back into your cheeks," Ruby said more softly but with a trill of hope in her voice.

Gina was genuinely touched with the way her friends were so sincerely concerned about her, and she couldn't help but feel grateful for the way they were so invested in helping her get past this terrible rut into which she'd gotten herself. Despite a strong desire to continue to hide away and indulge in unhealthy habits, she had an even stronger desire to put all of that behind her. She'd become sick to death of wallowing in such stagnant circumstances.

Dwight surely would have been disappointed to see what had become of her. If for no other reason, her desire to think of making him proud urged her to press forward toward making a better life for herself.

A somewhat awkward silence descended over the three women until Ruby began to fill it by reminiscing about how close they had all been since childhood, and Emerald soon joined her in talking and laughing about memories they all shared. Perhaps it was the only topic they could think of to try and distract Gina from any nervousness she might be feeling, or perhaps they wanted to remind Gina of the history they shared so that Gina would know they had her best interests at heart. Their motives were likely a little of both. But Gina couldn't deny her enjoyment at hearing them speak of fond memories.

Despite their dramatically different stations in life, the children of the widowed head cook—Mrs. Axton—had shared lessons with Gina during their childhood, and thus they had all become playmates, a situation that would have been repellent to many who belonged to the upper classes. But Gina's widowed father had been nothing but pleased that his daughter had other children with whom to spend her time. He was fond of Emerald and Ruby and their older brother Garnet—who far preferred going by the shortened version of *Garn*—and the four of them had become inseparable. No one was ever certain why Mrs. Axton had chosen to name her children after precious gems, although the cook often tended to call attention to the fact, declaring that they were her greatest treasure.

After the cook had passed away from a sudden illness, leaving the three siblings orphaned, Gina's father had taken a more serious approach to his responsibility for them. They were all old enough to work and he gave them each some simple employment, enough for them to learn how to work and earn their keep, but not so much that they didn't have time to play and become educated as children should be. When Gina had accepted Dwight Everleigh's proposal of marriage, her father had aptly made the decision that these three servants of his household should go with Gina, because he knew they would take good care of her, and she was comfortable with them. As long as the three siblings could remain together, they were unanimously pleased with the idea of settling into a new home where they could continue to work with Gina and maintain their well-established friendships. Gina's father believed she would be happier if her lifelong friends were under the same roof, and Dwight had been more than happy to accommodate her father's plan. Garn worked in the carriage house, just as he'd done previously, and he was also Gina's personal driver, which meant he accompanied her wherever she went. Emerald and

Ruby shared the duties of caring for Gina while also doing other odd tasks in the kitchen and laundry, which had allowed them to not feel cut off from the rest of the household. And neither of them wanted to feel idle; it was common knowledge that Gina didn't need the full-time attention of two maids, but she did appreciate that one or the other of the sisters was almost always nearby.

The conversation settled into silence once again as the carriage moved on toward the village, but Gina's mind became preoccupied with her gratitude for Garn and his sisters and how well they looked after her. She turned her attention to the passing scenery and found herself so thoroughly enjoying the experience of just being out that she felt a sudden dread over her inevitable return to her rooms and the self-inflicted prison they had become. She reminded herself that it was a very big house with beautiful grounds and gardens, and she didn't have to remain secluded, but then she recalled how difficult it had been just to walk from her rooms to the door where the carriage had been waiting. She finally determined that it would be a good idea to share a conversation with the sisters about her feelings and enlist their aid in coming up with suggestions that might help her make some positive changes in order to ward off such dread and discouragement. But since the carriage was slowing as it approached the narrower road that led through the village, Gina put her thoughts away for the moment and looked out the window at the familiar row of businesses that hadn't changed a bit during her months of confinement. Then she realized something was different, and she felt compelled to comment.

"Where is everyone? The high street is usually so busy this time of day." She recalled the countless visits to town she'd shared with Dwight; it was something they'd enjoyed doing together, and they'd been on kind terms with many merchants and villagers. She suddenly felt the urge to cry but quickly pushed the urge away; she'd shed far too many tears, and even if she felt the need to grieve, this was neither the time nor the place.

"There's a town meeting taking place at one of the pubs," Emerald informed her. "It happens every month on the first Tuesday at this time."

"We thought it might be easier for you to be here if there weren't so many people out and about," Ruby added. "Some of the shops are closed but not all of them. We know for a fact that the bookshop is open because the owner goes to these meetings but leaves his daughter to mind the store."

"Well, aren't you all very clever!" Gina chuckled, amazed at the relief she felt, knowing she wouldn't be facing the usual number of people, even if just stepping out of the carriage and into the bookshop was not likely to result in any significant number of encounters. "I confess that I feel more at ease over knowing this."

"Excellent!" Ruby said at the same time Emerald declared, "We *are* clever, indeed!"

The carriage came to a gentle halt directly in front of the bookshop that Gina had once visited occasionally with Dwight. He had sometimes been kinder and more attentive toward her when they'd been in public; perhaps that's why such memories were more tender for her. She looked out at the familiar display in the window, the door which had been painted a lovely red, and the inviting sign on it which she'd always loved: *Books are pathways to adventure. Come inside and find your newest adventure today.* Gina thought of all the adventures she had shared with Dwight by reading together and discussing the stories they enjoyed. It was something they'd always had in common, and sadly enough was perhaps the only truly positive aspect of their marriage; but in that moment the memories were pleasant for Gina, rather than sad or confusing.

The carriage rocked as Garn jumped down, and a moment later the door opened. Gina hesitated to step out, wanting to indulge in her quiet musings. Feeling the expectancy of the three siblings, she simply said, "I need a moment, if that's all right. The memories . . ."

The sisters nodded with understanding and remained silent; Garn leaned a shoulder against the side of the carriage, assuming a stance that implied he could stay there all day if necessary. And that's when Gina heard the cry of a baby.

"Did you hear that?" Gina asked, lifting her head abruptly to look out of the open carriage door, expecting to see someone passing by, carrying a baby. But there was not a person to be seen in any direction, which was proven by her quick, urgent perusal out of each window while the others did the same, silently indicating that they *had* heard.

"Something's not right," Garn said, now standing with his back to the carriage and his hands firmly on his hips, looking back and forth, up and down the street. Gina was as glad for his declaration—which expressed her own belief—as she was for the way he seemed determined to find the source of the soft but undeniable intermittent cries of a baby.

"You ladies wait here," he ordered as if he were about to go into battle. "Don't get out until I come back." He closed the carriage door as if that might keep them safer, which Gina thought was a bit humorous. He was looking for the source of a crying a baby, not the sounds of a brawling mob in the street.

They waited for several minutes, which felt much longer, while Ruby and Emerald began making nervous comments and speculations over what might be taking him so long, and why they were even so concerned about a crying baby to begin with.

"Surely a mother is simply nearby attempting to soothe her little one," Ruby concluded.

"He's likely just trying to help," Emerald added. "Perhaps she has other children and is having some difficulty."

Gina said nothing but felt inexplicably nervous. She could still hear the occasional but soft cries of what sounded like a very young baby, which implied that it was some distance away. All three women leaned toward the window when the crying noises seemed to be·moving closer very quickly. They could hardly see anything except Garn rushing toward the carriage; then he opened the door, stepped inside, closed the door, and sat down abruptly next to Gina, which forced her to scoot over a bit. She noticed that he sounded out of breath just before she realized he was holding a wiggling bundle wrapped in a little blanket that looked clean but very worn.

"I think she was abandoned," Garn said, easing back the blanket to expose the plump, wrinkled face of a very tiny baby. All three women gasped as he added, still breathless, "I found her in the alley between the bake shop and the butcher; both places are closed so I doubt anyone would even be there to hear her—not until later, at least. I looked all the way to the back of the alley, behind the buildings, and up and down the street. There's not a soul in sight. She was just tucked up close to the wall in a crate, near the back door of the butcher's shop. And this was tucked in the blanket." He held up a piece of paper imprinted with crude writing, which implied the writer of the note was not very well educated. Gina snatched it out of his hand to read the brief message: "*Please love her and take care of her.*"

"Lord, have mercy," Emerald prayed aloud, which was immediately followed by Ruby and Garn muttering, "Amen."

Over the span of a few seconds, Gina felt as if time stopped while she mentally recalled and examined seemingly hundreds of memories of her hope that she and Dwight would have children together and make them the center of their lives. With sadness, she recalled the dwindling hope each month when evidence came once again that she had still not conceived. She had come to feel a decline in her value as a woman, and even as a wife when she had wanted a child so desperately; and she knew that Dwight very much wanted a son to carry on his legacy and his name. And the very fact that she'd not been able to have a child to carry on the Everleigh name and bloodline had been a deep source of shame for her—something she'd never been able to talk about, not even with her closet friends and confidants. The sisters knew of her sorrow over the matter, but the painful, festering shame over not being able to become a mother—the most elemental expectation of a married woman—brought with it an undeniable social stigma and too tender a heartache for her to speak of. Even though she'd never uttered aloud her feelings on the subject, she absolutely knew in her heart that her grief over Dwight's death had been greatly enhanced by the fact that she'd not only lost her husband, she'd lost the hope of ever having a child. She'd mournfully mused over what it might be like to have been blessed with a child who needed her, who would have given her a reason to get out of bed, and who would have given some kind of meaning and purpose to her life. She'd imagined herself with a child so often that it seemed the most natural thing in the world to simply reach out and take the baby from Garn, holding it close as if she'd just found a missing part of herself. Peace and fulfillment washed over her with such immediate force that she absolutely knew this was no accident or coincidence. Gina and her dear, trusted friends had been meant to be in this exact place at this exact moment, because this baby was meant to be hers.

"What are you doing?" Garn asked in astonished response to the way Gina was cuddling the baby and cooing at her. "We can't just . . . *keep* her. We've got to inform the police or something. This is—"

"Surely Garn is right," Ruby said.

"Indeed, he is!" Emerald insisted.

Gina just looked into the eyes of the tiny infant, who seemed to be looking back at her as if she too comprehended a kind of celestial connection between them. Her mind swirled frantically with the choices before her. She had absolutely no idea what was legally involved with finding an abandoned baby. If Gina turned this child over to the police, would she ever see her again? Would this beautiful baby end up in some horrible orphanage? The very idea made Gina shudder. She considered the possibility of officially adopting this little girl, but again she had absolutely no idea what might be involved in such a process. However, it only took common sense to realize that an *adopted* child would never be as entitled to the privileges of the Everleigh name and fortune as would a child with Everleigh blood. She also knew the general attitudes of people enough to believe that an adopted child would likely always be looked down upon and shunned by polite society, and that could likely be as damaging to a child as an orphanage—emotionally, at least. Besides, Gina's home was not under her control. Dwight's cousin was the titled owner of Stonebridge Manor, and she could never bring home an abandoned baby without his approval and support. She didn't know him all that well but suspected it was possible that he might *not* be supportive of such a rash decision.

It took only a few long moments of thought for Gina to be certain of what she needed to do, although she felt the need to talk it through with her friends. Without looking away from the baby, Gina said, "You all know the story of Moses from the Bible."

"Yes," they all said in a variety of confused tones.

"The mother who gave birth to him couldn't keep him," Gina went on, "because it wasn't safe to do so. But God guided him into the arms of a mother who could give him the best of everything."

"What in the name of all that is holy are you saying?" Emerald demanded in a voice that startled the baby, but she didn't cry. "You can't just *keep* it!"

"And why can't I?" Gina looked up at Emerald with all the fierceness that she felt. In that moment she believed that if anyone attempted to take this baby from her, she would be hard-pressed not to cause them bodily harm. "We found her abandoned in an alley. *We* found her. This is the first time I've been out of the house in months, and no one else is around *at all*. We heard her crying, we found her, and the note is an obvious indication that the woman who gave birth to this beautiful girl could not care for her; its wording is an obvious plea for someone to do what she cannot do. And *I* can do that; *we* can do that." She looked around at the gaping faces of her silent friends and added, "We simply need to come up with a reasonable explanation for how this came to be, something that everyone in the household and community will accept without question. And no one—no one—but the four of us ever need know the truth. This is *my* baby now, and that is all there is to it. God clearly left her for us to find so that she would be in my care, and I know I can depend on the three of you to help make certain she remains with me forever."

"You know," Garn said, his tone mildly cynical, "the story of Moses didn't turn out so well for him in the end. The truth came out and he was exiled."

Gina didn't feel at all put off by Garn's caution. She simply retorted, "God had a plan for Moses, and He surely has a plan for this beautiful girl. I've been praying for peace and purpose, my friends, and that's what I feel now. Please, just trust me . . . and help me . . . and surely all will be well."

"We'd do anything you ask of us, Gina," Ruby said gently. Her siblings agreed, and Gina told them everything she had been thinking regarding the impossibility of taking the baby to the police or attempting to officially adopt her. Thankfully, they all agreed and began to discuss how they would go about convincing the occupants of Stonebridge Manor that Gina had left the house for the first time in months and was coming home with a baby—her baby.

CHAPTER TWO
the baronet

ONCE THE SIBLINGS ACCEPTED THAT Gina would not be swayed in her determination to keep the baby and raise it as her own child, they were full of ideas about how they could convince others that Gina had been pregnant and had given birth. In fact, the three of them talked so quickly back and forth that Gina could barely keep up. The fact that Gina had not left her rooms since her husband's funeral could now be explained as her not feeling well due to pregnancy; not telling anyone would obviously be perceived as a result of her being lost in grief. And she certainly had been lost in grief—even if her grieving had been confusing and unusual—so that part was easy. The fact that Gina's appetite had increased dramatically during these last months could now be attributed to pregnancy rather than the real reason, which was simply her desire to drown her misery in the comfort of food. And Gina's added weight was now a blessing because it would validate the story that she had been pregnant and had simply not wanted anyone to know except for her two maids who were also her closest friends. As all these elements combined to create the perfect story, Gina was even more convinced that God's hand had to be involved in this situation; surely this had all been divinely orchestrated.

"And how do we explain the actual birth?" Emerald asked. "And the fact that you *cannot* be seen by a doctor after you return home, because it would be glaringly evident that you have *not* given birth."

"Oh, that's easy," Ruby said with a surprising amount of enthusiasm, as if she were beginning to enjoy this scheme they were devising. "Before our mother died, she assisted with the birthing of some babies in the household and in the village. Her mother had been a midwife."

"Oh, I'd forgotten!" Emerald said, her eyes lighting up. It was as if they were all gradually warming up to what seemed obvious to Gina. There were so many little pieces of this puzzle coming together and making sense that every passing moment made it seem even more inevitable that this was meant to be. "We went with Mama more than a few times to help her; I think she had the hope that one or both of us might become a midwife. But she passed, and we turned our focus toward becoming more involved in caring for you." She nodded at Gina. "And everything else drifted away."

"But it's perfectly feasible," Ruby went on, "to say that Emerald and I together have enough knowledge and experience that we made certain all was well throughout your pregnancy, and that we helped deliver the baby."

"Here in the carriage?" Garn snapped, making it evident he had not yet been convinced that this was a good idea.

"Why not?" Ruby asked her brother, showing an unusual amount of assertiveness, evidenced by the unusual rise in volume of her voice. "Babies come when they're ready to come."

"So . . ." Garn said, "on the first day that Gina chooses to leave the house in months, she goes into labor in the carriage, right here on the high street, and—"

"Yes, exactly," Emerald said. "We simply need to do a few simple things to make certain everything appears the way we need it to appear. And after we return to the house, we can be firm on the fact that Gina only wants me and Ruby to care for her in her recovery, because she has an aversion to the doctor."

"Well, *that* is certainly true!" Gina declared. "He was dreadfully callous and cold when he came to talk to me about Dwight's death. I would never want him attending to me with something as intimate as childbirth."

"There you have it," Ruby said, and the two women embarked on a perfect plan to create the appearance of Gina giving birth in the carriage.

The street was still quiet and devoid of any people when Garn rushed into the bookshop to frantically ask for the assistance of the young woman who would be minding the shop while her father was at the town meeting. His sisters had carefully instructed him to behave as if he were panicked, to report that his mistress was in labor in the carriage, and to ask for string, scissors, towels, and boiling water. He returned quickly with everything except the boiling water, stating that since the family who owned the bookshop lived behind the business, there had been easy access to all he'd requested, and the water was on the stove. Garn remained outside the carriage in keeping with the tradition that a man would never be present for the birth of a child; and besides, his sisters were taking care of their mistress very well. When he gratefully received the boiling water from the helpful young woman, he told her according to Emerald's instructions that they would return the linens after they had been laundered.

"I'm just glad to help," Gina heard the young woman say nearby on the other side of the carriage window, where the curtains had now been drawn. "Is she going to be all right?"

"I've been assured all will be well," Garn said to her.

Ruby whispered to Gina, "Now would be a good time to make some kind of sound to indicate that you are in pain."

Gina initially felt startled by the request but quickly realized that it would go a long way toward making their scheme convincing. With a few more whispered instructions from the sisters, Gina did her best to groan painfully as if she were bearing down and pushing hard in order to deliver a baby. She repeated the performance a couple of minutes later, then the young woman thankfully returned to the bookshop so that Gina and her little troupe of friends and performers could just wait a short while longer before returning home with the baby she had supposedly given birth to.

Once the sisters agreed that enough time had passed, comically stating that Gina had been blessed with a brief labor—especially for a first baby—Garn returned the scissors and the empty pot to the young woman with instructions to tell her that the scissors had been cleaned with the boiled water. Garn returned to report that he'd been humbly appreciative and very convincing, and the young woman—whose name he had kept forgetting to ask in his nervousness—had been thrilled to hear that a healthy baby girl had been safely delivered, and that Garn could now drive the carriage back to the manor.

Before Garn got onto the box seat to begin the drive, he listened through the window to careful instructions from his sisters about how he needed to put on a careful ruse about needing to clean the interior of the carriage once they returned. The only explanation they gave was, "Childbirth can be a messy business."

During the drive back to the manor, Gina held her new little daughter close to her, looking only at her sweet face while she listened to Ruby and Emerald discussing the practical matters of carrying out all the proper appearances.

"Oh, my!" Ruby said with an element of alarm in her voice that made Gina look up. "We'll need to get a wet nurse; clearly Gina will not be able to feed the baby. How do we—"

"Mama said that occasionally a woman just doesn't produce enough milk to feed their baby and they need assistance." Emerald seemed calm and confident regarding the problem. "We will simply state that we've observed this to be the case and I'm certain Mrs. Darby will be glad to help us find someone and arrange all the accommodations."

Gina couldn't be certain what exactly that meant; she was only grateful that Emerald and Ruby had the foresight to think of all the necessary details in order to make this work. Gina's mind was mostly focused on the baby in her arms, and how an enormous emptiness inside of her felt suddenly and completely filled. While the baby looked up at her with the same seeming fascination that Gina felt, Gina silently prayed that God would protect this child, and that His blessings would be with them in all of the scheming taking place, with the hope that everyone beyond her friends would be convinced that this was indeed the child of Gina and her deceased husband. She found it strange to think of asking for God's help in creating such a deception, but her mind snapped quickly back to the story of Moses, and she felt an indescribable peace in believing that God had known this child needed a home and a loving mother who was in a position to properly care for her and give her a good life, and He had led Gina and her friends to the abandoned infant, because it was surely meant to be.

Gina thought of the poor woman who had just given birth to this child, likely in secret to avoid having anyone know—otherwise the absence of her child would surely be questioned. Was it a young woman who had gotten into trouble? Or was it perhaps a woman who had been assaulted or taken advantage of and left to deal with the consequences on her own? Whatever the case might be, Gina prayed for this woman, that her heart might be comforted regarding her desperate need to give up her child, and the unfathomable heartache she surely had to be enduring at this very moment. She prayed that the woman would be healthy and strong after having given birth—especially since she'd likely had no assistance or medical care if she'd kept the baby a secret.

Gina was startled from her deep thoughts and silent prayers when the carriage slowed, and she realized it was approaching the main entrance of Stonebridge Manor.

"We all know what to do," Emerald announced with a nervous tremor in her voice.

"Do we?" Gina asked, realizing she should have been paying more attention to all they had been saying throughout the brief journey from the village.

"Don't you worry," Ruby told her. "All you have to do is behave as if you're weak and in pain from just giving birth. We'll do all the explaining and arranging, and we'll do our best to keep the rest of the staff at a distance."

"Thank you," Gina said with sincerity, momentarily locking eyes with these precious sisters who were so good to her in every way, although she never could have imagined such a situation where they would become engaged in such scheming to assist and protect her in this unexpected endeavor.

Only a moment after the carriage came to a halt, Garn opened the carriage door and said softly that he would be carrying Gina up to her room.

"You can't possibly," Gina insisted, knowing such a feat couldn't be easy, even if she hadn't put on extra weight. "Surely I can just walk slowly with your assistance, and—"

"Are you questioning my masculine strength?" Garn said with a smirk and a wink just before Ruby took the baby from Gina's arms and Garn eased Gina into his, not giving her time to protest any further. He truly did prove his strength as he carried her inside after Emerald opened the door, all the while juggling the armful of supposedly soiled linens they had borrowed from the young woman in the bookshop. Garn carried Gina up the stairs, with Ruby and the baby following, and Emerald coming along with the linens. Gina attempted to appear weak in Garn's arms in case anyone might see them, but she saw no evidence that their return from town had even been noticed. This was verified when she heard Ruby say quietly, "I don't see a soul around. That's good, I think."

"Yes," Emerald added. "We'll get you settled into bed and Garn can go *clean* the inside of the carriage before anyone is the wiser."

Ruby went on, "And since I always launder your clothing and linens as it is, I can do a fair job of creating the appearance that these particular linens have assisted us in childbirth."

"You're all so clever I can hardly bear it," Gina said and heard her voice crack as she was suddenly overcome with the reality of all that was happening, and the reasons for it. "I'm so grateful for your help . . . all of it."

"I daresay the lot of us would do almost anything for you," Garn said, sounding out of breath once they reached the top of the stairs, but he still managed just fine with getting Gina to her bed where Emerald dropped the linens on the floor so she could pull back the covers and Garn could set her down. Emerald removed Gina's shoes and helped tuck her in before Ruby placed the baby in Gina's arms.

Garn took only a long moment to catch his breath before he hurried out of the room, muttering over his shoulder, "Got to get the carriage cleaned. Childbirth is a messy business." The comical way he quoted his sisters made them all chuckle before the door to the bedroom was closed and the three of them all hurried to help make everything appear more believable before any other servants came to the room.

Emerald put the supposedly soiled linens in Gina's dressing room, along with other items that needed to be laundered. Since—as Ruby had reminded her—she was always the one to personally see to Gina's laundry, no one would be the wiser. Emerald left the room to inform Mrs. Darby that Gina had given birth, and Gina was encouraged by Emerald's reassurance that she felt completely confident in being able to handle the situation well. As soon as Emerald left, Ruby helped Gina change into a nightgown and found a clean towel to wrap the baby in, hiding the blanket she'd been wrapped in until it could be burned without anyone noticing. The baby would need bathing, but that would require heated water from the kitchens, and they could do no more without assistance from others in the house. Gina could well imagine Mrs. Darby's astonishment, and her calm ability to take on any kind of challenge and make certain that every need was met. Gina felt confident that despite the overall surprise of everyone in the household upon learning that Gina had been hiding a pregnancy all these months—due to her overwhelming grief and her aversion to the local doctor—they would all be pleased on her behalf and happy to assist her in any way. This baby would indeed have a good life, and Gina's own life had just changed dramatically for the better. It was nothing short of a miracle.

⸙

Three days later, Gina couldn't remember life before the bizarre arrival of her daughter, whom she had chosen to call Janine, because Ruby had once read in a book that the name meant *Gift from God*. Gina was content to not venture out according to habit while she kept up the ruse of recovering from childbirth, but now she preferred to have all the draperies open so that the summer sun could fill her bedroom with its brilliant light through a stretch of days that were unusually cloudless. And when it rained, Gina found a new beauty in the rain drizzling down the windows. Everything was more beautiful now that she had this precious little girl to care for and to call her own. Janine had fine, lovely features and wisps of dark hair, and Gina believed her to be the most beautiful baby ever born. While she kept a prayer in her heart for the mother who had given birth to this baby, she felt no concern about any future problems arising. She simply hoped this woman would feel comfort and somehow know that her child would be well cared for and given every possible advantage in life.

Overcome with an unfamiliar happiness, Gina recounted all the wonderful things that had occurred in the wake of Janine's arrival. Ruby and Emerald had both reported with some amusement how different members of the staff had responded to the news of Gina's secret pregnancy, and the ironic timing of her giving birth in the carriage the first time she'd left the house in months. Mrs. Darby was convinced that the very effort she'd made to go out had surely brought on her labor, and Mrs. Chester had proclaimed multiple times that it was no wonder Mrs. Everleigh's appetite had increased so dramatically, as was common with pregnant women, and that as soon as she was up and about more she would surely get back to her normal self in no time. Gina was pleased with such observations and how they strengthened her story, and she was even more pleased with the way she no longer felt the need to eat excessively to help herself feel better. Holding her sweet Janine and caring for her was all the comfort she needed.

It had also been reported to Gina that the highest-ranking members of the staff were in complete agreement with Gina's request to not see the local doctor, since they didn't like him either. Therefore, it seemed a common consensus that everyone was glad that Ruby and Emerald had learned some midwifery from their mother, and they were able to care for the widow of Dwight Everleigh during her confinement, delivery, and recovery.

Gina was pleased with the sudden flow of little clothes, and blankets, and other necessities for a baby. A lovely cradle had been found among some old things in a storage room in the house, and it had been cleaned and brought to Gina's room for the baby to sleep in. The sisters reported to Gina that Mrs. Darby had immediately sent an order to a shop in the village for a great many other things that she knew would be needed for an infant, and there were also gifts that came from some members of the staff, and even some of the villagers. Gina was overwhelmed by such kindness, and she made certain that a list was kept of those who had been so generous so that she could write notes of appreciation and have them delivered at the first possible opportunity. It was also reported to her that Mrs. Darby had concluded—and therefore announced to everyone—that Gina had clearly been in a state of grieving and melancholy following her husband's tragic demise, which had kept her from informing anyone of the expected baby; therefore, it was understandable that she had not had the presence of mind to see that she had gathered all the necessary items to care for a baby. Ruby had aided the explanation by telling the housekeeper that the baby had also come earlier than they had calculated, which also explained why it would have been born while out on a rare excursion, because Gina surely wouldn't have gone out if she'd had any suspicion that her outing would bring on labor.

Garn came to visit a couple of times to see how they were getting on, and he reported with amusement that the talk among those who worked in the stables and carriage house was much the same. Gina was grateful for the support of her friends, as well as Mrs. Darby and many others. And she marveled over and over that she'd been blessed with this remarkable miracle; the timing of finding little Janine the way they did could be nothing less than a miracle, and the more she thought about it, the less she could deny that fact.

The fast spread of gossip among the household, which always reached the village quickly due to much interaction with comings and goings, proved to be an added blessing when a wet nurse was quickly acquired. Mrs. Darby had been reported to say that some women simply weren't able to feed their babies as well as others, and there was not a thing wrong with getting help when it was needed. Even though Mrs. Darby had not yet come to see the baby or personally check in on the new mother, Gina felt the kindness and support of this dear woman through the reports of her maids, and she was profoundly grateful. With word spreading through the village that Mrs. Everleigh had given birth to a baby girl and needed a wet nurse, a woman came forward the day after the strange events that had brought little Janine into Gina's arms. Elaine was a widow a little over forty years old who had two grown children, both married and on their own, and a four-year-old son who had been born not long before her husband's unexpected death. Around the time she had been weaning her son from breast-feeding, her sister had died in childbirth, and the father of the baby—and four older children—had been left in a terrible situation. Elaine and her young son had moved in with her brother-in-law's family so that she could feed and care for the baby. Amazingly, Elaine had been weaning her little nephew who was now nearly two, and she was just at the stage of still producing milk even though the child no longer needed to nurse. She'd come to the manor house of her own volition and had met with Mrs. Darby, explaining her recent desire to no longer remain in her brother-in-law's home. She had observed that the older children had become very adept at looking after their little brother when their father was working. She considered the opportunity to be a wet nurse at this very time to be a blessing and hoped they would be willing to hire her, especially since a room for her and her child would be provided, along with a salary as well as all their meals. Mrs. Darby had been impressed by Elaine and hired her immediately, but only after Ruby and Emerald had been given the opportunity to meet her and offer their approval, since Mrs. Darby considered Gina's maids would know her well enough to determine whether Elaine would be a good fit to work closely with Gina in caring for the baby. Ruby and Emerald reported that they liked Elaine very much, and the new wet nurse and her little son had moved into the servants' dormitories by the end of the day.

Gina was pleased to know that this problem had been solved so quickly when it could have been an extremely difficult challenge. To her, it felt like yet another piece of evidence that the hand of Providence was guiding the situation, and she was glad to know that the opportunity was a blessing to Elaine and her young son. Gina also thought a great deal about the fact that if gossip had spread through the village about Gina having a baby and needing a wet nurse, that the mother who had given birth to Janine would surely have heard the news, and would secretly hope that somehow this baby was hers and would know that she was in good hands.

Gina met Elaine soon after she'd finished her supper on the day following Janine's birth. Thus far the baby had been given small amounts of goats' milk, which she sucked from the corner of a clean towel that had been dipped into a bowl. Ruby escorted Elaine into the room, where Gina was in her bed, propped up with pillows. Janine was peacefully asleep on Gina's chest so that the baby's head was tucked against Gina's neck, as if it they were simply meant to be connected in this way.

Gina immediately felt comfortable with Elaine. Before introductions had been completed and the woman had offered an appropriate curtsy, Gina took note of her well-rounded figure and the way her dark-brown hair was streaked with silver as if an artist had painted the color of age into her locks so gracefully that it seemed a symbol of kindness and wisdom. Her hair was cleverly braided back from her brow and twisted and pinned up in a way that also seemed artistic, especially when Gina knew this woman surely styled her own hair and didn't have the luxury of a skilled lady's maid to assist her. Elaine's dress was a drab gray, but there were creamy-colored flowers embroidered around the neckline and the cuffs, adding a feminine and bright touch. Gina knew that Elaine had either done this needlework herself, or she was close to someone who had done it; such embellishment was costly. Yet Elaine wore it as if she simply wanted to feel more feminine and unique; her very countenance declared that she didn't need any kind of artistic hairstyle or fancy apparel to feel completely confident about herself as a woman. Her smile gleamed with kindness as Ruby invited her to sit in a chair near the side of Gina's bed. She did so but kept her back straight, resting her hands in her lap. Ruby sat down some distance from the bed, as if she intended to make certain all went well, but she would allow the two women to share their conversation without any intrusion from her.

"It is a fine pleasure to meet you, Mrs. Everleigh," Elaine said. "I understand you need some assistance that I am able to give. I'm glad to have met with the approval of the housekeeper and your maids; nevertheless, I want to be very clear that my sharing in the care of your daughter is a sensitive matter for a mother, and it's important that you feel comfortable with me. May I be forthright and say that with my experience of having done this before, it's important that I be allowed to take charge of the baby's feeding schedule? Beyond that, you are her mother, and it is your right to oversee her care and to have the final word regarding your daughter."

"Thank you," Gina said. "Janine is my first child; therefore, I admit I am not skilled in caring for a baby. I welcome your advice and expertise, and I appreciate your willingness to respect my place as her mother. I daresay there are those who would swoop in and want to take control, and I could not tolerate such an attitude."

"Nor could I," Elaine said, and Gina noted that the woman was well educated. Her speech and the way she carried herself indicated very ladylike manners and demeanor. Gina felt curious regarding her upbringing and other facets of her life, but they would surely have ample time to become acquainted as they worked together to care for Janine. "Do you have a nanny?" Elaine asked.

"No," Gina said. "The housekeeper expressed a firm desire—which was communicated to me through my maids—that we hire a nanny to help care for Janine. There's not been a baby in this house for a generation—as she put it. However, I want to care for Janine on my own as much as possible; therefore, I haven't made a decision regarding that yet."

"I admire your wish to care for your daughter," Elaine said with a smile that radiated kindness and respect. "I know that nannies are common among those of your class, and I believe that a mother of *any* class needs to have time away from her baby to refresh herself, and to be relaxed in knowing that the baby is safe and well cared for. I also believe that when children are cared for by their own mother, they are more likely to be well adjusted and confident. Of course, there are exceptions to every such belief, but that has been my observation."

"I appreciate your insights," Gina said, feeling delightfully comfortable with Elaine. She wondered what she would have done if the wet nurse who had been hired by the housekeeper was a woman Gina didn't like; she could only be grateful that such was not the case. "You clearly have a great deal of wisdom."

Elaine let out a short, humble laugh. "I've spent most of my life caring for children—my own and many others. Although I'm certain there is a great deal I do *not* know; good common sense fills in the gaps most of the time, I think."

"Indeed," Gina agreed.

"As for the matter of a nanny," Elaine said. "It's my opinion that since I will be feeding little Janine, and I am being paid very well for employment that will be nothing but a pleasure for me, that I am more than happy to assist with her care in any way that you might need—again always respecting your desires and preferences as her mother."

"That's a lovely idea," Gina said. "I would be very grateful for your help as well as your guidance."

Elaine nodded and smiled, seeming pleased. Then she appeared mildly nervous before she said, "I believe you are aware that I have a young son. Mrs. Darby was kind enough to allow him to come here and live with me for as long as you need me, and she has told me that there are maids in the house who are happy to watch over him while I assist you. I wonder, however, if you would feel uncomfortable with my keeping Tommy close by during certain times of the day. He is very well behaved, and I can find things that will keep him quiet and occupied in the sitting room or one of the rooms across the hall, so as not to disturb you. It's just that . . . an infant requires feeding so frequently that . . . I would be away from Tommy a great deal if he were not . . ."

Gina felt completely comfortable with Elaine's request; she completely understood a mother's desire to keep her child close. A subtle nod of approval from Ruby cemented her confidence in saying, "Of course you may keep Tommy nearby." Elaine smiled again and sighed with great relief. Gina continued, "There are so many fine rooms in this hallway alone that go unused, I think it would be far more prudent if you and Tommy used rooms across the hall rather than staying in the dormitories. Then you can be nearby when Janine needs feeding, and Tommy can be near his mother and be comfortable in a room of his own where he can settle in."

"Oh, you are most kind!" Elaine declared as if she hadn't imagined such an agreeable arrangement. But now that Gina had thought through the situation, she couldn't imagine having the woman who would be feeding Janine being some great distance away in this huge house, and she certainly didn't want her own needs—and her baby's—to come between a mother and child.

They talked a few minutes longer, discussing more details of the arrangement. Janine woke up and began to fuss, and with Gina's permission, Elaine took the baby and efficiently unbuttoned her bodice and began to feed Janine, who instinctively knew exactly what to do. Gina felt mildly jealous, observing this tender way of nature that she would not be able to share with her daughter, but the feeling was quickly suppressed by the depth of her gratitude for having been blessed with the miracle of this beautiful little girl coming into her life.

And with Elaine here to help her, it seemed that everything had fallen into place perfectly. There was only one matter that she feared facing, and five days beyond Janine's remarkable arrival in the household, news came to her that she could no longer avoid the inevitable.

"What is this?" Gina asked as Emerald entered her bedroom and handed her a sealed note.

"I should think it's obvious," Emerald said with a mild scowl.

Gina turned the note over to see a wax seal of dark green holding the folded edges of paper in place, and scrawled on the other side in a familiar, elegant hand, was one simple letter: G. There was only one person who would send such a formal communication within the walls of the house in which they both lived, instead of just sending a verbal message with one of the servants. And there was only one person who had ever called her simply *G*. Dwight's cousin and the heir of Stonebridge—and its accompanying title—had lightly called Gina by the initial G the first time he'd met her, and he'd rarely called her anything else. Gina found his company agreeable. However, since marrying Dwight and coming to live at Stonebridge, Gina scarcely saw him. The house was enormous, and he enjoyed traveling a great deal. Still, this was *his* house, and a huge, unexpected occurrence had taken place. She had known it was only a matter of time before he would want to speak with her.

Gina took a deep breath before she broke the seal and unfolded the page of fine parchment, which read: *G, I have been made aware that congratulations are in order. I would very much like to call on you and my new little cousin this afternoon. If five o'clock is not a good time for you, send word. Otherwise I will see you then. Sir Radcliffe*

"What is it?" Emerald asked.

"Sir Radcliffe wants to see me and the baby . . . at five o'clock."

"Good to get it over with, I'd say," Emerald said, her face looking a little grim, which didn't help Gina's mood at all.

"Yes, I'm certain it is," Gina said while Emerald busied herself with putting away some clean underclothing in the drawers of Gina's bureau. Gina looked at the note again and muttered, "How is it that he can be so casual as to write *G* on the front, and sign his own name so formally?"

"He *is* a baronet," Emerald said as if Gina might have forgotten. "I suppose he can do whatever he likes, and however he likes to do it."

"I suppose," Gina said, her mind wandering through strange, vague moments of the past while Emerald tidied the drawers and refolded clothing items that had surely been fine just as they were. But Emerald and Ruby were both perfectionists when it came to making certain Gina's belongings were in their proper place and cared for; and they were equally fastidious regarding Gina's care. She felt remarkably blessed to have them in her life and to share such closeness and trust with those who helped meet her needs day in and day out. And she was also grateful that their closeness went back enough years that they had been aware of every aspect of her meeting Dwight Everleigh, and their courtship and marriage. And that meant they had also been privy to Gina's every encounter with Dwight's cousin, Sir Radcliffe Everleigh, Baronet.

Gina had met Dwight and his cousin when the two men had been staying in the London home owned by the newly titled baronet, about a year following his father's death. They had gone to London at the encouragement of many friends who were certain that both men needed to engage in more social activity in order to help put the death of Radcliffe's father behind them. Gina and her father had been staying with a friend of her father's in London who had invited them to spend the social season in his home, certain he needed to be of assistance in finding Gina a husband. Gina hadn't at all expected that the wish of her father's friend might come to pass, but as soon as she'd met Dwight and his cousin, they had attended many social functions together. And it hadn't been long before Dwight had asked permission of Gina's father to court her, and his permission had been gladly given. Radcliffe had attended socials with many different women, but Dwight had only wanted Gina by his side. Still, Gina had come to know both men rather well; however, she felt a little intimidated by Radcliffe. Still, he had always been kind to her, and he'd shown nothing but pleasure and support in Dwight's desire to marry Gina. Since Dwight lived in the same home with his cousin, she had understood upon their marriage she too would be living under the same roof with Radcliffe. But he had always allowed them to do as they pleased, and since he traveled and socialized a great deal, they had seen him very rarely. Yet when he *had* been around, Gina had shared many stimulating conversations with him about things in which Dwight had exhibited no interest. They shared a mutual respect at the very least, and she believed him to be a good man.

Gina knew that Radcliffe had been devastated by his cousin's untimely death, but despite their mutual grief, Gina had refused his multiple requests to see her when she had locked herself away following the funeral. He'd finally given up, and in truth she'd hardly given him a thought for months—until she'd unexpectedly brought a baby into his household. Naturally, she couldn't help wondering how he would respond. And now he had informed her that he intended to come and see her. His note had given her the option of changing the time of his visit, but the wording of it seemed to carry an unspoken declaration that he would not be turned away. In truth, she wanted to see him. The perspective she'd gained since little Janine had come miraculously into her life had helped her see that she very much owed Radcliffe an apology. Nevertheless, she also believed he would be extremely glad to have this baby in his home. She couldn't think about the guilt she felt in her deception; Radcliffe would believe this was the blood child of his cousin, that Dwight had left something of himself behind. And she could never tell him the truth. Gina considered how quickly she had become comfortable with the story that her friends had helped her construct, and she settled her mind firmly on keeping to that story no matter what might happen.

As soon as Gina had finished having her tea, Ruby made certain that Gina's hair was brushed, and that she was sitting comfortably in the bed with a stack of pillows behind her. Gina was glad that she'd bathed just yesterday, and that Emerald had assisted her with washing her hair. She felt more confident, knowing that she was clean and as well-groomed as possible while being confined to bed. She'd become very good at following the guidance of the sisters on how to accurately pretend that she was weak and sore from having given birth, but in facing Radcliffe for the first time in months, she didn't want to look anything but her best.

Just a few minutes before five, Elaine brought Janine to Gina and laid her in the crook of Gina's arm. The baby had been fed and had fallen asleep wearing a fresh nappy and gown, and she was wrapped up tightly in a little blanket.

"Thank you," Gina said, smiling up at Elaine who smiled in return.

"A pleasure, m'lady," Elaine said. "I am going to take Tommy on a walk outside to give him some fresh air; hopefully, allowing him to run for a while will help him be a little less rambunctious." She chuckled softly. "I hope he's not disturbed you with—"

"Not at all," Gina assured Elaine. "I've hardly heard a peep, and you mustn't worry about it. He's very well behaved, and I'm glad to have you close by, but I wouldn't want you to be without *your* child."

"You're very kind," Elaine said, and they exchanged another smile before Elaine left, promising not to be gone very long, and reassuring Gina that she would be in the sitting room with Tommy when she was needed.

Gina thanked her, then realized she was alone with her little daughter the very moment the clock across the room chimed five times. Her heart quickened but she couldn't discern whether that was the result of anticipation or dread.

She reminded herself that she had no reason to be nervous about a visit from Radcliffe—except that she had consistently avoided him for months, and now she was deceiving him about the source of this child she had brought into his home.

Gina pushed that and every other thought out of her head when she heard footsteps in the hallway, and a moment later Radcliffe appeared in the open doorway, knocking lightly on the door to alert her to his presence, even though she was already looking at him. For a long moment they simply exchanged a silent gaze. Gina felt suddenly self-conscious about the extra weight she had gained. Sitting in bed and mostly beneath the covers, only her face was visible, but she knew that it appeared far rounder than it had the last time he'd seen her. Glad to recall that he would likely attribute her changed appearance to pregnancy, she focused her attention on *him*. He too had changed. She'd never known him to wear a beard, but he was sporting one now—although the dark hair on his face was neatly trimmed and only enhanced the hardy features of his well-favored appearance. The equally dark hair on his head was a little longer, combed back from his brow and hanging nearly to the bottom of his neck. He was dressed typically in dark breeches and a crisp white shirt topped by an elegant waistcoat and contrasting cravat, which was tied perfectly around the high collar of the shirt.

Gina's already quickened heart rate increased even further, and she felt a strange fluttering in her stomach that she'd not felt since early in her marriage to Dwight. She felt immediately overcome with a strange kind of guilt that she would react to Radcliffe's appearance in such a way, but she only had to remember that she was carrying out a huge charade regarding the baby in her arms for one measure of guilt to be completely smothered by another.

"Hello, G," he said with the hint of a smile that only enhanced that inner fluttering.

"Hello, Rad," she replied with equal familiarity; they had once been very comfortable and casual with one another even though she had found him intimidating at times, and she saw no need to try and change that now, despite all the changes that had taken place in their lives.

CHAPTER THREE
lies and secrets

W HEN R ADCLIFFE REMAINED STANDING IN the doorway, Gina was struck by the obvious.

"Please . . . come in," she said, motioning with her arm toward a comfortable chair that had been kept near the bed for Gina's visitors, even if that only consisted of the three siblings and Elaine. "Sit down."

"I hope I'm not imposing," he said before making a move. "If this is not a good time to visit, I would be glad to come back when—"

"No, this is fine," she said and motioned again toward the chair with her free arm.

Radcliffe walked to the chair but didn't sit down; instead, he leaned over slightly in an obvious attempt to get a look at the baby. Gina moved the blanket back a little so that he could see Janine's face more clearly.

"Oh, she's lovely!" he said, genuinely pleased. "I daresay I can see a wee bit of Dwight in that little face."

Gina felt astonished by the comment but managed a little chuckle that suppressed her inclination to gasp. She felt certain Radcliffe was seeing something he wanted or expected to see, rather than there being any remarkable coincidence of resemblance. She considered her response carefully and said, "I have trouble seeing any resemblance to anyone; I've only come to see *her*."

Radcliffe finally sat down, crossing one leg over the other. "She's a beautiful baby. I confess that I've not seen many babies in my life, but she looks beautiful to me."

"And to me," Gina said, brushing her fingers over the baby's wispy dark hair.

"So," Radcliffe said as if the word were meant to be a grand preamble to something particularly important, "this is quite a secret you've been keeping, G. However did you manage?"

Gina felt proud of herself for the way she was able to hide any hint that she was nervous about his mention of her keeping secrets. She cleared her throat softly and simply said, "I'm sorry for that. I just haven't been myself since we lost Dwight, and . . . I didn't want anyone to know that . . ." Gina considered the next words she might say and found a way to make them less dishonest. "That . . . I had wanted a baby so badly."

"You always were a very private person," Radcliffe said as if it were a compliment. "I can understand why you might want to keep the circumstances to yourself. I'm glad that your maids are so skilled and gracious, and that you had all the help you needed during a difficult time."

"I'm glad for that too," she said. "I'm very blessed."

Radcliffe chuckled and shifted slightly in the chair as if to make himself more comfortable. "I understand it was quite the affair—giving birth in the carriage and all. I know that many consider it inappropriate for such things to be discussed between those of the opposite sex, although we are both mature adults, and I daresay I'm capable of not embarrassing you too badly." He chuckled again.

"No, you won't embarrass me," Gina said and meant it. She impulsively repeated something she'd heard Ruby say more than once, given her previous experience with midwifery. "A woman has no ability to maintain any pride or decorum when nature takes over during the birthing process

"I can well imagine that's true," he said thoughtfully, "although in truth I can't begin to imagine what a woman goes through to bring a child into the world."

Gina's silent response was that she couldn't imagine it either, but of course she couldn't even hint at any such thing. She hoped and prayed a day would come when she would forget that she hadn't given birth to this precious baby, and that thoughts of Janine's true origins wouldn't intrude upon her continually.

Following a long moment of silence, Radcliffe cleared his throat as if doing so might expel any awkwardness in their conversation. "What will you call her?" he asked.

"Janine," Gina said, looking down at the baby's sweet face, which was lost in slumber.

"That's very nice," Radcliffe said and seemed to mean it.

"Oh, look!" Gina said with delight. "She's dreaming!"

Radcliffe stood and leaned over Gina and the baby just in time to see Janine smile in a way that a baby so young would never do while awake. Radcliffe chuckled and continued to watch the baby with fascination while

Janine's breathing became more audible and she scowled in her sleep, making both adults laugh softly; she then smiled more broadly and Radcliffe asked, "What do you suppose she's dreaming about?"

"Heaven, perhaps," Gina said, having contemplated that very question many times.

"Perhaps she was with her father there," Radcliffe said and returned to his chair.

"Perhaps," was all Gina said, hating any reminder of her need to continue this complex charade in order to preserve the appearance that Janine was hers, and hers alone.

Fortunately, the awkward silence that followed was brief. Radcliffe diverted the topic by asking, "And how are you feeling, G? You look well."

"Do I?" she asked but didn't wait for him to answer. "I confess that I feel much better than I did before Janine came." She had mentally prepared herself to use words that would keep her lies to a minimum; Janine had *come* into her life, as opposed to having been born to Gina. Knowing that Radcliffe couldn't possibly look at her and not be aware of how different she looked—in contrast to the last time he'd seen her—she impulsively decided to simply address the matter rather than avoiding it and feeling embarrassed while she wondered what he might be thinking. "I'm well aware that my appearance has changed a great deal through these months since we lost Dwight." She forced out a chuckle, attempting to keep this light, even though she didn't feel any humor regarding the matter at all. "I confess that I have been eating far too much, which my maids have assured me can be common for some people when they are grieving."

"Surely an increased appetite is normal for a woman who is with child," Radcliffe said matter-of-factly.

Gina couldn't tell him that she hadn't actually *been* with child; she tried to keep to the truth as much as possible. "Perhaps," she said. "However, many women don't gain as much weight as I did. But I'm feeling much better . . . emotionally . . . and I feel ready to move on . . . for Janine's sake, if not my own." She paused, a little taken aback by how comfortable she felt talking this way with Radcliffe. Their conversations had always been easy, but then Dwight had always been a part of them; she couldn't recall if she'd ever spoken privately with Radcliffe before now. If such a thing had happened, it had never been anything personal, and this conversation was *very* personal. She hoped she wasn't saying too much, but she felt the need to clarify. "I'm looking forward to being up and about so that I can resume the habit I once had of going for long walks, which I'm sure will do me good. And I'm no longer feeling the need to eat nearly so much." Focusing again on Janine's precious little face while she slept, Gina added, "Caring for my little angel is far more gratifying than any of Mrs. Chester's cakes and biscuits."

"I'm sure you're right," Radcliffe said with a chuckle, "although one cannot deny that Mrs. Chester's cakes and biscuits are truly a delight."

"Yes," Gina let out a short laugh, "that is certainly true. Although I'm certain it would be far better for me if Mrs. Chester had put a limit on the amount of food she was sending to my room." Realizing how that sounded, she clarified, "But of course she is certainly not to blame; she only sent what I requested."

"And she didn't know you were expecting," Radcliffe said. "None of us did." He sounded disconcerted, and she realized that he was likely very unnerved over the sudden arrival of a baby in the household—and Gina couldn't blame him. Committed to keeping up the proper façade, she simply said, "Again, I'm sorry about that." Making a general statement rather than one that might sound more dishonest, she added, "I can see now how one should share the happenings of their lives with those around them—whether it be sorrow or joy. I should not have locked myself away like that."

"Losing Dwight that way was understandably difficult," Radcliffe said. "I don't believe you owe me an apology for shutting yourself away. I'm simply . . . adjusting to the fact that my cousin has left a child behind." He laughed pleasantly. "I daresay having a baby in the house will liven things up a great deal, and I think we could all use some livening up."

"I'm certain we can," Gina said and felt another layer of guilt arise unexpectedly, adding to the weight of the guilt she already felt for all her deception regarding the baby. Radcliffe's words echoed through her mind about how understandably difficult it had been for her to lose Dwight; in some ways it certainly had been—but now that some time had passed, and perhaps more specifically, now that Janine had done so much to change her perspective— she was able to see even more clearly how much she had been lying even to herself regarding the state of her marriage. Her grief over Dwight's death was complicated at the very least, mostly because there were hefty amounts of guilt and relief mingled with her sadness—one likely being the result of the other. She took a long glance at Radcliffe, wondering why she felt the sudden urge to unburden herself about the truth regarding her marriage with Dwight, but a fresh fluttering in her stomach added to her guilt and she hurried to look away, doubting she could ever tell him such things, and even if she could, now was certainly not the time.

Gina was relieved when Radcliffe spoke, once again easing the possibility of awkward tension between them. "I spoke with Mrs. Darby about the things you might need in order to care for a baby. She told me you have a cradle." He glanced toward it and smiled. "I do believe it was mine."

"Oh, how quaint!" Gina said with a small laugh.

"She also told me there is a lovely crib stored away for when the baby gets bigger, and it can be made ready before she needs it. And apparently you are well supplied with clothes and such for her."

"Until she grows," Gina said lightly, "which I understand happens very quickly."

"And you know that Dwight left plenty of money behind for you to be able to purchase whatever you need or like," Radcliffe said, his tone quite serious, "and if you ever need *anything* else," he implored even more intensely, "all you have to do is ask. I will make certain you and Janine always have everything you ever need or want."

"Thank you," was all she could think to say. The conviction of his words was so strong that it had quickened the beating of her heart. "We are both very blessed that you still consider this our home, and that you—"

"Of course it's your home!" he said as if he couldn't comprehend that she would think otherwise.

"I know, but . . ." Gina took the opportunity to say something that she'd considered a great many times, but had never discussed with him, "I know that you took Dwight in when he lost his father. And I know that his father's debts left him with very little, and—"

"Regina," he said, and she knew he intended to say something he considered extremely important because he rarely used her full given name, "Dwight *did* lose his home due to his father's debts, but he still maintained a significant fortune, and you came here with a fine dowry as well. It was not a sacrifice to invite Dwight to live in my home when it's large enough for a dozen families. And I don't have to tell you that I was always fond of his choice in a wife." He winked at her and she hoped he couldn't see the blush she felt rising on her face. "I was worried after Dwight died that you might decide to return to live with your father, and I want you to know that I'm glad you stayed, and I hope you will always consider this your home."

Gina didn't want to discuss the reasons she would never want to return to live in her father's house, and she didn't want to point out that his comment regarding always making this her home implied that she would never marry again, because if she did she would obviously move to the home of her new husband. But Gina couldn't comprehend ever wanting to commit to marriage again, especially when it had been such a tumultuous and confusing experience for her. Now that she had Janine, and she had the comfort and security of knowing that Radcliffe would always provide a home for her—and that she had plenty of money with which to support herself and her child otherwise—she felt content to think of living out her life in this place and raising her daughter with every possible safety and comfort, and also enjoying the freedom to make wise decisions and enjoy a good life.

"Thank you," Gina said again. "You're very kind."

"Not at all," he insisted. "That's just how it should be. You're family." He cleared his throat softly. "Now, back to the point I was trying to make . . . I wanted to get a gift for you . . . for the baby . . . and so I spoke with Mrs. Darby about what you might need. She informed me that a perambulator would be quite necessary, especially for someone such as yourself who enjoys long walks." He chuckled. "Silly name, I think, for something so simple as a little carriage for pushing a baby around. Nevertheless, the perambulator we have in storage—which was likely mine—is in extremely poor condition. So . . . with the assistance of an exceedingly kind shopkeeper who knows how to find just about anything, I have ordered one and it should arrive within a week. I hope it will be here by the time you feel up to getting out."

"Oh, that's a lovely gift!" Gina said with enthusiasm. "I'd not even thought about it, but of course I can't carry her everywhere I go—especially as she gets bigger." Without realizing what she was doing, she reached a hand toward him and he quickly took hold of it and squeezed gently. "Thank you, Rad! You're so very thoughtful!"

"Well, I hope you like it," he said. "I chose red. You like red, don't you?"

"You remembered!" she exclaimed with delight. "Red is indeed my favorite color. Thank you!" she said still again.

"You are most welcome," he said and surprised her by lifting her hand to his lips, keeping his eyes connected to hers while he kissed the back of her fingers.

Gina's reaction to the gesture was so intense that she feared Radcliffe might hear the pounding of her heart or the sudden and almost violent fluttering in her stomach. While she was silently acknowledging that she was indeed attracted to her husband's cousin—and the guilt that came with such an acknowledgment—she couldn't bring herself to draw her hand away, or to stop looking at him. He was slow to lift his lips from her fingers, and even slower to let go of her hand—and the very fact that she was glad for it only increased her confusion—and yes—guilt. Dwight had not been gone so many months.

According to respectable society, she should remain officially in mourning for quite some time yet; one year and one day following his death was considered minimally appropriate. Such interactions with a man before that time would be perceived as entirely improper. Both doors to her room were wide open, and she knew that either Ruby or Emerald—or both—were in the sitting room, simply because it was the decent thing to do while Gina was visiting with a man in her bedroom. But her maids had no idea of the lingering gaze taking place between Gina and Radcliffe at that moment, nor did they have any inkling of Gina's most personal feelings—both regarding the reality of her marriage to Dwight, and what she had just begun to realize about her attraction to her husband's cousin.

"Perhaps . . . " he said, looking away as if it had taken great willpower to do so, which made Gina wonder if he might be experiencing some kind of attraction to *her*; recounting all he'd said and done in the last few minutes let her know it was possible. She felt both giddy and terrified over the very idea—but mostly she felt confused. How could he look at her like this— overcome with the results of months of self-neglect and eating too much— and see a woman to whom he might feel attracted?

Gina waited for him to complete his thought, but that one word seemed to have become lost in his mind and she saw his brow crease as he looked in the direction of the windows while he was apparently trying to gather his words. He finally looked at her and said, "Perhaps I should go and let you rest." Gina couldn't think of a way to tell him that she'd like him to stay, that she was enjoying his company; any words that came to her mind sounded forward and presumptuous. She was relieved beyond all practicality when he added, "May I come back? I assume it must be tedious for you being confined to bed while you heal. And I confess I'd very much like to see this little one when she's awake."

"I would truly like that," Gina said, giving him a smile that she hoped would add conviction to what she'd said. He stood up and she added, "Thank you for coming. I very much enjoyed our visit." She wanted to tell him that she'd missed him, even though she'd not realized it until he'd come into the room not so many minutes ago. She settled for saying what she felt was more appropriate. "It's been far too long. We should not be strangers living in the same house."

"I agree wholeheartedly." He bowed slightly, then said with a smile, "May I call again tomorrow at the same time?"

Gina nodded in return. "I'll look forward to it. Thank you again for taking the time to visit."

"My pleasure entirely," he said, then bowed once more and left the room.

For more than a few minutes, Gina looked toward the door through which he'd exited, while she attempted to make sense of all she was feeling—and the reasons for it. Her thoughts went to Dwight and she wished desperately that she'd not been so secretive regarding the truth about her marriage. There had been wonderful moments with Dwight; she had some sweet and precious memories, and she sincerely believed that he had loved her. But she had also experienced a great deal of confusion from the way he had behaved toward her. He'd often been angry with her for reasons she couldn't understand, and his attitude had frequently been demeaning and insulting, despite her having made every effort to be the best possible wife to him. Her inability to conceive a child had added fuel to his disdain toward her, and she'd constantly struggled with feeling wholly inadequate and unloved. She had certainly been shocked and horrified by his untimely death, and she had sincerely grieved over his passing at such a young age. But now that Gina was coming out of the dark isolation into which she'd imprisoned herself since his death, she was beginning to see more clearly that the most dominant emotions she'd been contending with, which had kept her so bound up and stagnant, had been confusion and guilt over the fact that—more than anything—she'd been relieved over his death. She considered the very idea to be utterly terrible—that a woman would feel *relief* to lose her husband to a tragic accident. And she still felt confused over the matter, but far too ashamed of how she felt to even dare speak of it—even to her most trusted friends and confidants. And now Radcliffe had suddenly appeared in her life again, bringing with him feelings she'd never experienced before. For all that she'd felt drawn to Dwight—and he'd been perfectly charming and kind prior to their actually becoming husband and wife—she had just realized in a matter of minutes that she had never felt so alive and so keenly aware of her senses. And ironically, she'd never felt so beautiful; even when in all honesty she had never felt less attractive in her life. Yet, Radcliffe's eyes had shown an admiration that she'd *never* seen in the way Dwight had looked at her. How could that be? Had she been such a fool as to believe that what little attention Dwight had given her during their courtship had been a sufficient expression of love?

Gina finally forced her mind to the present, reminding herself that she was still a woman in mourning—at least as far as anyone would be allowed to see or know. How she might feel inside was a secret she needed to hold carefully close to her heart. She had no reason to believe that Radcliffe's kindness toward her, or even the glimpse of what she'd believed might be a kind of attraction, would ever amount to anything. She would be wise to find contentment in being able to live out her life in this beautiful home, cared for by people who loved her, and blessed with the miracles that had brought little Janine into her life. For now, nothing else mattered. And if she lived out the rest of her life just as it was, she believed she could be thoroughly content and happy.

⤙⤚

Gina chose to keep Janine's cradle in her own room, near her bed, wanting to care for the baby as much as she could on her own, even though she couldn't feed her. Despite needing to maintain the ruse that she was sore and weak from childbirth, Gina was always the one to change the baby's nappies and to dress her whenever necessary. Gina insisted that Elaine sit near the bed while she fed the baby, and Gina enjoyed visiting with Elaine and getting to know her better, even during the times when Janine wanted to be fed every couple of hours during the night. But Gina stayed awake during those nighttime feedings, and once Janine was full, Elaine would turn the baby back over to Gina, who would hold Janine against her shoulder and pat her little back until little bubbles of air would come out of her in a way that always made Gina chuckle. Elaine had taught Gina that this was necessary for babies, and as always, Gina was grateful for Elaine's experience and wisdom. Janine would go back to sleep only after this had occurred, and as grateful as Gina was for Elaine's very necessary help, she was equally grateful to be the one who could hold her baby until she slept. Even though the many interruptions to her own sleep were challenging, Gina was able to nap during the daytime hours when the baby did, and she had made certain that Elaine's son was taken care of elsewhere each afternoon so that Elaine could also nap in order to keep up her own strength.

Overall, Gina had slept better since Janine had come into her life. Despite having to sleep in brief intervals in order to care for the baby, when she *did* sleep, she was able to do so more deeply, and she woke up with a better sense of rest than she'd experienced since Dwight's death. She believed that Janine's presence in her life had given her a great measure of peace and fulfillment that had been absent before, but she also believed that she was beginning to acknowledge feelings that had been causing her a great deal of confusion. Even though she had a great deal to sort out, she could see now that she'd been putting considerable effort into trying to push away feelings that needed to be examined thoughtfully, and it seemed that simply acknowledging that fact had already helped her feel more at peace.

The night following Radcliffe's visit, Gina came awake suddenly from a deep sleep, and it took her a long moment to realize that she'd not been awakened by the baby. In fact, she could hear Janine's even breathing, since the cradle was right next to her bed. Through another long moment, she assessed that her own breathing was shallow, and she was sweating even though the room was mildly chilly; the heavy rain sliding down the windows had eliminated any excess warmth of summer.

Assured that all was well, and soothed by the close presence of her baby and the coziness and security of her surroundings that protected her from the storm outside, Gina forced herself to relax and catch her breath while she willed her mind to recall what she'd been dreaming that had been so upsetting. It took some effort to remember, and when she did, her heart began to pound, and her breathing became even shallower as it became difficult to even fill her lungs with air.

"Heaven help me!" Gina muttered into the darkness as a very real fear settled into her. She'd dreamt that she'd been running in the dark through strange, unfamiliar woods, dodging back and forth to keep from colliding with the trees. Janine was in her arms, held tightly against her, crying fiercely, the way she would cry when she was hungry and not getting fed as quickly as she would like. But Gina felt such a strong sense of danger, as if the sound of the baby's cries made it impossible to hide from whatever or whomever was chasing her. She couldn't recall any other images from her dream, but she remembered well the feeling that had seemed to smother her: someone knew the truth, that Janine was not her child, and they were determined to make the truth known, see Gina undone, and take Janine away from her.

Gina forced herself to take long, even breaths while she reviewed all that had come together in a miraculous way to make it possible for her to have this beautiful little girl and raise her in an atmosphere of abundant love and comfort. Janine had been abandoned; the note left with the baby had been a plea for someone to care for her and love her, and that's what Gina was doing. She had no logical reason whatsoever to think that anyone would ever discover the truth, or that it would ever be a problem. Already the household and the village were aware of Gina supposedly having given birth to a daughter, and it had been well established and accepted as a fact. Beyond Gina's closest friends who had aided her in this deception, there was only one other person who knew the truth—and that was the woman who had given birth to a baby and left her in an alley—assuming that she had given birth without any assistance, and that no one had known of her pregnancy. Abandoning a baby certainly implied that to be the case, although Gina couldn't know for certain. She felt confident that the mother wouldn't want either her identity or her grievous act of leaving a baby that way to be revealed, due to the potential consequences that might ensue. But despite all of Gina's speculations regarding the circumstances of Janine's birth, she had no idea as to what had really happened and why, and she could never be certain that the truth wouldn't be discovered. Janine's real mother could very well have guessed that her child was the same one that had suddenly appeared at Stonebridge Manor on the very day she'd abandoned her baby, hoping she would be found and cared for. But did that possibility serve Gina well, or could it eventually cause her trouble? Gina was already so deeply steeped in the lie that she'd given birth to Janine that she could never undo what had been done. If she were discovered, the results would be disastrous. No one would ever trust her again, and Radcliffe would likely see her thrown out of his house. She had money of her own that would serve her well, but she had no desire to have to rely entirely on her own resources, and to live elsewhere without the security of this home where she'd grown to feel so safe and comfortable. Still, for all the uncertainties, Gina could do absolutely nothing to change the situation. She could only move forward with a prayer in her heart that she and her baby would remain safe and secure, and that their secret would never come to light.

While Gina tried to calm herself with thinking only of the positive aspects of the situation, Janine began to stir, making comical grunting noises that always preceded her coming fully awake and working herself into a state of crying loudly to demand being fed. Her cries always brought Elaine from across the hall so quickly that it seemed Elaine had some special ability to perceive Janine's need to be fed, so much so that she was always fully awake even before Janine reached the point of crying loudly. And yet Elaine had told Gina many times that she always slept well between the baby's feedings, which was surely due to the absolute exhaustion of assisting in the care of an infant throughout the nights.

Gina was glad for Elaine's company and the normalcy of the routine they'd developed, which helped immensely in pushing away the horror of her nightmare. After Elaine had gone back to bed and Gina had gotten Janine back to sleep and placed gently in her cradle, she felt hesitant to go back to sleep, not wanting to experience such horrible fear again. In her heart she knew the source of such a dream was surely the guilt she felt for all her deception regarding Janine, and surely there *was* a fear inside of her that the truth would be discovered, and not only would Janine be taken away from her, but every facet of her life could be adversely affected due to the exposure of her deep-seated deceit.

Despite her own resistance, Gina drifted quickly to sleep; her body's need for rest was clearly stronger than her fear of being assaulted with bad dreams. When Janine woke again to be fed, the room was becoming light with day, and Gina was pleased to note that she'd had no dreams at all. She quickly talked herself into enjoying the day before her, even though it was still raining outside. But she was safe and warm and dry here with her precious little daughter and every possible comfort and luxury. She also had Radcliffe's visit to look forward to, although she had to put a great deal of effort into suppressing her heightening enthusiasm. The guilt and confusion she felt were overwhelming regarding her feelings for Dwight, in contrast to what was coming to life inside of her with respect to Radcliffe. But there was nothing to be done about that. For the time being she was still considered a widow in mourning and recovering from childbirth. She would simply enjoy Radcliffe's visits for what they would appear to be to everyone else in the household—he was a friend and a cousin to her baby's father.

The day went well, and Gina enjoyed the way that Janine spent some time awake on the bed beside her without fussing. Her eyes were open more widely than they'd ever been before, and she seemed to just be looking around and taking in this world into which she'd been born. Gina was continually fascinated with her infant daughter and felt as if she could spend every waking minute just watching her and falling more in love with her hour by hour.

After remaining awake longer than usual, Janine took a longer-than-usual nap, which made it possible for Gina to do the same. She had a glimpse of the terrible dream she'd endured the previous night, but she'd come awake with a gasp before it had gone on for too long. Then she fell back to sleep quickly and didn't dream again before Janine woke up only minutes before tea was brought to Gina's room. She and Elaine shared tea while they visited and cared for the baby. Elaine watched over the baby while Ruby helped Gina feel presentable for Sir Radcliffe's visit, then left Janine on the bed at Gina's side, clean and fed and content, once again taking in her surroundings while she sporadically moved her little arms and legs.

Gina was completely lost in her fascination with her daughter when a quiet knocking startled her and she looked up to see Radcliffe standing in the frame of the open doorway, looking perhaps even more dashing than he had the previous day. The green paisley waistcoat he wore enhanced the matching color of his eyes, and Gina's heart quickened against her will, which prompted an unexpected tingling from head to toe. She fought to keep her expression from revealing her reaction to seeing him, and simply smiled as she said, "Do come in and sit down. Janine is awake and rather entertaining—at least *I* find her entertaining."

Radcliffe smiled, his eyes filled with curiosity, and he slid the chair as close to the bed as it would go before he sat down and leaned over so he could see Janine up close, resting his forearms on his thighs so that he could observe her comfortably. "Oh, look at those beautiful eyes!" he said, genuinely intrigued.

"Indeed," Gina said.

"I do believe she has her father's eyes," he added, and Gina pushed away the guilt that was never far away, always threatening to devour her.

"Perhaps," Gina said, trying to sound nonchalant. Perhaps she *did* have her father's eyes; there was no way of knowing for certain. Gina suspected this child's father was likely a scoundrel, given that her mother had been left in a position where she'd had no choice but to leave her baby abandoned in an alley.

"She's so tiny that it's almost difficult to believe she's real."

"I've thought the same thing many times," Gina said, loving the sincere interest Radcliffe exhibited toward the baby.

Gina was surprised when Radcliffe suddenly turned his eyes toward *her*, asking with sincere caring in his voice as well as his expression, "And how are you feeling, my dear?"

My dear? Gina's mind echoed silently. She checked herself against making anything out of the words, recalling that he'd referred to her that way more than once in the past. Through the entire course of courting Dwight, and living here as his wife, Radcliffe had always been kind and had treated her as family. Reminding herself to not allow her own silly feelings to distort the reality of their relationship, she simply said, "I'm able to get up and about a little more every day."

"I'm very glad to hear it," Radcliffe said, once again showing his remarkable smile. "I understand that you've relied entirely on your maids for your care—including that of your health throughout this experience. I will honor your wishes, G, but I must ask if you are absolutely certain you don't want me to summon a doctor to make certain all is well after such an ordeal?"

"You're very kind," Gina said without even needing to think about her response, "but I have complete faith in the skill and knowledge of my maids, and truthfully I don't feel comfortable with the doctor. I can assure you that if for any reason I believed there was a problem beyond the expertise Ruby and Emerald possess, I would see that you're informed."

"Fair enough," he said and sighed, still looking at her. "I confess that I find the doctor rather stodgy; his arrogance certainly snuffs out his ability to show any warmth or compassion toward his patients. He *does* have a great deal of skill and knowledge, but I've learned to only call upon him when absolutely necessary, and thankfully that's only happened a few times since such decisions became my responsibility."

"Have there been illnesses in the house I've been unaware of?" Gina asked.

"One minor case of pneumonia, and a couple of injuries," he said, "all among the servants, and all with excellent outcomes."

"I'm very pleased to hear it," Gina said, glad to know that despite the local doctor being exactly the opposite of kind and personable, he was at least competent. There was always the chance of being faced with illness or accidents; they were a natural part of life. And she was glad to know—especially now that she had a child to care for—that good medical care was available. But given the intimate nature of childbirth—even if she had only been *pretending* in that regard—she would far prefer to be cared for by such kind and tender women as Ruby and Emerald.

The remainder of Radcliffe's visit was filled with their mutual admiration of little Janine, some trivial conversation about simple goings on among members of the staff, and a couple of recent social events, which Radcliffe had chosen *not* to attend.

In response to his vehemence on that matter, Gina asked, "Would you not wish to socialize with—"

He interrupted sourly, "With people who hold no interest for me whatsoever?" He made a scoffing sound. "There is no one who would attend such functions with whom I am not already well acquainted. The gentlemen are all shallow thinkers and boorish at times, if not downright vulgar; their company is intolerable, and certainly not a place where I would ever find a friend. The ladies are simple-minded and have nothing to discuss amongst themselves beyond acquiring the latest fashions and catching themselves wealthy husbands. Any attempt I've made to converse with such ladies has been worse than trite and utterly meaningless. No, G. I will not be attending any such events." He smiled toward Janine whose eyes were turned in his direction, but she was still so tiny that she didn't appear to actually be able to focus on anything she might be looking at. "I would far rather spend my time with this little lady." He chuckled and put his smallest finger against the baby's hand; she immediately grabbed onto it, which made him laugh with perfect delight. "I daresay she likes me."

"I'm certain of it," Gina said, wanting very much to continue the conversation about his attitudes on socializing. Certainly, she was curious; but she also couldn't deny some measure of relief to think that he would rather be spending time with her and Janine than be out looking for a wife among the most elegant and wealthy ladies in the county.

"May I ask you something?" she ventured to say. "If you consider it too personal a question . . . you surely don't need to answer."

"You may ask me anything you like," he said as if the idea pleased him very much, then he added with a wink and a smile, "although I reserve the right to maintain silence."

"As you should," she said and took a deep breath, hoping she would not come across as presumptuous or nosy. "I was only thinking that . . . with what you just said about your feelings over the socializing in the area . . . you must be very lonely."

Gina saw something pass through his eyes that was so dark and heavy she almost felt afraid. Only then did she recall that Dwight had once—and only once—made mention of a betrothal in Radcliffe's past that had fallen apart in a way that had been deemed rather scandalous by the community. Gina knew absolutely nothing else, and she certainly didn't feel as if it were her place to ask for clarification about such a topic, at least given the current nature of their relationship. She found herself hoping that the nature of their relationship might eventually become such that she *could* ask more personal questions, then she forced the very idea away, certain that it was either ludicrous or at the very least not the right time for her to even be entertaining such thoughts.

"At times," he said, not sounding at all irritated to be answering her question, although she felt certain he would avoid even mentioning the secretive incident from his past that had surely contributed largely to his loneliness. "I'm not opposed to being alone; in fact, I far prefer that to being in the company of people who are pretentious and self-absorbed. The estate keeps me busy, and as you know, I enjoy riding and taking long walks, and I also enjoy taking advantage of the many beautiful rooms in this house."

"Of course," Gina said, recalling how Radcliffe had never seemed to prefer one particular room over another, but rather held to an attitude that many lovely rooms should be equally used and enjoyed. Gina recalled that without the assistance of a servant, she and Dwight had often had difficulty knowing where to find him, and where tea might be served on any given day. Gina had enjoyed the unpredictability and adventure of the matter, silly as it might be; Dwight had only complained and spoken ill of his cousin, but never to Radcliffe's face.

As silence took over, they exchanged a warm smile and a long gaze; just warm enough and long enough for Gina to believe that he truly might be feeling some measure of attraction toward her. Even while it was difficult to imagine such a thing being possible, the evidence before her was undeniable. The very fact that she wanted such to be the case made her want to disregard the possibility; she'd had too many disappointments to dare hope too deeply that something good and wonderful might come into her life. She looked toward Janine and scolded herself for such a thought when this baby was such a miracle—as long as she ignored her nagging guilt over the fact that Janine's young life was already surrounded by lies. And Gina wasn't certain she would ever be free of the fear of being found out.

CHAPTER FOUR
the new maid

OVER THE COURSE OF THE following two weeks, Gina was up and about more, taking the opportunity to walk vigorously within the confines of her rooms in order to build up the strength she had lost through months of being so idle. She found it an interesting contrast that she'd spent so much time not wanting to leave the security of her rooms, and now she felt terribly anxious to get outside and enjoy the summer weather and also to take Janine out with her, certain that fresh air on a warm, sunny day would be good for the baby—and Emerald and Ruby agreed.

Whenever any other servants came to Gina's rooms to deliver tea or meals or for any other purpose, she made certain that she was sitting in bed or in a nearby chair as a woman recovering from childbirth should be doing. She was grateful for the guidance of Ruby and Emerald regarding what would be considered the normal time of recovery, and how she should go about the proper pretenses in order to continue her ongoing façade in making everyone believe that Janine was her natural daughter.

Radcliffe continued to visit every day, and their conversations became gradually more comfortable, even though they didn't talk about anything too personal or deep. He seemed both thrilled and terrified when Gina suggested he hold the baby, but after he'd done so once, he wanted to hold Janine each time he came. When Gina had passed the point where a woman would naturally be up and about more, she began to receive Radcliffe's visits in her sitting room, where she wore a dressing gown over her nightgown, mostly because she only had a couple of dresses she could fit into. Nevertheless, Gina could already feel herself becoming slimmer. Now that she'd taken to eating a great deal less, and she'd spent a significant amount of time each day engaged in vigorous walking—even if that was only circling around the rooms in which she lived—she could already feel a difference and believed that she would be able to get back into her old clothes before long. She had a lovely variety of dresses hanging in her wardrobe, and Ruby and Emerald had helped her assess that some of them might fit her, considering the fulness she'd already lost, and given their gathered skirts and high waistlines. With a few minor alterations, Gina knew she had clothes she could wear outside of her rooms, and she could see in the mirror that her face was slimming down to the features that were more familiar and attractive.

The day the perambulator arrived, Radcliffe was so excited for Gina to see it that he carried it all the way up the stairs, declaring after he'd breathlessly set it down in front of her that it was more awkward than heavy.

"Oh, it's beautiful!" Gina exclaimed, delightfully examining the comfortable spaciousness for a baby to lie down—or sit up once they'd gained that ability. And there was a hood that could be folded up to cover half of the carriage, or folded down to be out of the way, depending on whether the baby needed protection from the sun. There was also a wide handle with which to push the contraption, and large wheels that greatly resembled those of a horse-drawn coach. For this reason, Radcliffe determined they should call it *the coach*, since he still insisted that the name *perambulator* was a bit ridiculous and far too cumbersome for an apparatus that was designed for a baby's comfort and a mother's convenience.

Gina found *the apparatus*—as Radcliffe had called it—to be completely clever, but also beautiful. The red fabric that entirely covered the outside looked like something that would be used for a very fine and elegant sofa, and the edges were adorned with narrow lengths of cream-colored lace, which added a feminine appearance that Gina believed suited her little Janine perfectly.

"Now that you've seen it," Radcliffe said, his hands on his hips while he admired his generous gift, "I'll take it back down the stairs and leave it near the side door where you can take it easily into the gardens."

"That would be lovely when we're ready to venture out," Gina said, "although I think I'd like to keep it here in the meantime. I rather like being able to look at it, and perhaps I can help her become accustomed to sleeping in it."

"Excellent plan," Radcliffe said and plopped down comfortably into a chair. He'd become noticeably comfortable with his visits, and Gina was glad for it. She enjoyed his company far more than she wanted to admit. She was glad for his attention, his winks and smiles, and his occasional long gazes, which always quickened her heart and made her skin tingle. But she still couldn't be certain that his attention meant anything more than simply his fondness toward the widow and child of his deceased cousin, or perhaps his desire for a friendship that didn't require socializing with people he disliked. While Gina became more and more aware of her own attraction to Radcliffe each time he came to visit, she became less and less certain that *his* feelings toward her were rooted in anything more than a simple desire for friendship and company. Still, Gina enjoyed his visits and remained appreciative of them; even if they only and forever simply remained as friends, she was glad to have such a friend and to know that he would always see that she and Janine were cared for and had a good life. As long as she didn't think about the possibility of Radcliffe finding out the truth about Janine's true origins—and the tangled web of lies that had been constructed to hide the truth—she believed she could live out the remainder of her life just as it was and be happy and content.

On the day that Janine turned one month old, Gina was able to fit into one of her favorite day dresses, and she actually felt pretty as she studied her reflection in the mirror while Ruby styled her hair. Most of the excessive weight had left her face, and she looked more like the woman she'd been before Dwight's death—although she felt freer and happier than she'd been throughout the course of their marriage.

Since Radcliffe had known the previous day that she planned to finally leave the house with Janine—provided the weather cooperated—he had carried *the coach* down the stairs where it would be waiting for her to use. Gina had decided to take her first excursion on this one-month anniversary of her baby's birth, since Ruby and Emerald both believed it was a normal amount of time for a woman to recover and be out and about. She had been thrilled to come awake after three nighttime feedings and find the room filled with brilliant sunlight, especially since there had been a great deal of rain during the past week. Rather than wearing little slippers, she chose to wear short boots that laced up over her ankles since the ground was likely wet. But given that it was the middle of summer and the sun was out, the day would be delightfully warm; perfect for Janine's first excursion outdoors.

Once Gina was all ready and Janine had been bathed and dressed and fed, Gina resisted the proffered assistance of the women who helped care for her and the baby, and she went down the stairs holding Janine in her arms. Being outside of her rooms already felt delightful, but she couldn't hold back a small laugh when she found Janine's little coach waiting near the doors that led out to an enormous patio, which stretched toward the elaborate and well-groomed gardens that were a fine asset to Stonebridge Manor. She was easing the baby into the coach when she heard footsteps on the tiled floor of the hallway and looked up to see Radcliffe approaching. As always, his appearance took her breath away, but she forced herself to breathe evenly as she smiled at him, hoping that his being here might mean what she wanted it to mean.

"I confess," he said lightly without offering any kind of greeting, "that I pressed the servants for gossip about exactly when you might be going out, hoping that I might accost you and convince you to allow me to venture out with you. However, I completely understand if you prefer to be alone, and I will leave you in peace to—"

"I would very much enjoy your company," she said.

Radcliffe smiled, bowed slightly, and held the door open while she pushed Janine outside in her grand mode of transportation. Gina paused once she had gone past the patio and the shade of the house and emerged into the sunlight. She closed her eyes, lifted her face skyward, and took in a deep breath of fresh air. "It's been far too long," she said.

"Indeed," Radcliffe replied, and before she had her eyes open, she felt him replace her hands with his so that he could push Janine. He began to walk, and she walked beside him at a slow pace, as if they shared the desire to take their time and enjoy this outing.

They walked in silence for more than a few minutes before Radcliffe said, "May I ask you a somewhat personal question, G? You certainly have the option not to answer."

"Of course," she said; short of anything to do with her deception regarding Janine, she couldn't think of anything she wasn't willing to discuss with him.

"Do you still miss Dwight terribly?" he asked, his tone of voice sounding as if her answer was particularly important to him.

Gina resisted the urge to search his face for evidence as to the motive behind his question. She just kept walking, glad that Janine was sleeping soundly, and pondered her answer for a long moment before saying truthfully, "My relationship with Dwight was at the very least . . . complicated; therefore, my grieving over his death has been the same."

Gina felt Radcliffe looking toward her, and she sensed his surprise, even though she continued to force herself to only look straight ahead, perhaps not wanting him to see the confusion in her eyes. What she'd just said was already treading into feelings she'd never shared with anyone. But she trusted Radcliffe, and she'd longed to be able to speak with someone about the true nature of her marriage to Dwight. She only hoped she wouldn't regret being so forthright about it with Radcliffe; perhaps he would not take kindly to anything that might paint his cousin in anything but a favorable light.

"That . . . certainly makes me more curious," Radcliffe said. "I wanted to believe the two of you were happy together . . . except . . ."

"Except?" Gina pressed, now looking at him boldly as she desperately wanted to know what he apparently wanted to say, but at the same time feeling hesitant. "Please tell me. I always thought that no one else could have ever seen the . . . challenges; if you *did* notice something, I think it might help me feel a little less . . . confused."

"Well," Radcliffe drawled as if stretching out the word might give him more time to consider his words carefully, "there were simply moments when . . ." he cleared his throat gently, as if that too might help him come up with the most appropriate way to express something that was clearly uncomfortable. Gina's heartbeat quickened over the very possibility that someone else had noticed Dwight's less-than-congenial attitude toward her; but perhaps she was getting ahead of herself. She reminded herself to be patient and hear what Radcliffe had to say before coming to any conclusions. "Well," he said again, "if I'm to be entirely honest, and you should know I firmly believe in absolute honesty, there were times—a great many times, in truth—when I did not at all like the way he spoke to you. I was quite astonished—not only that a man would address his wife in such a way—but that he would do so in such a casual manner in front of other people, almost as if he *wanted* people to know he treated his wife badly; or perhaps he was completely unaware of how . . . *atrociously* . . . he was behaving." He paused then added, "Forgive me if that sounded too critical of him . . . or too presumptuous; that was simply my observation."

Gina took a few steps while Radcliffe's words settled into her, then she suddenly felt a little light-headed and was grateful to see a bench nearby, which she immediately took advantage of and sat down, never more glad than now to know that a great many benches were scattered throughout the enormous gardens so that those enjoying strolls here might have a place to sit and relax wherever and whenever they might decide to do so.

"Are you all right?" Radcliffe asked, following her. He situated Janine's little coach next to the bench and sat beside Gina, sounding concerned enough to believe that she might be on the brink of death. "Did I speak out of line, G? Have I upset you?"

"Not at all," she managed to say while her mind whirled like a cyclone with a thousand thoughts and memories of her experiences with Dwight, most of which had been confusing and had often left her feeling unloved and unworthy of anything good in her life and perhaps even less than sane at times. But she had no idea where to begin to express such thoughts to Radcliffe,

despite how forthright he had just been about his observations of Dwight—
which had been surprisingly accurate.

If only to break the ensuing silence, Gina finally managed to say, "It's just
that . . . I've never spoken to anyone at all about how difficult it was to be married
to him, and . . ." She hesitated and looked up at Radcliffe to see genuine concern
in his eyes, his brow furrowed with something akin to anger; she suspected his
anger was aimed at Dwight, although she couldn't be certain. It took a great deal
of courage for her to take a deep breath and go on, not certain how he would
respond. "I suppose realizing that you observed things between us that . . . I
had falsely believed no one would have seen . . . is somehow . . ." She hesitated
while keeping a close eye on his expression, sensitive to any indication that
this conversation might be making him uncomfortable; or worse, that it might
incite him to believe that their growing friendship was not such a good idea. "I
sincerely don't know how to describe what I'm feeling, Rad, other than to say
that . . . I'm overcome . . . confused . . . but I've felt that way to some degree
ever since Dwight's death. No," she corrected, looking at the green grass on the
ground in front of her, "since our marriage. He changed dramatically after the
marriage, as if he'd been playing a part in order to win my affection, and once we
had exchanged our vows, he no longer needed to pretend. At times he was truly
kind, and those were the times I held onto, with the belief that this part of him
would become more prominent. Unfortunately, the opposite occurred. With
time, he only became more distant from me, more impatient, more . . . unkind.
And he would often say things that left me so . . . confused; I often wondered
if I was going mad, if there was something wrong with me because I couldn't
make sense of what he said . . . and the way he could somehow always manage
to make every little thing that made him unhappy seem like my fault. He even
went so far as to behave as if I were actually concocting schemes to destroy his
happiness, and he would purposely blame me for the most ridiculous things,
and . . ." Gina stopped when she realized she was surely saying far too much.

"Go on," Radcliffe encouraged.

But Gina was quick to reply, "I've already said a great many things that
are surely better left unsaid. Forgive me. I'm certain it's best for both of us to
remember the good in Dwight and to honor his memory."

Gina heard Radcliffe clear his throat and prepared herself for a gentle
reproof concerning her attitudes about his cousin; Dwight certainly never would
have approved of her speaking so boldly about *anything*. She found it ironic
that he'd never had any difficulty demeaning *her* character, and he'd certainly
never defended her when other people in social situations might have uttered

disparaging remarks aimed at her. She steeled herself to be assaulted by words from Radcliffe that would be difficult to hear and digest, but she had become rather good at doing just that. She could deal with her disappointment later.

"My dear G," he said in a voice that was so surprisingly tender it drew Gina's eyes toward him, "I do not believe for a moment that death somehow magically erases all of the less-than-favorable characteristics of any human being. Of course, no one of any character is going to speak ill of the dead publicly, and funerals always seem to be brimming with tributes to a person's glowing and admirable qualities, even if that person was mostly deplorable in life. However," he actually held up a finger as if to make his point very clear, "I believe it is extremely important—if not mandatory—for those who were closest to the deceased, for those who knew them best, to be honest with themselves about the reality of that person's character." He sighed deeply and looked away, although he seemed to be looking at nothing in particular. "I confess that what you've said very accurately describes how I felt following my mother's death. I was an adult when she died, but only just, and I was faced with a great deal of confusion as I heard everyone around me speaking of her as if she were saintly and practically perfect, when my personal experiences with my mother had always been tainted by her disdain and disapproval." He looked again at Gina. "She said terrible things to me, Gina, and she always made it clear that she'd been glad to have nannies and governesses to care for me because she wanted as little to do with me as possible."

Gina couldn't keep herself from gasping. "That's terrible!"

"It *was* terrible," Radcliffe said matter-of-factly. "I was blessed to have a father who was much more tender and compassionate, and he was also a man of integrity and good common sense. I look back now and realize that he went to a great deal of effort to shield me from my mother's difficult nature, and to speak to me about the disparaging things she'd said to me to help me understand that her attitudes were rooted in her own internal issues, which had nothing to do with me." He chuckled wryly, with no sign of humor. "I shudder to think what kind of man I might have become without his intervention. But I suppose," he sighed and looked again at Gina, "that my experiences in coming to terms with my mother's ill-treatment have made me more sensitive to the same kinds of behavior in others—and I saw it far too clearly in Dwight. I was concerned for you, G, even before the two of you were married. I didn't consider it my place to intervene in any way, although there were many times as I observed the way he treated you that I wished I had."

Gina was so overcome with his kind explanations and perfect compassion that she couldn't get a sound out of her throat and was relieved when he went on. "I've wanted to have this conversation with you ever since Dwight died, but . . ."

"But I had made myself quite unavailable," she stated, wishing now that such had not been the case; she likely could have spared herself a great deal of grief and confusion if, a long time ago she'd heard what Radcliffe was now saying.

"Yes," Radcliffe said with understanding in his tone, "but I was also confident that with time you would come to terms with his death enough to talk about it . . . and given the friendship—however marginal it may have been—that we've shared since the day we met, I was also confident that we *could* eventually have this conversation. I know that the things I've said may likely take some time to settle in for you, and that's all right. We need never speak of it again if you choose, although I believe it's far better to speak of our difficult emotions to someone we can trust rather than holding them inside. And I hope you know that you can trust me to keep any confidence, and that I am here should you ever feel the need to talk through all that's happened and how it's affected you."

"Thank you," she said. "You are truly kind, Rad; you always have been. And I *do* trust you."

"I'm very glad to hear it," he said, sounding pleased. "There is one more thing I would very much like to say while we are on the topic, and then we can put the matter to rest for now. I've thought about my situation a great deal; I suppose my efforts to overcome my mother's ill-treatment gave me a strong desire to understand why she would have behaved that way. I tried to speak with every one of my living relatives—some of whom have since passed—about the situation, and most of them were surprisingly cooperative. I pieced together the fact that Dwight's mother and my mother were very similar in their behavior, and I believe she treated him rather badly, although Dwight was not fortunate enough to have a father who possessed the strength of character or power of insight enough to compensate—as my father did. That might explain why Dwight behaved the way he did, which is something we could discuss further after you've had some time to think about it; I know I'm spewing a great deal of information, which is surely overwhelming. But to conclude my point . . . I wondered why both my mother and Dwight's mother would be so much alike when they were not related in any way. And then I discovered through conversations with my father, and some aunts and uncles, that my grandmother—the mother of my father *and* Dwight's father was very much like the women they had married. I do not begin to understand the reasons behind such human behavior, G, but I can't help but find it fascinating that two men who were raised by a very difficult mother both gravitated toward marrying women who had personalities similar to their mother—and I'm absolutely certain they were not consciously aware of any such connection when they were seeking out a wife. In my father's case, he made every effort to counteract the impact of his mother *and* his wife, but in the case of Dwight's father, I believe he only succumbed to it and allowed himself to be controlled by it—and so Dwight came into adulthood—and marriage—entirely unaware of how his own behavior had been negatively impacted by the influence under which he'd been raised. It might sound strange, but . . . well . . . forgive me for being so terribly analytical about all of this, but it just seems to be the way I am . . . and . . . I think somehow that Dwight may have been unkind to you because he'd been so deeply hurt by his mother, but he never could have stood up to her—and so you unwittingly became some kind of . . ."

When he hesitated to find the right word, Gina provided a word that she'd often silently used to refer to herself regarding how her husband had treated her. "Scapegoat?" she suggested, then explained. "I believe you might be correct, Rad. I always felt as if I were being punished for things that had nothing to do with me . . . as if he brought an enormous amount of resentment and unhappiness into the marriage with him, and I had somehow become his . . ."

"Scapegoat," Radcliffe said while she was trying to think of a different word to describe how she'd felt; but that was certainly the most accurate description.

Gina looked at Radcliffe and said what she believed needed to be voiced after everything he'd told her. "Thank you . . . for being so candid with me about your thoughts and observations. I very much like the fact that you are so insightful about many things. I recall you and I sharing many analytical conversations while Dwight simply read the newspaper or just ignored us. It seemed he never had any interest in analyzing anything." She sighed and went on. "You have given me a great deal to think about, and I confess that it is somewhat overwhelming . . . but not in a bad way by any means. I want to heal . . . to feel better about myself . . . to be . . . happy. Your insights have been helpful, Rad. Thank you for making the effort to share them with me. I'm grateful."

"I'm glad," he said with one of his heart-stopping smiles. More lightly he added, "And I'm *especially* glad that you still want to be my friend after I just rambled on and on in some crazy attempt to summarize months—if not years—of thoughts and ideas into a brief conversation."

"I daresay I would go mad without your friendship," Gina said, resisting the temptation to admit that she would far prefer their relationship held the possibility of becoming something far beyond friends. "And nothing you said sounded remotely crazy. If *you* are crazy, then I am surely mad beyond any hope." This made him laugh and she laughed with him.

Their conversation seemed finished, and Radcliffe peeked beneath the hood that shaded the baby before he whispered, "She's sleeping . . . well . . . like a baby." He eased away from Janine so as not to disturb her before he chuckled. "She seems to enjoy being outdoors."

"I daresay she is oblivious," Gina said. "Sometimes it can be difficult to get her to go to sleep, but once she does, she can sleep practically anywhere, and nothing seems to disturb her. Ruby and Emerald tell me that won't last; they say most children become overly sensitive to noise when sleeping; therefore, I should enjoy this stage while it lasts." Gina sighed and looked around. "However, *I* am very *much* enjoying being outdoors. It's been far too long. I should not have shut myself away from the world like that. I suppose I was so lost in my own . . . complicated emotions that I didn't feel capable of going beyond my rooms, but I wish now that I had."

"There's no need to regret the past, my dear," Radcliffe said.

"I'm certain you're right, but I daresay I can learn from it. We should all strive to learn from the past, don't you think?"

"I wholeheartedly agree."

"Then I vow to never do anything so foolish again."

"I will hold you to that, G," he said with a small laugh, and she liked the implication that they would be involved in each other's lives enough in the future to be able to hold each other to keeping their promises.

Together they strolled a while longer, talking of trivial things, until they came to the little stone bridge that crossed a wide stream, which wound its way through the gardens. The bridge was lovely and quaint, and barely wide enough for Gina and Radcliffe to walk over it side by side as he skillfully kept Janine's little coach in front of them. Suddenly, Gina felt compelled to stop in the middle and look down over the railing to the water running beneath the bridge.

"I'd actually forgotten this was here," she said. "I love this bridge! I can't say why exactly, but I've stood here a great deal just contemplating life, I suppose."

"I've done the same," Radcliffe admitted. "Perhaps it's the sound of the running water that has a soothing effect."

"Yes," Gina agreed, "and it's occurred to me that perhaps bridges have a metaphorical meaning in our lives. Are we not crossing bridges of one kind or another all the time?"

"I'd never thought of that," Radcliffe said, sounding intrigued, "but I do believe you're right. Whatever the reasons, this bridge is a fine addition to the gardens; the finest perhaps."

"It is indeed," Gina agreed, then shared another thought she'd had frequently. "Given that the bridge is constructed from stone and has clearly been here a long time, do you suppose the house was named after the bridge, or the bridge was built to complement the name of the house?"

"That is a very good question, G," he said with a little chuckle, "and I have absolutely no idea. Both have been here for generations, so I doubt we'll ever know. I would say that the bridge *and* the house are equally splendid, and I'm grateful to be able to live here and enjoy them."

"I too am grateful for that," Gina said, and they stood there for a minute or two in silence, just listening to the water as it slid beneath the bridge and moved on to some unknown destination.

Janine began making her silly grunting noises, which implied she would soon be awake and in need of nourishment. Gina had no trouble saying to Radcliffe, "She'll be needing the wet nurse very soon. We should hurry back."

"Of course," Radcliffe said, and they returned to the house. Radcliffe offered to carry the baby up the stairs, which Gina appreciated since she was still a bit out of shape and tended to get out of breath easily. And Janine was wholeheartedly fussing now, which meant she was doing a great deal of wiggling.

At the door to Gina's bedroom, Radcliffe eased the baby into her arms, thanked Gina for a delightful excursion, and quickly asked if she would join him for tea in the summer parlor.

"I would love to," she said, thrilled with the invitation—not only because it meant spending more time with Radcliffe, but it also implied that he wanted to spend more time with her. She knew that Elaine and the sisters would take good care of Janine while she spent an hour away. "I will see you then. Thank you for a lovely outing."

"The pleasure is all mine," he said, bowing slightly before he hurried away.

Gina wanted to watch him as he left, but Janine was now demanding to be fed. She entered her bedroom to find Elaine there waiting, and Janine was quickly satisfied by being given what she needed.

Gina went about her normal routine while she counted the hours and minutes until tea, all the while reviewing in her mind what Radcliffe had said earlier regarding his observations of Dwight and the possible reasons for his behavior. She felt very much drawn to Radcliffe's tendency to think deeply. She found herself comforted and perhaps even validated by the things he'd said, and she had a desire to discuss the matter in more depth, even if she wasn't certain exactly what she might say, or what opinions of his she might like to know.

Less than an hour before Gina would meet Radcliffe for tea, both Emerald and Ruby bustled into Gina's bedroom where she was sitting near the window reading a novel, while Janine slept soundly in her cradle nearby. Gina immediately picked up on an aura of anxiety in both women as Emerald carefully closed the door so as not to wake the baby. But it was clear that she also wanted privacy. The sisters then both stood in front of Gina, each wringing their hands in a way that was so similar there could be no doubt that they were siblings, even if they bore little physical resemblance to one another.

"What has got the two of you so concerned?" Gina asked, unable to imagine what could possibly be so upsetting. "And please . . ." Gina motioned with her arm, ". . . sit down."

They did as she asked but remained at the edge of their seats, continuing to wring their hands, while neither of them uttered a syllable.

"I'd be very grateful if one of you would tell me whatever it is you've come to tell me," Gina said.

The sisters looked at each other and nodded, as if they shared a secret and unspoken understanding. They both looked at Gina, and Emerald spoke in a voice that was uncharacteristically soft; she clearly didn't want to be overheard, despite both doors to the room being closed. "Mrs. Darby hired a new maid," Emerald reported. "She moved into the dormitories yesterday afternoon, and she'll be working in the laundry."

Gina took this in—along with the anxious silence that followed—and asked, "Is this an unusual occurrence? Is there a reason that—"

"Just now," Ruby whispered, "she was sharing tea with Mrs. Darby and some of the staff—including ourselves—who often have tea on the early shift." Gina was well acquainted with the schedule of the household, and the way the staff alternated shifts with their meals and tea so that someone was always available to assist members of the family with *their* meals and tea.

"And . . ." Gina made an impatient gesture with her hand as she drawled out the word.

"The new maid—her name is Bernice—was asking a great many questions about the new baby in the household."

"What?" Gina gasped and put a hand over her suddenly pounding heart. The behavior of her maids now became perfectly understandable.

"Far too many questions," Emerald added. "I believe she thought she was being discreet, but even Mrs. Darby appeared a little put off by her supposedly innocent curiosity regarding the fact that there's an infant living here."

"What do we know about this . . . Bernice?" Gina asked breathlessly.

"She comes from the village," Emerald reported, still speaking very quietly—especially for her. "She says that she's been working with her father in his bakery all her life but has grown tired of it and felt the need for a change. But . . ." Emerald put a hand over her mouth as if she couldn't bear to speak what she was thinking.

Ruby continued where Emerald had left off. "But if she's the woman who gave birth to Janine, and she heard the rumors of your having a baby . . . in the carriage right where she'd left her little one to be found by someone else . . . it's not unlikely for her to have guessed the obvious."

"Still," Gina said, surprised at the calmness of her own voice when she felt such unbridled panic, "if this woman abandoned her baby, she wouldn't want to be found out. What purpose could she have in coming here and making trouble?"

"Perhaps she has no intention of making trouble," Ruby suggested. "Perhaps she simply wants to be near her child, even though she knows she can never claim any rights to her."

"Still," Gina said, "if she suspects that Janine is not my baby . . ."

"We've all told a great many lies in order to make others believe that Janine is your child," Emerald said. "We always knew the woman who gave birth to this child might suspect the truth, but I don't think any of us anticipated that she might end up working here at the manor."

"Perhaps she remained hidden nearby after she'd left her baby in the alley, waiting to make certain someone found her," Ruby said, sounding alarmed. "Perhaps she witnessed everything; we saw no one in the streets, but if she was hiding . . ."

"And perhaps," Emerald said with more confidence than fear, "we are making something out of nothing. Perhaps Bernice is simply curious and asks too many questions about *everything*. The entire village knows that Gina had a baby; such is always the case when a child is born into this kind of family. We are far better off to not be making any fuss at all, which might draw attention to the fact that we suffer from any measure of guilt or fear; even if we *do*, we can't let on or we will surely give ourselves away. There is nothing we can do except to continue as we have been doing. We will take good care of Janine and remember that Bernice cannot say or do anything that would not bring about far more trouble to herself than to any of us."

Gina appreciated Emerald's wisdom and confidence and took in a deep breath, which she let out slowly, attempting to blow all her worries and fears out into the room where they might disintegrate. Janine was *her* baby; God had sent this precious little girl into *her* life, just as He'd guided Moses into the arms of the Pharaoh's daughter. She *knew* it! And she needed to trust that God would keep her sweet Janine safe, and that all would be well. Working herself into a frenzy would certainly do no good, and exhibiting even the tiniest bit of concern or defensiveness in front of any member of the household might only make herself look guilty. She needed to be even more careful about putting forth her best acting skills, and she reminded the sisters of the same—and asked that they also remind their brother, who was the only other person in the household who knew the truth. They all felt confident that Garn would never betray their secret, and with mutual conviction they made the decision for Ruby and Emerald to do their best to remain informed on Bernice's attitudes as well as her character. Otherwise they would all go about their business as they had been doing since the day Janine had arrived in their home.

⁂

Gina very much enjoyed sharing tea with Radcliffe. Only a few minutes after they'd exchanged greetings and had sat down together, each holding their cups and saucers while their tea cooled, Gina remarked, "It's so nice to be having tea somewhere besides my rooms. I confess it's become rather tedious."

"Then perhaps we should make a habit of it," Radcliffe said and took a careful sip before he set down his cup and saucer and selected a couple of small cucumber sandwiches, which he put onto a delicate little plate. "It seems silly for two adults who live under the same roof to *not* share meals and tea—although I confess that I enjoy having breakfast in my rooms because I tend to stay up far too late reading and therefore I'm not an early riser."

Gina laughed softly. "Nor am I. Even before Dwight's death, I always tended to be slow about getting up in the morning and making myself presentable, but since Janine has come along, with all of the nighttime feedings and such, I am *very* slow about being ready to leave my rooms."

"Then perhaps we could share lunch and supper—and tea, as well—but only if that suits you. And perhaps there will be days when it won't work out for one or both of us, but I would very much enjoy your company, G—if that's agreeable to you."

Gina let her glance linger far too long on Radcliffe, enjoying the effect he had on her. In fact, her fingertips tingled so intensely that she marveled over her own ability to place a small sandwich and a fairy cake on her plate. "I would enjoy that very much," she said. "I'm certain my maids and Elaine can care for the baby long enough for me to do that—I would even go so far as to say they would all be pleased with me leaving my rooms more often; they've been nagging me on that very issue for a long while."

"We shall make a habit of it, then," Radcliffe said, seeming pleased, but Gina wondered if he was pleased because he simply wanted the company of a friend with whom he could share comfortable conversation, or if he had any of the feelings for her that she had for him. Only time would tell, for certain, which meant that every opportunity she had to spend time with him would help her determine the truth of his feelings toward her. For now, she chose to simply enjoy his company and the fact that her desire to be in his presence had lured her out of her rooms and away from her old habits.

They relaxed and conversed long after they'd finished eating the variety of delights Mrs. Chester had sent from the kitchen. Gina found great pleasure in his company—perhaps too much, she told herself. She was still officially in mourning, and even though relief was her most prominent emotion regarding Dwight's death, it was mandatory for her to keep up the proper appearances so as not to damage Radcliffe's social reputation, if not her own. Although she was more concerned about *him*. He'd never been anything but good to her, and she owed him her deepest regards. She couldn't even allow herself to think about the fact that everything he'd been led to believe about Janine was a lie. She only knew that he could never know the truth. *Never!* For now, she only wanted the opportunity to spend time with Radcliffe every day so that they could get to know each other better, and any possible outcome seemed too far into the future to be worthy of any concern.

CHAPTER FIVE
the letter

The weeks of summer settled comfortably into a life more pleasant than Gina had ever experienced. Even though it was typical for the weather to give them more rainy days than sunny ones, Gina took advantage of every day when the sun offered its favor to take Janine out for lengthy walks in the gardens. Gina became particularly good at timing her little excursions when the baby had been fed and was content to nap in her little coach so that Gina could stay outside and soak in the sunshine for as long as possible. On such days she generally went out once in the morning and again in the afternoon, and she *always* found her way to the little stone bridge where she would stand for a few minutes and contemplate the bridges in her life while she listened to the sound of the running water flowing beneath her. She was glad that Radcliffe seemed to enjoy sharing the ritual, since it wasn't uncommon for him to join her, as if he regularly interrogated the servants in order to know when she was setting out so that he could be there at the door waiting for her. Either that, or he spent a great deal of time waiting at that particular door on the chance that she might go out, although she knew him to have major responsibilities and she couldn't imagine him being willing to waste so much time. Nevertheless, she was always glad to see him and enjoy the pleasure of his company. He never joined her without first making it clear that he didn't wish to intrude if she preferred to be alone, and she appreciated his kindness in respecting her wishes, but she was always able to tell him with complete honesty, "I appreciate your companionship. I have far too much time alone."

"As do I," he often said before they ventured out into the gardens.

"Autumn is beginning to show hints of appearing," Gina commented as they ambled slowly between rows of late-blooming roses. "Whatever will we do when it's too cold to bring Janine outside?"

"We will find a way to enjoy our time indoors," Radcliffe said, "just as we have on rainy days."

Gina quickly recounted pleasant memories of the three of them visiting in the library or any number of parlors in the enormous manor house. Janine's little red coach had been used for long walks up and down the vast hallways of the ground floor, and had served as a perfect place where Janine could safely sleep in whatever room Gina chose to enjoy, often with Radcliffe there for company. Janine often joined them for lunch or tea, depending on the baby's mood. And with Janine starting to get strong enough to hold her head up and staying awake more during the days, Gina often held her daughter in one arm while she skillfully managed to enjoy drinking tea and eating with the other. She was at first surprised when Radcliffe offered to hold the baby during tea, and it was somewhat comical seeing him learn to keep the baby comfortably relaxed in the crook of his arm while he managed to feed himself. But no one found it more humorous than Radcliffe, and he quickly adapted, declaring that he very much enjoyed holding the baby and assisting in some tiny way with her care.

Gina loved watching them together, even though that meant having to fight extremely hard to not imagine them *always* being together. It took no effort at all to look into the future and see Radcliffe raising Janine and being a father to her, and Gina wouldn't be at all surprised if Radcliffe were having the very same thoughts. But Gina didn't want to get her hopes up, and always at the back of her mind was the fear of Radcliffe discovering the truth—that he shared no blood with Janine at all, and that Gina had constructed a terrible web of lies to conceal the reality. She couldn't imagine ever being able to tell him the truth; but on the other hand, she couldn't imagine ever marrying a man—and bringing a child into his life—without him knowing all there was to know. Therefore, Gina became very efficient at pushing away all thoughts about the future, and simply enjoying these precious summer moments while they lasted.

While Janine slept contentedly, Radcliffe guided Gina to a bench that had become their favorite due to the way it was nestled beneath an old tree with branches that seemed to speak of the history they had witnessed. She loved the way she and Radcliffe could talk endlessly about any topic. They were both avid readers, and even though they preferred quite different kinds of books, they loved to share with each other what they were reading, and doing so always provoked stimulating conversation. Gina preferred novels, but she loved to deeply analyze the characters of these stories, and their reasons for behaving the way they did. Radcliffe always had interesting things to say on such matters, and they usually found themselves comparing the decisions and behaviors of fictional characters to challenges in their own lives, and behaviors they had observed in people they knew.

For all that Radcliffe enjoyed discussing novels with Gina, he preferred to read about factual topics from which he could learn all kinds of things. He loved the way books could open his mind and offer him an ongoing education. He'd enjoyed his time away at university when he'd been younger, although he'd been an avid reader long before then and ever since. He read books on history and science and other places in the world. He'd read every book in the enormous library of the manor—and that was a lot of books. He was continually ordering books with the help of the proprietor of the local bookshop, and he was always excited when his orders would arrive. Gina grew to admire him more and more as she listened to him talk with enthusiasm about things he had learned; she felt as if she could spend her entire life hearing about the knowledge he'd accumulated inside his mind, and never grow bored. He took his responsibilities regarding the estate and his title very seriously, and he never allowed his desire to read to interfere with anything that required his attention. And he was adamant about his belief that no book could ever replace the need for human beings to interact with one another. Gina knew he was implying that he set a high priority on his growing friendship with her and Janine, and she felt sure from other things he'd said that he'd spent periods of his life experiencing a great deal of loneliness, and he never wanted to be so isolated again. Gina knew how he felt and told him so, and that too was a topic of deep conversation, and something which gave them a common bond.

As usual, the moment when Janine began to express signs of discomfort, they headed back to the house, wanting to get her to Elaine so she could feed her before she became too upset. The moment they were inside the door, a maid approached holding out a small silver tray, which held a letter. Gina assumed it was for Radcliffe, since he received written communications far more often than she did, but while she was lifting Janine into her arms, she heard the maid say, "For you, m'lady."

"Oh," Gina said with some surprise, "thank you." She then felt a little flustered since Janine was fussing and her attempts to bounce the baby and soothe her didn't leave a free hand.

"May I?" Radcliffe asked, nodding toward the letter.

"Of course," Gina said, already knowing it was from her father; in all the years she'd lived here, she'd never received a letter from anyone except her father, and those were not necessarily a regular occurrence.

Once relieved of her assignment, the maid curtsied slightly and walked away. Radcliffe walked with Gina toward the stairs, looking at the letter in his hand as he said predictably, "It appears to be from your father."

"No one else ever writes to me," she said as Janine's fussing became more vocal and they both quickened their pace. "I'm certain it will be filled with all the usual complaining; well, I don't know if it's complaining, really, but he only writes to tell me of the circumstances in which he's living, and they are not at all favorable. I daresay his letters are all nearly identical."

"Why are his circumstances not favorable?" Radcliffe asked, with as much concern as if she'd told him the house was on fire and they were all in imminent danger. But Janine was wailing now, wanting to be fed, and Gina just tossed Radcliffe a sideways nod, a form of communication he'd come to know well while spending time with an infant. He knew that it meant the baby's needs had to be met and then they could finish whatever it was they might have been discussing.

As always, Elaine was waiting and ready to feed the baby, and Gina left Janine in her capable hands while she and Radcliffe went to Gina's sitting room where they sat with the doors open. Gina always wanted to be nearby so that she could care for Janine as soon as she'd been fed and changed. If she were not with Radcliffe, she would have changed the baby herself, but Elaine had insisted weeks earlier that Gina should enjoy her visits with Sir Radcliffe and that she would see to the more basic necessities of caring for the baby when Radcliffe was around.

The moment Gina and Radcliffe were seated, Janine's crying from the next room ceased, and Radcliffe said, "If the matter is none of my business, you know that you are free to say so and I will respect your privacy. However, I can't deny feeling some concern from what you said. Will you tell me why your father's circumstances are not favorable, and why his letters are only repetitions of the situation?"

Gina sighed. "I have no issue with telling you, except that I've never found any reason to burden you with the challenges of my family."

"I don't consider anything you share with me to be a burden," he insisted, and Gina felt warmed by the sincerity of his statement.

Gina sighed again. "I believe you're aware that when I married Dwight, I was eager to leave the home in which I'd been raised."

"I do recall that," he said, "but I never knew the reasons; I didn't feel it was my place to ask. I also recall that when we met in London—when you were staying with an uncle, I believe—you were not pleased about having to return home when the time came."

"No, I was not," Gina said and looked down at her hands clasped in her lap. "I was never close to either my brother or my sister, and yet they were always *very* close to each other. They always seemed to have a bizarre sense of mischief in common, and extraordinarily strong personalities. I would go so far as to say that they are overly intrusive and assertive to the point of being obnoxious. My mother did well at keeping their behavior more under control, although I believe that it was difficult even for her. After she passed, they just . . . seemed to take over the house. My father is kind to a fault; I don't think I've ever seen him stand up to them, and it's only gotten worse over the years. My brother is very much in control of the household and the estate, even though my father is in good health and certainly of sound mind. My brother is very much influenced by my sister who is nothing less than conniving and manipulative." Gina couldn't hold back a visible shudder, which Radcliffe clearly noticed. "The two of them are always scheming about one thing or another. And they put a very high priority on their social standing, and in fact have a very large circle of friends—mostly because they host a great many extravagant social events, which always end in everyone becoming intolerably drunk, while the staff are treated badly and left to deal with consequences that should not be their responsibility. My father has quite literally given up any effort to try and rein them in. He's simply . . . miserable and lonely, and—"

"Then he must come and stay with us," Radcliffe interrupted with enthusiasm, and Gina was so stunned she literally couldn't speak. Thankfully, he kept talking, which deflected attention away from her shocked silence. "It's the most obvious and simple solution, G. The day you exchanged vows with Dwight you became family to me, and that means your father is also family. If he's so very miserable in his present circumstances, and the two of you miss each other as you do, then he absolutely should be here with us. You know as well as I how enormous this house is. There are seemingly countless rooms closed off with the furnishings covered. It's not as if I'm intending to host some grand event that would require overnight accommodations for dozens of guests. Your father could practically have an entire wing to himself, and he could express his own preferences regarding such things. He's your father and deserves respect for that reason alone. You've told me he's a good man, and for that he deserves even more respect. Should he not be able to live out the remainder of his life in peace? Should he not be here where he can be a part of your life—and that of his granddaughter?"

All of this made perfect sense to Gina, despite her ongoing surprise that Radcliffe would be so kind and generous. But the mention of her father's *granddaughter* caught her off guard—although she was careful not to let on to that fact. Keeping up these pretenses was something that would always be a part of her life and she hoped to become more comfortable in putting up the proper front in order to keep Janine safe and properly cared for.

"You look as frozen as a statue," Radcliffe said to Gina, startling her from a myriad of thoughts.

"I . . . I'm just . . . so surprised," she admitted. "You certainly have no obligation to take on my father."

"I assure you it would not be a burden in any way," Radcliffe insisted.

"Well, he's certainly wealthy enough to provide for his own needs," Gina stated. "The problem is the way my siblings have taken over the house, and the way they're so unkind to him. Of course, my brother will inherit the home eventually anyway, and I think my father has come to loathe the place. But until my father's death—which we all hope is still a great many years away—my brother has no access to his money except for the generous allowance he's been receiving for years. The money used for the management of the household and estate was very wisely put under the legal control of the head butler and the overseer a long time ago, and my father's trusted solicitor sees that everything is kept honest and in order." Gina drew in a long, slow breath and let it out even more slowly, as if that might help her think more clearly, and Radcliffe seemed to sense her need to do so. "I've suggested to my father more than once that he should just . . . move elsewhere . . . make a life for himself away from this ridiculous situation, but he's always insisted that despite the circumstances, he didn't want to leave his home."

"Listen to me, G," Radcliffe said, intensifying his gaze on her, "and be completely honest with me."

"Of course," she said and resisted the urge to add that she would never be anything but honest with him. She could never explain that she was committed to total honesty except for the source of Janine's existence. But she kept her thoughts and her focus on him as he continued.

"Is there any reason that having your father here would cause stress or difficulty for *you*? I don't want to create different problems by trying to solve this one when I know little about the situation."

Gina considered the question carefully, grateful for Radcliffe's insight and concern. She then answered confidently, "My father and I have always been close. We have certainly had our disagreements, and occasionally we get frustrated with each other, but that's normal, is it not? I have missed my father and I know he misses me. I can't foresee any potential difficulty with having him live here . . . especially when he would be able to have his privacy and live according to his own preferences. He's a good man; he would always be respectful toward you—I'm certain of it. Nevertheless, I must make it clear that you are under no obligation whatsoever to do this."

"I *want* to do this, G," he said firmly. "I sometimes wonder why I was born into such a life, why I was blessed with so much when others have so little. I try to find ways to help make the lives of others better, but . . . I still sometimes feel at a loss as to how I can make a positive difference in this world. Let me do this for your father . . . for you."

Gina looked at him searchingly, as if she might be able to discern whether his desire was sincere. She was surprised at how easily she was able to perceive that he was a decent man who only wanted to do good—and the very fact that he was willing to do this for *her* implied a devotion to her happiness that couldn't help but warm her heart.

"I cannot deny that it would be a great joy to me to have my father here, and I do believe that he would be much happier. Your kindness and generosity have left me quite overcome."

"Think nothing of it," Radcliffe said, as if having her father come to live in his home was nothing more extravagant than requesting that the cook prepare her favorite dessert.

"There is one thing we must take into consideration," she said.

"And what is that?" Radcliffe asked as if he'd made up his mind to do this and there was nothing that would deter him.

"It must be my father's choice. Perhaps, despite the difficulty of his present situation, he won't want to leave his home. Even though he's not necessarily a prideful man, I can understand why any man might struggle with his pride in having to leave his home behind and live under someone else's roof."

"Of course," Radcliffe said. "You are insightful and wise . . . and sensitive, as always, G. Write a letter to your father and explain the situation in detail."

"I will," Gina said, "if you're absolutely certain."

"I would not have offered if I'd had any doubts about following through on my offer," he insisted.

Gina told herself to take him at his word, which reminded her that Dwight had often left her confused and unsettled by changing his mind about something, or insisting he'd never said things that he'd absolutely said. But Radcliffe was not Dwight, and now that she'd allowed his offer to settle in, she couldn't help feeling thrilled over the prospect of having her father come and live here.

"Very well then," she said, "I will write a letter immediately and we can send it out with the next post and—"

"On the contrary," Radcliffe said, "I will deliver it personally with the hope that he will be convinced, and I will bring him and his personal belongings back with me."

"Oh, surely it's not necessary for you to take the time or go to the trouble to—"

"Regina," he said firmly, "there is nothing here that those I've hired to manage my business cannot see to while I am gone for a few days. What? A week at most. I know very well where your father lives; I visited there with Dwight a number of times, did I not?"

"Yes, you did," she agreed, recalling those memories with fondness. Dwight had been much kinder and more charming prior to their marriage, and Radcliffe had always been pleasant company.

"Your father knows me well enough; we played cards together and had a good many conversations. I will deliver the letter directly into his hands and do everything in my power to persuade him and assist him."

"I daresay my brother and sister would be only too eager to assist him in leaving the house," Gina said, disgruntled. "I hope that such an offer will come as a relief to my father. And again, you are most kind and generous. I don't know how I could ever repay you for all that you—"

"There's no need to think like that," Radcliffe said and impulsively kissed Gina on the brow. It was so quick and unexpected that she didn't have even a moment to anticipate it before it was over, but the touch of his lips left a tingling sensation that spread over her face. "You are precious to me, G," he said, looking into her eyes in a way that enhanced that tingling sensation. At such moments, she felt certain he was as drawn to her as she was to him. But she hardly knew what she might say to help her clarify whether that was true.

Radcliffe then left the room abruptly, saying on his way out, "I'll leave you to write that letter while I make arrangements for my travel. Now that I've made up my mind to do this, I very much want to be on my way as quickly as possible."

"Thank you," Gina said. He tossed a quick smile over his shoulder and was gone. But his enthusiasm and kindness seemed to remain in the room like some kind of invisible, pleasant fog that crept into every corner and crevice, leaving Gina with the hope that perhaps—after many difficult years—her life might actually have the possibility of all that she'd ever dreamed it might be.

Gina had no difficulty writing a suitable letter to her father, explaining everything, especially when she didn't have the slightest concern about the possibility of it ending up in someone else's hands. Knowing that Radcliffe would deliver it to him personally made it easier to be forthright in her written words, imploring her father to come and live here with her and her daughter. She'd written to tell him of Janine's birth, apologizing for not having told him that she'd been expecting. But it had been easy to rehearse the deception she had created around the entire situation of her life since Dwight's death until the day when Janine had miraculously come into her life. Her father had written a lovely letter in return, filled with joy on her behalf, and his own joy over having become a grandfather. He had written that he would look forward to meeting his granddaughter, but he'd been vague about when that might be, and Gina knew that he didn't necessarily like to travel, especially alone. That thought hadn't occurred to her until long after Radcliffe had set out in one of his many carriages with her letter in hand. She could almost believe that he had been inspired with the idea to go and get her father personally; she truly believed he would be more likely to come with Radcliffe accompanying him than he would if it meant traveling nearly two days' distance alone.

Within hours of Radcliffe's departure, Gina missed him terribly. She had the company of Ruby, Emerald, and Elaine, as she always did, and she enjoyed telling them about Radcliffe's plan to personally go and get her father. They were all pleased with the idea and agreed that Radcliffe was a fine man and they all felt blessed to be in the employment of a man who was fair and generous.

"You've been spending a great deal of time with him," Emerald said. All four women just happened to be gathered in the sitting room, relaxing and visiting while Elaine fed the baby. This was not an uncommon occurrence, but Emerald's comment took Gina off guard. For all that she and Radcliffe *had* been spending a great deal of time together, no one had commented on the fact until now.

"Yes," Gina drawled, smiling toward her maid and friend. "Is there a reason you think that should not be the case?"

"Not at all," Ruby answered for her sister. "Only that . . . you very much seem to enjoy spending time with him and . . ." She let out an odd little nervous laugh that got Gina's attention because it was so unusual; only then did she realize that the sisters were exchanging a conspiratorial glance.

Elaine saved Gina from having to know what to say when she stated matter-of-factly, "I think what they're wondering is whether you have any kind of romantic interest in Sir Radcliffe, because the entire household is gossiping about their belief that *he* has romantic feelings for *you*."

Gina drew in her breath so sharply that it made her cough, and then she couldn't stop. Emerald rushed to pour her a glass of water from a nearby pitcher, and Gina did her best to sip it slowly between coughing spasms, embarrassed by the coughing fit but glad for the time it gave her to measure her response to such a candid—but awkward—turn of conversation.

Gina finally got control of her throat with one final cough and stated firmly. "I have absolutely no idea whether Sir Radcliffe has any such feelings toward me. He's certainly never said a word to indicate anything beyond friendship— which is how it should be." Gina let out a disgruntled chuckle completely lacking in humor. "I detest the thought of the household gossiping about such things."

"There's nothing malicious or unkind in what anyone is saying," Ruby clarified. "It's only that . . . everyone who works for him can't help being curious about his life—and yours, of course. There's been a fair bit of drama in the household since you lost your husband. I do believe everyone wishes you well."

"Everyone?" Gina echoed before she considered that her thought might be better left unsaid. But the curious glances of the others forced her to go on, although she made certain her tone of voice held no hint of concern; Ruby and Emerald understood the deeper implications, but Elaine knew nothing of Gina's secret. "Do you believe the new maid—Bernice—wishes both of us well? I doubt she has met Sir Radcliffe directly; I've never met her. Yet you've told me she's been unusually curious."

"Oh, I believe she's just a curious sort," Emerald said with a confidence that didn't seem at all contrived for the sake of keeping up pretenses regarding the situation. "From the few times I've encountered her personally, she seems rather amiable."

"Indeed, she does," Elaine interjected. "I get the impression that her situation prior to coming here was not a good one, although she's vague about the reasons. I do believe she's grateful to have such fair employment that includes good living accommodations." Elaine smiled toward Gina and added, "I know that I do."

Gina smiled at Elaine, humbly grateful that this woman who was necessary for Janine's survival had turned out to be so kind and comfortable to be around.

"Yes," Ruby said, "I believe Bernice is a fine young woman, and although I haven't asked her personally, I do believe she would want the best for you *and* for Sir Radcliffe." She tossed Gina a comical glare. "I daresay you're trying to divert the topic of this conversation. You say that you have no idea how he feels about you, but how do *you* feel about *him*?"

Gina took in another sharp breath as if the question pierced something secret inside of her, perhaps as frightening as the possible discovery of the truth about Janine. But she was careful to not start coughing again. She cleared her throat and said with only a little indignation, "Since I've not yet been widowed a year, I do believe such a question is completely inappropriate."

"We are not talking about whether or not you would consider publicly courting a gentleman," Emerald said. "We are only talking about how you feel. I do believe you consider all of us trustworthy enough to keep in confidence anything you tell us, and you also know we all care a great deal for you. You *have* been spending a great deal of time with the baronet; we can't help wondering how you feel about him. Do you only consider him a friend, or . . ."

Emerald didn't finish her sentence, since the question was obvious. The room became taut with silence while all three women looked curiously toward Gina; regardless of how much the household may or may not have been speculating over this topic, these three women who personally assisted Gina had certainly been discussing it. Gina hurried to state the facts plainly. "I enjoy Sir Radcliffe's company very much. He and I have shared a comfortable acquaintance since I first met him and his cousin in London years ago, and I confess that we have become friends more recently. Beyond that, there is nothing to tell. Even *if* such feelings existed, it would be entirely inappropriate to acknowledge them when I am still officially in mourning. However, allow me to make it perfectly clear that there has been no indication of anything at all beyond friendship. We both loved Dwight and we both lost him. He's very fond of Janine." She cleared her throat again in a way that she hoped would put an end to the conversation.

"Not only Janine, I think," Ruby said with a little giggle.

"Indeed," Elaine said, and then all three of them were giggling.

"Oh," Gina huffed, trying to keep her tone light to cover her rising embarrassment, "the three of you are intolerable!" This made them giggle more and Gina just joined them, hoping they couldn't detect any signs that she was very much attracted to Sir Radcliffe, and that she missed him greatly. She hoped and prayed that all would be well with him throughout his journey, and that he would be able to convince her father to come and live here at Stonebridge. The more she'd thought about the idea, the more comfortable—and even excited—she had become. She knew her father could be happy here, and the idea of Janine growing up with a grandfather who loved her filled Gina with joy. She fought away her ever-present concerns about the truth being discovered by imagining a day, years into the future, with her father and her daughter playing together in the gardens. Recalling her own childhood memories made the scene easy to see in her mind, and she couldn't comprehend how devastated she would feel if her father chose not to come. The idea had only come up very recently, and already its possibilities seemed to hold a great portion of her happiness in the balance.

Knowing she could do nothing to influence her father any more than she already had, Gina focused instead on enjoying every moment of being Janine's mother, always keeping a prayer in her heart that all would be well for her and those she loved.

⚜

On a pleasant afternoon, six days after Radcliffe had left to personally deliver Gina's letter to her father, Ruby rushed breathlessly into Gina's sitting room to declare, "The baronet's carriage is approaching."

"Oh, my!" Gina popped to her feet as if some external force had propelled her.

"Hurry along," Elaine said, who was sitting nearby feeding the baby while little Tommy played on the carpet at her feet. "I'll see that all is well here."

"Thank you," Gina said and took only a long second to glance in the mirror and make certain her hair was still in place. "Oh, I do hope that . . ." She couldn't finish due to a sudden breathlessness.

"Yes, we know," Ruby said. "Now you must go, but don't forget to breathe. Fainting on the way down the stairs would not turn out favorably."

Gina tossed Ruby a comical scowl but heeded her advice as she rushed out of the room and toward the stairs, forcing herself to walk at a reasonable pace while she consciously drew her breaths in and out so as not to arrive in the foyer breathless and possibly light-headed. She arrived at the bottom of the stairs just in time to see three male servants step out through the enormous front door onto the wide drive that had been constructed purposely so that carriages could stop near the entrance. Gina wondered if someone had been informed of the baronet's pending arrival, or if one of the footmen—whose job it was to always be near the door to receive callers—had spotted the approaching carriage and had summoned others to welcome their employer and bring in his luggage. Gina was proud of herself for having arrived without any noticeable breathlessness, but she still attempted to draw in a few deep breaths and blow them out slowly in a possibly futile attempt to calm herself. The recent inquiries of her three friends concerning her feelings for Radcliffe almost made her blush as she had to acknowledge her excitement over the prospect of seeing him again, and how dreadfully she'd missed his company. Her anxiousness increased due to the unanswered question regarding whether her father had chosen to come home with Radcliffe. The possibility of seeing him as well made her heart beat so quickly that breathing evenly became even more of a challenge.

Gina heard the crunch of footsteps on the fine gravel that covered the enormous circular drive in front of the house, mixed with voices as the footmen and the driver exchanged greetings and instructions. She recognized Radcliffe's voice, and a tingling of her skin was suddenly competing for attention with a fluttering in her stomach. She put one hand over her quickened heart and another over her middle, silently willing both to be calm. A moment later, Radcliffe appeared through the open doorway, removing his hat as he entered the house. For the brief second she had to observe him before he saw her, she was freshly taken aback by his handsome demeanor and the way his fine manner of dress created an overall masculine effect that seemed like a work of art personified. Gina was grateful that she had been able to fit into a blue chiffon day dress that had once been a favorite, topped by a little blue jacket of a darker shade. It occurred to her that in a strange way she felt more like herself than she had since she'd married Dwight, which gave her the odd sensation of wanting to go back to that time and once again be the fair young lady who had the possibility of making a fine marriage. She wished now that she had focused her attention more toward Radcliffe back then, that she had been more sensitive to the signs that she could see in retrospect of character traits in Dwight that had been less than favorable. But Dwight had been extremely assertive about his affection for her, and she had been blinded by his charisma and possessive attention. Now, she longed to have Radcliffe see her as a lady who might win his favor; then she quickly shoved her thoughts to the present the very moment he saw her standing there. He smiled in a way that required no words to let her know that he was as pleased to see her as she was to see him. The very idea made it necessary to remain conscious of every breath so that she didn't make a fool of herself.

"What a lovely vision to greet me upon my return," Radcliffe said, taking her hand to kiss it, allowing his lips to linger against the back of her fingers longer than necessary.

"It's so very good to have you back," she said. Radcliffe's assertion of being glad to see *her* made it easier for her to admit how nice it was to see *him*.

"It's good to be home," he said with a long sigh that didn't diminish his enthusiasm. "Has Janine missed me?" He chuckled with delight. "I've certainly missed *her*," he said, then winked at Gina. "Almost as much as I've missed her mother."

"We have both missed you very much," Gina said, and Radcliffe finally let go of her hand.

Their eyes locked for a long moment as if they were each trying to assess the thoughts and feelings of the other, and each perhaps afraid to say too much—or not enough. Gina broke the silence by looking past Radcliffe's shoulder toward the door, asking the obvious question, "Did my father . . ." She hardly dared finish, fearing her own disappointment if he'd decided not to come.

"Oh, he's here!" Radcliffe said with enthusiasm and a warm laugh as he glanced toward the door. "I believe he's regaling the footmen with tales of our adventures."

Gina listened more carefully to the voices just outside the door and laughed immediately after hearing her father's laughter among the little group of men. "Ah, so he is!" she said and laughed again with deep relief. She then looked inquisitively at Radcliffe. "You had adventures?" she asked. "Did something go wrong?"

"Not at all," Radcliffe said. "We simply encountered some interesting people along the way. I'll let him tell you all about it; I wouldn't dare deny him the pleasure."

They both turned toward the open door, silently waiting for the men to finish chatting so that Gina could greet her father. When Gina knew it would be at least a minute longer, she said to Radcliffe, "Thank you . . . for doing this for me . . . for us. I'm so incredibly grateful."

"It is nothing but a pleasure and a privilege, G," he said with an admiration in his eyes that she could never mistake for friendship. She looked down in order to keep her thoughts straight, knowing she needed to consider this new evidence in his behavior. Could it be possible? Truly possible that he *did* want their relationship to go beyond friendship? She couldn't think about that now. Reminding herself of what he had just said, she asked, "Did you have any trouble convincing him to—"

"Not a bit," Radcliffe said. "I don't know if I've ever seen a man happier than he was when he read your letter."

"Truly?" she asked with a burst of giddy laughter.

"Truly," he replied, his echo of laughter implying that he found delight in her response. "We had one meal with your brother and sister while the servants were packing your father's things. Of course, I've met them on more than one occasion in the past, but I'm certain I simply wasn't paying much attention to their behavior. After what you'd told me, I was keenly observant, and I can assure you that they are nothing if not far worse than you described. I've known a great many self-absorbed, arrogant people in my life, but . . . oh my goodness. It's no wonder you didn't want to live under the same roof with them. And no wonder your father has been so miserable. He assured me that he'd long ago taken to keeping everything of real value to him in his own rooms because he didn't feel like the house was any longer his, and he didn't trust that his belongings would be respected elsewhere—which made it extremely easy for his things to be packed quickly so that we could be off."

"And did the journey go smoothly?" she asked. "Besides your adventures?"

"Very well, indeed," Radcliffe said. "I find your father a delight, G. He's a kind and generous man. Reminds me very much of his daughter." Radcliffe winked. "I do believe that—"

He stopped when Milton Elliott walked through the door, holding his hat in his hand, looking mildly nervous and deeply humble as he took in his daughter's gaze. Gina had not seen her father since the funeral; he'd only been able to stay one night, and she'd been so lost in her shock and confusion that she recalled very little of their brief time together. He seemed to have aged even since then. There was more gray hair dominating the light brown hair at his temples, but his clean-shaven face was still mostly wrinkle free, and his lean build was evidence that he still rigidly adhered to his regimen of long, brisk walks every day, no matter the weather.

"Oh, my dear, precious girl!" Milton finally said as if he'd had sufficient time to just look at her and now he couldn't hold himself back from engulfing her in an embrace so tight that it seemed to be for the purpose of expressing every bit of the love they'd not been able to share since she'd married Dwight and left her father's home.

"How are you, my dear?" he asked, finally relinquishing his embrace only to take hold of her shoulders a moment after a maid seemed to magically appear to take his hat. He nodded and smiled toward the maid, then looked into Gina's eyes as if he might find the answer to his question without her having to speak.

"I am very well!" Gina said with enthusiasm, certain her eyes would echo her words, since it was absolutely true. "And I am far better now that you are here. What a tremendous blessing this is!"

Milton's brow furrowed and his eyes showed concern. "Your letter said that it would be . . . a blessing for me to come and live here. I hope that you meant it, Regina. I never *ever* want to be a burden to you, my precious. Nor do I wish to cause any trouble for Sir Radcliffe; he's been so exceedingly kind and gracious and—"

"And I've told you at least a dozen times," Radcliffe interrupted, reminding Gina that he was still standing nearby, "that it's not a bit of trouble. I'm only glad that we could rescue you from that mausoleum that used to be your home."

Gina was a little shocked by such a derogatory description, and Radcliffe clearly noticed her expression. He pointed at her father and said, "His words; not mine."

"It's true," Milton said. "The situation has only become steadily worse, and I had truly begun to feel as if I might lose my mind. The timing of your offer," he nodded toward Radcliffe, "couldn't have been more perfect. A year ago . . . or even a few months ago . . . I don't know if I would have been willing to leave. But I have come to see and feel that it's no longer a home to me, and I don't have the motivation or strength to attempt to control the situation. I'm getting old and I just want to enjoy what's left of my life. Coming here is surely the answer to many prayers, even though I had never even considered such an option—except perhaps the idea of coming here for a lengthy visit."

"Well, you should have done that a long time ago," Radcliffe said, putting a hand on Milton's shoulder, and the two men exchanged a comfortable smile that made it evident they'd gotten to know each other very well throughout their journey together. "And now you know you never have to leave."

"A miracle indeed!" Milton said, then he looked at Gina and added, "Now, where's my granddaughter? It's high time I met her; don't you think?"

Gina suppressed the familiar guilt that arose inside her every time she was reminded of her deception. Her father had every reason to believe that Janine was a child of his posterity who would carry on his bloodline, and Gina was purposely deceiving him into believing it. But she swallowed the lie with all its accompanying guilt and self-reproach before she smiled and took her father's hand, leading him toward the stairs. "The wet nurse was feeding her when you arrived. I daresay your granddaughter is ready for company by now, and she's likely as excited to meet you as you are to meet her."

This made Milton chuckle as he walked by Gina's side up the stairs. "May I come along?" Radcliffe asked, falling into step behind them. "I've missed her dreadfully."

"Of course," Gina said. "Perhaps we should just have tea brought to the sitting room. I daresay that neither of you will want to leave Janine's company before then."

"Perhaps we should have our supper brought there as well," Radcliffe said with a chuckle, and Milton laughed with him, as if he very much liked that idea. Gina was simply overcome with the reality of having her father here—and knowing that he always would be—and having Radcliffe back; she truly had missed him, and her heart was full to think of the evidence she'd seen in the foyer that his feelings for her might be what she'd been hoping, and that perhaps enough time had passed that he was willing to show them more freely. Oh, how she hoped that was the case!

CHAPTER SIX
confessions

WHILE SHE LOUNGED COMFORTABLY IN her sitting room, observing her father and Radcliffe sitting on the same sofa, taking turns holding the baby while they admired her, both making fools of themselves by making silly noises and ridiculous faces in their attempt to get Janine to look at them or show some kind of response, Gina felt happier than she believed she had ever been. She repeated what Elaine had taught her, that an infant Janine's age might be able to see what's close to their face, but they were still too young to show any real response. Janine smiled and scowled a great deal in her sleep, as if she dreamt often and with great emotion. But while awake, she did little more than simply look around with a lazy kind of interest in her surroundings or cry if she felt any hunger or distress. The moment Janine began to fuss, the men were all too eager to turn her over to Gina's care. She managed to keep Janine content for a little while by walking with her and holding her in her most preferred positions. But it soon became evident she was hungry, and like magic, Elaine appeared with little Tommy at her heels. As always, she was ready to take the baby and satisfy her hunger. Milton had met Elaine when she'd turned the baby over to Gina earlier, but Tommy hadn't been with her. Now that Milton had sighted the little boy, he immediately became playful and got right down on his knees to greet the child with a kind voice and animated gestures that made Tommy giggle. Elaine seemed pleased and heartily agreed with Milton's request that Tommy stay and play while she took care of the baby.

Gina observed the interaction between her father and little Tommy for a few minutes—while Radcliffe did the same—and it was easy for her to imagine how it might be to have her father here in the same home while Janine grew from a baby to a child to a young woman. With any luck and God's blessings,

Milton would be there when Janine got married, and when she became a mother herself.

Gina was startled from her reverie when Radcliffe said, "There's something I've been wanting to show you, G. I think now would be a good time, and I believe Tommy and your father should join us."

Milton obviously overheard and said, "Are we going for a walk?"

"Yes, we are," Radcliffe said with enthusiasm.

"Very well," Gina said, wondering what kind of surprise Radcliffe had brewing. He was clearly excited to show them whatever it was he'd mentioned. "Just let me tell Elaine that Tommy is coming with us so she won't worry."

Gina walked across the hall and peeked into Elaine's room just long enough to softly tell her that they were taking Tommy for a walk. Elaine seemed pleased and Gina headed out, walking at Radcliffe's side with her father and Tommy coming behind them, holding hands while Milton asked the boy questions about the sounds that different animals made. Tommy's responses and imitations were not only comical, they were evidence that his mother had taught him a great deal on the subject.

Gina wondered where they were going, especially when they passed the top of the stairs and remained on the same floor. In fact, they hadn't walked far at all before Radcliffe stopped and opened a door with a great deal of aplomb. "I give you . . . the playroom," he said with a dramatic laugh. Gina entered a room she'd never seen before, taking in a sharp breath at seeing its magical beauty. Along one wall were a great many large windows, and opposite was a wall beautifully painted with brightly colored animals. There were some strategically placed sofas, little tables, and comfortable chairs—obviously meant for the adults who would spend time in this room while children played. But the focus of the room was the enormous number of toys, some on the floor and many artfully arranged on beautifully crafted shelves.

"I was thinking," Radcliffe said, "that this room should be aired out and cleaned, given the fact that Janine will grow quickly into needing a place to play, and we have little Tommy here who often seems rather bored—well behaved, mind you," he added, winking at Tommy, "but bored, nevertheless. Perhaps his mother could sometimes feed Janine here, and she and Tommy would be welcome to use this room any time they like. What do you think, G?"

"Oh, it's lovely!" she exclaimed, turning a circle in the center of the room so that she could take it all in. "It's perfect! I had no idea such a room existed, but I think your ideas are exactly right. Elaine will be helping us for a good, long time yet, and Tommy should have a place to play. I hadn't even thought about having a playroom for Janine, but of course it will necessary in time. It's brilliant, Radcliffe, truly!"

"I'm glad you like it," he said, while Gina noticed that Milton and Tommy were already examining a collection of toy soldiers on one of the shelves. "The room hasn't been used since I was a child. I ordered a few new toys, but most of what's here was mine."

"I daresay that makes the room all the more special—sentimental," Gina said.

"I'm glad you think so," he said, smiling at her while his gaze took her in unabashedly, prompting a distinct tingle that rushed over her from head to toe. For a moment she felt as if he'd just given her this room as a gift; it might as well have been wrapped in a fancy box with a neatly tied bow on top. And she wondered if the possible deeper implications that came to her mind might be something he'd considered as well, or if it was only *her* thoughts that had gone there. Was his offering of the playroom he'd used as a child simply a matter of obvious practicality, or was his effort in this more personal? He seemed to be saying that he never wanted Janine to leave his home, which meant of course that Gina would always stay as well. Now that her father was here, with the implication that he would stay for as long as he lived, Gina could see a puzzle falling into place with the pieces all fitting together very nicely. She hoped that Radcliffe's thoughts were the same as hers, and that she wasn't defining the situation in a way that was based solely in her own hopes and wishes.

"They appear to be having an enjoyable time," Radcliffe said with a smile, motioning toward where Milton and Tommy were now quite comfortable sitting on the carpet, lining up the toy soldiers according to the different colors of the little painted-on uniforms. "Perhaps we should have tea *here*." He motioned toward the little tables and comfortable places to sit. "Make yourself comfortable, and I'll go and make certain Elaine can find us and that tea is brought here when it's time. I won't be long."

"Thank you," Gina said and watched him leave the room, far too aware of the way the silky fabric of the back of his waistcoat accentuated his masculinity so perfectly, and of the way his hair hung down over the high collar of his white shirt and the striped cravat tied there that was only partially visible due to the perfect length of his hair—just long enough to look well-groomed and entirely fashionable. He left the room with an air about him that was the perfect combination of humility and confidence; he'd always carried such an air, but Gina had been too focused on Dwight—or herself—to notice what a remarkable man Sir Radcliffe was and had always been.

Gina sat down at one end of a pale-gray brocade sofa near one of the room's many windows and settled easily into the comfort she found. She imagined this to be the perfect place to sit for many hours a day while her child—or children—played. She allowed herself to genuinely wonder for the first time since Dwight's death if she would have more than one child. She'd not been able to conceive during the years she'd been married to Dwight, and he'd exhibited no restraint in making certain she knew that he blamed her for the problem. Gina had enough common sense to know that it was possible that the medical conditions that might possibly prevent conception could be rooted either in the mother or the father. But Dwight had not been willing to take any responsibility for the possible fifty percent of the problem, and he'd had no compassion toward Gina and her heartache over not being able to have a child. And compounding this was his tendency to blame her for that fact, as if her ability to make him a father had become her only value as a woman. Janine had miraculously come into her life despite that problem, but Gina had no idea whether or not she *was* responsible for not being able to conceive; therefore, if she married again, she had to believe there was a fifty-percent possibility that Janine would be her only child—and that of the man she married. While it was becoming easier to imagine herself one day marrying Sir Radcliffe—especially given his growing attention to her—she wondered in her heart if she could carry the deception regarding Janine's origins into marriage. The very thought was so disconcerting and created such a painful inner dilemma that she pushed it away and focused on the lovely scene of her father playing toy soldiers on the carpet with Tommy. She felt a peaceful satisfaction to think that her father had wanted grandchildren for years, but Gina had been unable to have a child, and her siblings had shown little interest in even getting married; it was as if their relationship as brother and sister, with all of its shared selfishness and scheming, was all they would ever need. Gina believed her brother would marry eventually—mostly because he very much wanted an heir to his fortune, although his desire was based purely in vanity and arrogance rather than in any paternal yearnings. Gina doubted that her brother would ever hold a wife in higher favor than his sister, and Gina also doubted that her sister would ever marry and leave the home where she was completely comfortable and very much in control. But now that Gina's father was here, the deplorable attitudes and behavior of her siblings no longer affected her and her father. And as an additional blessing, her father had gained a playmate—a little boy who was very much in need of a kind male figure in his life. Gina believed she was witnessing the beginning of a fine friendship between the two, especially given the amount of laughter as well as serious conversation taking place between them regarding the imaginary battle raging on the carpet. Building blocks of different shapes and sizes were discovered in a box on one of the shelves, and they immediately began building walls and fortresses, which enhanced the enjoyment of their battle. Tommy was so enthralled that Gina wondered if he had ever played with anything more than the few, simple toys she had observed him carrying around with him. Her father was so equally enthralled—and looked so happy—that she felt a quiet thrill to realize that he was finally here, and he would be staying. Over time she would surely become accustomed to his presence in the house, but right now it almost felt like a dream, one from which she never wanted to awaken.

Radcliffe returned to report that he'd successfully accomplished his tasks, and Gina's heart quickened just to see him enter the room. But when he sat beside her on the sofa, the mere inches between them did not feel sufficient to keep her from sensing a kind of warmth radiating from him. She was glad when he quickly took notice of Milton and Tommy playing together, even though they hardly noticed Radcliffe's return, given how intently they were focused on their imaginary game.

"Isn't that delightful!" Radcliffe said to Gina in a voice that was little more than a whisper.

"It is indeed!" she replied in the same tone. "I daresay you are a worker of miracles, Sir. Having my father here is a blessing I don't believe I ever thought possible, and your having this room made available for us to use was so truly kind and thoughtful."

"I just want you to be happy, G," Radcliffe said, and she realized he was looking at *her* rather than at the cozy vision of Milton and Tommy playing together. The moment she allowed her eyes to connect to his, she wished she had restrained herself from allowing it to happen. She had sensed during the weeks they'd been sharing so much time together that he held some kind of affection for her, and deep inside she had hoped that it might be love as opposed to simply the comfort of being friends or cousins by marriage. But that idea also held some fear for her, knowing that he was a good and honest man, and she was the author of an enormous web of lies that had been constructed within the walls of his home. But seeing the unconcealed adoration in his eyes now, nothing else seemed to matter—at least for the moment. She wondered what might have changed since he'd left less than a week earlier to go and retrieve her father. The evidence of his affection for her had previously been subtle and difficult to discern, and now it was as if he'd removed all curtains and veils that had guarded the evidence of his feelings, and she felt as if he were silently challenging her to dispute what she could see so clearly in his eyes.

Unable to tear her gaze away and brutally aware that she was also unable to speak, Gina was relieved when Radcliffe said, his voice even softer as if he didn't want to take any chances on being overheard, "What are you thinking, Gina? I do wish you would tell me."

It was easier for her to speak, given that she had a specific question to answer, and she had no trouble turning it back on him. "I was wondering what *you* are thinking, Rad."

"Can't you guess?" he asked, one corner of his lips twitching upward slightly, while one of his dark eyebrows rose into a slightly mischievous arch. "Is it not obvious?"

"Perhaps," Gina admitted, "although I confess that I might be afraid to speculate aloud when I might be wrong."

He looked mildly nervous, but only for a moment. Then it seemed as if a layer of courage enveloped him and his gaze became almost audacious. "Then perhaps it's time I tell you how I feel, so you don't have to wonder, and I won't need to continue putting so much effort into trying to conceal my feelings—and also trying to guess yours." He took a deep breath and added, "I adore you, Gina." He sighed as if he'd just put down an enormous burden and he felt great relief to be free of it. Gina's heart raced in response to his confession, pounding so loudly that she could hear her own pulse beating in her ears. "I think you are a remarkable woman in every respect, and I've never known such a fine and lovely lady." While Gina still felt dazed and a little unsteady over what he was saying, he took her hand and pressed it to his lips, continuing to hold her gaze with his while his lengthy kiss was accompanied by a gentle squeeze of her fingers. He finally lifted his lips from her hand but didn't let go of her fingers as he lowered his voice to a whisper that was even quieter. "I realize this is neither the time nor the place to discuss such things, and I do hope that I haven't shocked you too terribly by making such a confession. I only ask that you . . . think about what I've said, and . . . perhaps we might be able to steal some time alone later . . . and . . . talk."

Gina saw him become uncharacteristically nervous and realized he had admitted to something that had left him feeling vulnerable. While she longed to ease his concern and let him know that he was not alone in his feelings, she was more grateful than she ever could have expressed that he was giving her time to mentally process what he'd just admitted to, which would allow her to carefully consider the best way to respond. She had no doubt about her feelings for him, and she knew that winning the favor of such a man—and the possibility of marriage to him—was surely one of the best things that could have ever happened to her. But the other best thing that had happened in her life was tangled up in terrible deception. She felt certain that if Radcliffe knew the truth about exactly how Janine had come into their lives he would surely never want to speak to her again; he would rightfully feel taken advantage of and sorely betrayed by her lies, and she wouldn't blame him in the slightest. And yet, how could she even consider engaging in the possibility of any kind of serious relationship with him when such deception existed between them? How could she spend the remainder of her life always on guard with her own husband so that he would never discover the truth? The very idea made her cringe; in fact, there was no possible course in this matter that *didn't* make her cringe—or feel downright terrified. She only hoped that by the time she and Radcliffe had the opportunity to talk later as he'd suggested, that she would be able to come up with some kind of reasonable explanation of her feelings for him that would still allow her the time and freedom to consider the possible impact of the truth about Janine's existence on their potential relationship.

Gina nodded and smiled at Radcliffe, saying quietly, "Of course." She was relieved that his expression made it clear that he'd perceived her implication that she was pleased with what he'd admitted—and what he wanted to discuss.

At that very moment, Elaine came in through the open doorway, carrying Janine, and Radcliffe hurried to let go of Gina's hand before Elaine might notice. Elaine stopped and turned to look in every direction, much as Gina had done earlier. She let out a little laugh and said, "What a perfectly magical room!" Her eyes then went to her son who was playing so contentedly with Milton that he hadn't even noticed his mother entering the room. "Oh, how delightful!" she said, and her face seemed to quite literally become brighter.

"Yes, it is, isn't it," Gina stated. Elaine crossed the room and eased the baby into Gina's arms, while Gina whispered to her, "It seems the two of them might need each other."

"Indeed," Elaine said, observing Tommy and Milton again now that her arms were free of the baby. "That is very delightful, indeed."

"Please, sit down," Gina said. "Tea will soon be here for all of us. And we wouldn't want to interrupt whatever is going on over there." She laughed softly. "It seems like very serious play." She turned more toward Radcliffe and asked, "Is that a contradiction? Serious play?"

"Not in my opinion," Radcliffe said, watching the *serious play* taking place, wearing a childlike smile, as if the scene conjured up pleasant memories of his own childhood spent in this room.

The remainder of the day was utterly delightful as Gina observed her father blending so easily into their usual routine that she found it difficult to imagine his not having been there the previous day. And she was so glad to have Radcliffe back; she'd genuinely missed him, and it was evident that he'd missed her. As they shared tea, visited, and passed Janine around so she could be held and admired, Gina couldn't avoid the frequent, not-so-subtle glances that Radcliffe regularly sent in her direction. It took great willpower to suppress her nervousness over the fact that they were going to speak later—in private—about his earlier confessions and the feelings they had shared. Gina wasn't certain what she might say to him, other than firmly believing she needed to be honest—but her commitment to honesty regarding her feelings for Radcliffe felt deeply hypocritical when she considered that she felt nothing less than desperate about keeping her secret hidden regarding Janine's true parentage. The possibility of a future with Radcliffe made her happier than she'd ever been, and the possibility of him discovering the truth made her feel sick inside. While a part of her believed he *should* know, she pushed that thought away, reminding herself that admitting to their mutual attraction was just one small step with many unknown factors ahead of them. If and when the possibility of marriage came up, she would need to firmly decide whether she intended to keep her secret from him, or if she could hope that he would still be accepting of her and Janine if he knew the truth. For now, she simply did her best to enjoy the day, although at supper her nervousness increased, knowing from what Radcliffe had said earlier that he likely would not let the day end without continuing their conversation.

Since Elaine had suggested that Gina enjoy the evening with her father and the baronet, she'd offered to care for Janine on her own and insisted that Gina not worry about what time she came upstairs for the night. After supper, Gina and the two men went to the parlor closest to the dining room where they talked and laughed for a long while—or rather Radcliffe and her father did most of the talking while Gina just observed them, amazed at how naturally comfortable they were with each other. How could she not think that this was a good sign regarding the possibility of sharing a future with Radcliffe? The house was certainly large enough for one to be able to mostly avoid relatives whose company they disliked, but if they could truly live like a family and bring joy to each other's lives, it would be a glorious thing.

Gina had almost forgotten about her commitment to share a conversation with Radcliffe until her father announced that he was ready to turn in for the night, given that the journey had worn him out. Milton stood and reached his hands toward Gina, who came to her feet and took them.

"My dear girl," he said, kissing her cheek. "What a joy it is to be here with you and your family! I've not felt so content since . . . well . . . likely since you married and left home. I've missed you dreadfully."

"And I've missed you, Papa," she said, squeezing his hands. "I'm so very glad you're here." She kissed *his* cheek and added, "You are welcome to ring for breakfast to be brought to your rooms in the morning, if you like, or you are welcome to join me and Janine in my sitting room. We're very much about slow mornings here, and then we join each other for tea and our other meals later in the day."

"And you always have the option to either have meals brought to your room, or to join us," Radcliffe added. "I want you to feel completely at home and do whatever is comfortable for you on any given day."

"Your generosity is most welcome," Milton said to Radcliffe before he nodded at Gina and added, "I suppose we will see what time I wake up and what kind of mood I'm in." He pointed quickly at Gina. "I know where to find you."

"Yes, you do," Gina said, "and if I'm not there, one of the maids will be nearby and know where I am."

Milton thanked both her and Radcliffe and wished them good night before he left the room. Gina's heartbeat immediately quickened at the sudden realization that she was alone with Radcliffe, and their intended conversation was about to take place.

"Alone at last," he said with a laugh that came out on the wake of an exaggerated sigh. He walked to the open door and closed it, which was highly unusual since they always left a door open when they were in a room together in order to maintain every appearance or propriety. Of course, they were both mature adults and had the right to share a private conversation, and she suspected that he didn't care if anyone might find the situation worthy of criticism; *she* certainly didn't care.

Gina sat back down, and Radcliffe sat on the sofa next to her rather than in the chair where he'd been sitting before her father had left. He immediately took her hand into his, a gesture that bridged this moment to their brief exchange earlier in the playroom.

"I must admit," he began, "that I've been rather nervous all day. I've not once in my life so openly admitted such feelings to a woman; therefore, such vulnerability is highly uncomfortable. I hope that doesn't sound odd or—"

"Not at all," she said, attempting to reassure him.

"I have suspected you might have feelings for me, G, but of course I can't be sure. Perhaps you only see me as a friend . . . or your cousin by way of your marriage to Dwight, but still . . . I had to tell you how I feel, even if it means hearing that you don't share my feelings."

He chuckled in a way that revealed the nervousness he'd admitted to, and Gina felt inclined to relieve him of his concern. "There is no reason for such anxiousness, Rad," she said, "although I feel rather like a hypocrite to say such a thing when I too have been nervous. But rest assured, you are not alone in your feelings. I have been wondering for weeks now if this conversation might ever take place, and very much hoping that it would."

"Truly?" he asked as if the Red Sea had just parted right there in the parlor.

"Truly," she said with a little laugh, practically giddy over the evidence that he was so thoroughly amazed to know that she cared for him as he did for her.

"Then there is much we need to discuss, G," he said, now more somber. "We are both well aware that it's not considered suitable for a lady to court or marry too soon following the death of her husband, and while I'm not terribly keen on worrying about certain abstract social guidelines, I do believe it is prudent to take time in such serious matters. I'm not by any means proposing marriage in this moment, Gina, but I do want to say that I hope it's a possibility, and I wonder if—just between you and me, and perhaps those few members of the staff we work with closely and trust implicitly—that we might enter into some form of courtship for the purpose of focusing our time together more keenly on learning more about each other and whether or not marriage would be a good decision. Of course I hope the outcome will be marriage, and if for some reason we decide that it's not, I do hope that our friendship will never be compromised, that we will be able to contend with our feelings maturely and remain close throughout life, whatever path our relationship might take."

"I agree wholeheartedly," she said, "with everything you've just said."

He laughed again with pure delight. "Oh, I would say that's a very good sign."

"I would like to add, however, that we have known each other an exceptionally long time. I do believe we each have a fairly good idea of the other's character, although getting to know one another better regarding more personal matters and beliefs is surely prudent."

"Agreed," he said and kissed the hand he'd been holding tightly, which provoked a pleasant tingle that rushed up Gina's arm. He then surprised Gina by looking down abruptly, but not before she saw something akin to shame come over his face like a shadow. "Before we go any further, my dear," he said, "there's something I must tell you, and I pray you don't think too ill of me once you know the truth."

Gina's heart quickened as she could imagine herself saying these very words to him regarding Janine; but she absolutely knew he couldn't be confessing to anything nearly as severe as lying about a pregnancy and the origin of a child. She swallowed carefully and said in a soft, encouraging voice, "It's all right. You can tell me anything. No human being is perfect, Rad. I'm quite certain there are things about me you would find disagreeable, and I would hope you'd be forgiving and bear an open mind regarding my own shortcomings. I would never offer you anything less than what I would hope for in return."

He looked up at her, his eyes showing relief while she wondered what on earth he might be trying to tell her. "I feel so much guilt," he said, "over the fact that I rarely felt anything but contempt for Dwight."

"Contempt?" she echoed, confused.

"In truth, he and I did not know each other very well before he came to live here following his father's death. He had nowhere to go and I was his only family. I felt it was only right that I provide a home for him. But I quickly realized he and I had next to nothing in common, and I practically loathed spending time with him; in fact, I went to a great deal of trouble to avoid him. And yet, he had a way of manipulating me into attending many social events with him, although I can look back now and see that he most likely wanted to take advantage of my connections, whereas he was a newcomer to the social circles of London." Radcliffe took a deep breath and added, as if he were letting go of a heavy burden, "I disliked him deeply, Gina, and I have struggled a great deal to come to terms with such feelings since his death."

Gina felt more than a little stunned by his confession, but attempted to assuage his self-imposed guilt by saying, "I too have struggled with many confusing emotions regarding my relationship with Dwight—both prior to his death, and since. Surely our response to his behavior is not something over which we should feel guilt. It's taken me a long time to come to such a conclusion, and it's been difficult; nevertheless, neither you nor I are responsible for the way that Dwight treated us."

"No, you're right," he said with a relief in his voice that contradicted a persistent guilt in his eyes. "Are you saying then that I should not feel guilt over the fact that . . ."

"That what?" she encouraged when he hesitated.

"That something changed in me the moment I saw you . . . that day I came to your room after Janine was born." His voice trembled slightly, and she realized she was hearing an even deeper confession. "I will never forget how I felt just standing in the doorway, seeing you for the first time in months. It was as if I were looking at my own destiny somehow, and . . . yet at the same moment as I was thinking of how I'd never before noticed how absolutely lovely and wonderful you are, I felt the weight of guilt come over me . . . that I would have such feelings for my cousin's widow. I've been struggling with these conflicting feelings ever since. I often think that—given the fact that I disliked Dwight very much—I should not care how he might feel about my falling in love with his widow, but on the other hand . . ."

Gina was grateful for the way he paused to try and gather his words. She was so stunned by what she was hearing she could hardly breathe, let alone speak. She couldn't deny the truth in what he'd said about his feelings toward Dwight. She could look back now with a more open mind and realize that she had sometimes sensed his disapproval of Dwight's subtle but undeniable lack of respect toward Gina, but perhaps she had pushed that away into the far recesses of her mind along with the unhappiness of her marriage and her inability to have a child—simply because she could do nothing to change any of it; therefore, even thinking about such things only brought on unbearable grief. But everything had changed with Dwight's death; she had been set free, even though she'd hardly dared admit such a rueful idea to herself, let alone anyone else. It seemed so crass to feel relief over the tragic death of a loved one, and she *had* loved Dwight, despite his many shortcomings. And yet it wasn't at all surprising how quickly her love had dwindled in his absence; with him gone she had been able to more clearly see how uncomfortable and even unsafe—if only in an emotional sense—she had always felt in his presence. Now, to hear that Radcliffe too had struggled with conflicting emotions regarding Dwight since his death was nothing less than comforting. He'd mentioned it once before, but what he'd just said went much deeper into his truest feelings on the matter. But far more surprising and wonderful was to hear that at the very same moment Gina had felt a strange, new attraction to Radcliffe, he had been feeling the same toward her. She had to mentally review his words to convince herself that he really had used the word *love*. She almost felt as if she were floating in a dream. And yet she could feel the sofa beneath her, and Radcliffe's hand in hers, reminding her that this was indeed very real.

Once again seeing stark vulnerability in Radcliffe's expression, she fought to gather her voice if only to ease his concerns. Overwhelmed as she was by his mention of love, she resorted to focusing on the more practical facets of their conversation. She had to take a forced deep breath and clear her throat before she was able to say, "There is no need for you to apologize, Rad. I have wondered myself a thousand times what I might have done differently, what signs I might have missed regarding Dwight's behavior because I was so naive . . . so blindly in love with him; or at least I thought it was love. Now I believe I was more in love with the idea of love and marriage, and by all social standards he was considered an excellent catch. I was being praised right and left by nearly everyone I knew for gaining the favor of such a fine man; I suppose I held to that description of a *fine man* and ignored the rest. My father expressed his concern to me, but he had also told me that he trusted me to make good choices for my life. I know now that he put too much faith in me, because I had no idea what I was doing. I can also see that a parent rarely has influence over the decisions of an adult child, and I think he knew that; I think he knew I was in love with Dwight—or at least I believed I was—and I was determined to marry him and there was nothing he could say or do to change my mind. Truly, Rad, I believed it was a good choice, and yet in retrospect I am appalled with myself for all that I ignored or chose not to see." Gina put her other hand over where Rad was still holding hers. "You have nothing to apologize for. It seems we were both very much in the same state of mind, and perhaps we both needed these experiences and this time for us to learn the lessons in life that God is trying to teach us."

"Perhaps," he said with the barest hint of a smile. "I never thought of it that way, but I confess that might actually help me feel better." He sighed loudly. "I know we can't change the past, G; we can only move forward from this moment. But I had to tell you the truth; I need you to know that I love you, and I no longer care what Dwight might think of how I feel . . . or how we go forward with our lives."

For several long moments Gina considered her words carefully, knowing they were important but also extremely sensitive. But his own confessions made it easier for her to say, "May I tell you something that's been difficult for me to reconcile?"

"Of course," he said, looking up abruptly, as if he were far more comfortable discussing her sensitive feelings, rather than his own.

"I've actually felt a great deal of confusion since Dwight's death . . . because I've had so much relief mixed in with my grief. And then I felt so guilty for being relieved; a wife surely should not feel that way over her husband's death."

"I don't believe at all that you should assign guilt to what you *feel*, G. It's only a matter of learning to understand *why* we feel something, isn't it? And

I believe you've done that. I admit it's a sad thing for a wife to feel that way over her husband's death, but that was surely due to *his* choices, not yours. I know—because I saw so much evidence of it—how hard you tried to be a good wife."

Gina had no warning that tears were threatening before they spilled down her face and there was no opportunity to hide them from Radcliffe.

"Oh, my dear," he said with perfect compassion as he took a neatly folded handkerchief from his pocket. And rather than handing it to her, he took it upon himself to dab at her cheeks to dry them. "There is no need for tears."

"I do believe these are tears of relief," Gina admitted, "even . . . joy, perhaps. To be able to express such complicated emotions . . . and to have you understand . . . means more than I can say. I've cried many tears of sorrow and confusion and grief. But this feels different." She laughed amid her ongoing flow of tears, which seemed to validate what she was trying to say. Fearing her nose would run, she took the handkerchief from him and pressed it there, not wanting to embarrass herself any more than necessary. When her tears wouldn't stop, which made it impossible to speak, Gina was pleasantly surprised with the way that Radcliffe guided her face to his shoulder, holding the back of her head with his hand, and placing his other arm gently around her back. The enormity of all he'd admitted to her about his feelings, along with the unburdening of her *own* feelings—overtook her with such ferocity that she found herself quietly sobbing while she tried not to think about how her vast quantity of tears would surely leave a great deal of moisture on Radcliffe's waistcoat.

Gina lost all sense of time while she wept within the safety and comfort of Radcliffe's assuaging and unassuming embrace. Her tears finally relented to silence, but she found his shoulder so comfortable that she felt no incentive to move, and he showed no sign of impatience for her to do so. Only when she began to fear that remaining in his embrace this way for too long might appear presumptuous did she force herself to sit up straight, using the handkerchief to clear away the remaining moisture clinging to her face.

"Forgive me," she said. "I'm not certain why all of that bubbled up in such a way, but . . ."

"You have no need to apologize," he said and surprised her by touching her face with his fingers. "It is my honor to share your tears with you, G." She smiled at him and he smiled back, but she didn't know what to say in response to such sincere gallantry—something Dwight had *never* given her. "I'm certain," Rad went on, "that I've likely said far more in this conversation than should be said in any *one* conversation, therefore I certainly don't expect you to offer any response this evening, but I do hope you'll think about what I've said, and . . . perhaps we can talk again soon . . . when you're ready. I don't want you to feel any pressure from me simply because *I* felt the need to unburden myself. We will go on as we have, and when you wish to talk all you have to do is—"

"I love you, as well, Radcliffe," Gina said emphatically, so there would be no room for him to doubt her sincerity. She heard him gasp softly, and she hurried to clarify herself. "I've always enjoyed your company, but my focus was entirely on Dwight."

"As it should have been," he said with a somberness that emphasized how much he believed that to be true.

"However," she went on, "when you came to my room . . . after Janine was born . . . I felt something for you I'd never felt before . . . and I've felt it growing every day since. I hardly dared hope that you would feel the same for me, but . . ." she laughed softly, "now I know that you do, and . . . I agree with everything you said about our . . . courting . . . in a private kind of way for the time being. I can't imagine anything more wonderful! You've already given me so much . . . made our lives so good . . . and now you've made me happier than I ever thought possible."

Radcliffe let out a small laugh and placed a lingering kiss on her brow, which took Gina's breath away as much as it made her tingle. He then looked into her eyes and said, "I do believe it's the other way around, G."

Gina's idyllic reverie was intruded upon by the recollection that she had constructed an enormous lie about the origin of her daughter, and she felt certain that if he knew the truth, the trust between them would be shattered, and no amount of love could ever repair such indelible damage. Seeing the undeniable evidence of love and adoration in his eyes, she wanted to believe that he would still accept her and Janine—that he would forgive her—but she couldn't be sure, and she wondered if she would ever be able to tell him the entire truth. And if she couldn't be completely honest with him about something that was at the very center of her life, how could she ever expect to share a life with him and have a free conscience?

Longing to simply enjoy *this* moment, and the hope that somehow everything might come together for them in every good way, Gina pushed her fears aside, certain she might drown in the relief that enveloped her when he kissed her brow once again, this time allowing his lips to linger there even longer. It was a gentleman's kiss, completely lacking in any kind of presumptuousness, and showing absolute respect for her. Their confessions of love were still too new for them to venture into the kind of kiss she longed to share with him. And she knew him to be entirely a gentleman, which made her doubt that he would even attempt to kiss her lips until there was an official agreement between them regarding their future. But the very fact that she knew he wanted to share such affection as much as she did, afforded her a lovely anticipation of exploring her relationship with him. If not for one exceptionally large problem, everything would be absolutely perfect.

CHAPTER SEVEN
discovered

GINA FOUND IT IMPOSSIBLE TO fall asleep as she recounted the conversations she'd shared with Radcliffe, which had left no doubt about their feelings for each other, nor their hopes and intentions. But her mind kept vacillating between the extreme of absolute happiness at the prospect of sharing her life here with Radcliffe, and her deepest fears regarding the lies she had constructed in order to have Janine in her life. Mixed into her racing thoughts and conflicting emotions was the wonderful reality that her father was now living beneath this roof, and having him here had already given her so much joy. He seemed happy and comfortable, and she didn't want to ever do anything to compromise *his* place here at Stonebridge Manor.

Gina finally slept from the sheer exhaustion of regularly getting up in the night to care for an infant. She and Elaine went through their usual nighttime routine of sharing the responsibilities for what Janine required, while they talked of trivial things to help keep each other awake. While Janine slept, Gina did as well, and it was only when Janine awoke in daylight that Gina got up and prepared herself for the day after Janine's needs were met and Gina had enjoyed an excellent breakfast in her sitting room, still wearing a nightgown beneath a well-worn but comfortable dressing gown that had been her favorite for years.

Gina was sitting at her dressing table in front of its big mirror while Ruby styled her hair when Milton knocked at the partially open door and asked with a pleasant laugh if he might visit with his daughter and granddaughter.

"Oh, do come in!" Gina insisted, pleased that she could visit with her father under such casual circumstances. "How did you sleep?" Gina asked, as he crossed the room toward her. "And how are you finding your new accommodations? Is everything to your liking or—"

"One question at a time, my dear girl," Milton said with a chuckle and kissed her cheek without interfering at all with Ruby's ongoing work on Gina's hair. "Hello, Ruby," he said, nodding and smiling at the maid. Of course, he remembered the three siblings who had not only worked for the family for years but had been playmates and then Gina's dear friends. Nevertheless, Ruby looked a little surprised by his greeting. "And how are you, young miss?"

"I'm very well, thank you, sir," she said, sounding only mildly nervous. "And you?"

"I'm very well," Milton said and dropped into a nearby chair that Gina knew to be wonderfully comfortable. It was also placed at a perfect angle near a large pair of windows so that it afforded a pleasant view of the lawn to the side of the manor, as well as the woods that stretched out in the distance. "And to answer your questions, daughter," he went on, "I slept like the dead; the bed is fine and comfortable, as are all my accommodations. The servants have been kind and immensely helpful. I enjoyed a delicious breakfast without so much as having to get out of bed, and I've been well cared for in every regard. I couldn't possibly ask for more." Milton smiled at Gina and she returned it even though she had to be careful not to move her head while Ruby continued to work on her hair. "Sir Radcliffe has even gone so far as to provide me with a personal valet who is a fine young man . . . as thoughtful as he is skilled. Kirby is his name."

"Oh, I know Kirby well," Ruby said. "We are on the same shift for our meals; he's well-liked and respected in the household."

"Yes," Gina added, trying not to sound affected by mention of the young man, "he worked as Dwight's valet, so I knew him well . . . although I don't think I've seen him once since Dwight's death."

"The baronet insisted on keeping him employed," Ruby explained, "although Kirby's admitted to feeling rather useless, or sometimes doing work that was far beneath his skills and abilities. I daresay he must be pleased to have the opportunity to once again do work that is more within his know-how."

"Then perhaps this is a blessing for both of us," Milton said. "I like him very much. Sir Radcliffe and I discussed the possibility of my bringing my valet with me—or any of the other servants if I felt that was appropriate. He generously offered to bring anyone into the household that would help me feel more at home. Nevertheless, in all honesty, it had come to feel as if every single soul in that household had been poisoned by the dictatorship of my children who have completely taken control. I was only too glad to leave and bring nothing with me except my most personal belongings. So, to conclude the answer to your questions, dear girl, I am pleased as punch in every respect. Last week I never could have imagined that *this* week my life would be so much improved—all thanks to Sir Radcliffe's kind heart."

"Indeed," Gina said, smiling more to herself in the mirror.

"He's a good man and a fair employer," Ruby declared, clearly comfortable now with being a part of the conversation, even with Gina's father present. Generally, the servants were expected to speak only when invited to do so, but those who worked closely with Gina knew that she paid no heed to that rule, and she always welcomed the conversation and any insights her maids had to offer. She only saw Garn on his occasional visits to check in on her and Janine, and sometimes she was able to join the three siblings as they visited, and he clearly knew the same applied to him.

"I'm extremely glad to hear it," Milton said, "and not at all surprised." Following a long moment of silence, an idea seemed to occur to Milton, and he asked with zeal, "Now, where is my granddaughter? I've missed her terribly since yesterday evening."

Gina laughed softly, loving the way her father had already fallen in love with Janine, and she had no doubt the two would bring each other great joy throughout the whole of their lives—or for as long as her father lived.

"She's there on my bed," Gina said, motioning with her hand in a way that didn't move her head. "This time of the morning she likes to just look around and is generally rather content. She seems especially fascinated with the light coming through the windows, more so than later in the day."

Milton hurried to the bed as if he couldn't get there quickly enough, and Gina could see in the reflection of the mirror how he sat down carefully before he began speaking to Janine in a funny voice, greeting her with very formal words that seemed contradictory to the tone in which he spoke them. He leaned closer to the baby and spoke softly to her about the warmth and light that the sun provided to the earth, and how it never went away even when it was hiding behind clouds that offered rain, which was equally important to the world in which they lived. He spoke to her as if he intended to spend his life teaching her about *everything*, and in a way that implied she was presently old enough to actually understand what he was saying. Gina found the scene touching to the point that she was almost brought to tears, and she was warmed by the way Ruby whispered in her ear, "If I say so myself, m'lady, bringing Janine into your life could only be right when you see the joy she already gives your father."

"It would seem that way," Gina replied in an equally soft tone that her father couldn't hear. Oh, how she prayed that her secret remained safe, and that the love and tenderness Janine brought about among those who were a part of her life would always remain intact.

⚜

Over the next few weeks, Milton settled in so naturally that Gina couldn't imagine how life had been without him there. She wished that she had initiated this move years ago, although she suspected that Dwight would likely not have been in favor of the idea, and she also believed that the situation with her father had needed to reach a point of being so terrible that he'd been ready and eager to leave his home; otherwise, he would have been resistant to such a move. But now that he was here, sharing bits and pieces of his days with Gina and Janine and Radcliffe, he seemed happier than she had seen him since her mother had passed away many years earlier.

Summer had clung desperately to their little part of the world with unusually warm days, which allowed for time outside. Sometimes Milton joined Gina and Radcliffe for their strolls through the garden with Janine, and sometimes he chose to relax inside. Gina thoroughly loved the way her private conversations with Radcliffe had changed so dramatically since their confessions of love for each other. When they were alone, they talked in depth about their beliefs, their preferences, their philosophies on life and the world. And it gradually became more and more comfortable to talk about the possibility of sharing their lives together permanently and officially. As always, Gina kept any thoughts of her deception regarding Janine pushed far to the back of her mind, and she was glad to find that it was becoming easier to do so. The longer that Janine was a part of their lives, and the more that everyone around her came to love her, the easier it became for Gina to believe with all her soul that this was where God had intended for Janine to be, and Gina was committed to giving her the best possible life.

Summer lost its battle for survival abruptly and harshly as heavy rain and cold winds arrived in torrents, removing the last of any dead leaves from the trees, and turning the lush shades of green from the lawns and gardens to varying hues of yellow and brown. The world outside took on a dismal appearance, but life inside Stonebridge Manor became all the cozier and happier as Gina became increasingly confident that her relationship with Radcliffe was forever, and they thoroughly enjoyed every moment they had together—whether they were alone and able to share deep conversation, or with her father who was always amiable and good company. And the three of them could never get enough of Janine; every day she seemed to change a little, and with the passing of weeks she had not only become chubbier and more alert to her surroundings, she was able to focus on the faces of those who were talking to her, and she began to respond with smiles and sweet cooing sounds, as if she were telling those who loved her some very important things, even though they were unable to understand.

It was great cause for celebration among Janine's admirers—her family members as well as the maids who helped care for her personally—when she was able to hold a little rattle in her dimpled hand and shake it furiously. And the day she first laughed created ripples of laughter among all who heard her. From that time forward, there seemed a continual effort to make Janine laugh, which caused every adult who interacted with her to become absolute fools— which in turn created more humor. The happiness that Janine radiated all around her was too great to be measured, but it filled Gina's heart with perfect joy; well . . . almost perfect joy—as long as she chose to not think about the secrets that she believed more and more would always remain unknown.

Gina also enjoyed her many opportunities to share conversations with her father. She was delighted at the evidence of how they had both come to a place in their lives where they could discuss life as adults, and she was continually impressed with her father's wisdom and keen perception; she'd always seen him as a good man, but her own life's experiences had given her a far more accurate lens through which to view the happenings and people around her—both in the present, and in analyzing the past for the purpose of trying to learn from it. She grew to love and admire her father in a way she never had, and little gave her more joy than seeing the precious relationship he shared with her daughter.

Milton also continued to spend time in the playroom with Tommy every day, and they became good friends. Gina or Elaine—or both—were always present and watching the two of them playing in a variety of ways was always entertaining. Sometimes Radcliffe joined them there when estate business wasn't monopolizing his time. He too enjoyed watching Milton and Tommy play, but he also liked to join them, and that's when the activities became especially entertaining. Gina had seen a side to Radcliffe she'd never known before as she'd observed his tenderness and silliness with Janine; but seeing him play with a little boy who was actually old enough to play brought out an entirely different kind of silliness that was completely endearing.

Once Janine had reached an age where, given their experience with babies, Ruby and Emerald declared that she was strong and healthy enough to be exposed to the outside world, Gina finally took the baby to church. She had to fight back a great deal of anxiety in preparing to go; the lies she had constructed around the fiction of Janine being her daughter plagued her more loudly when mixed with the reality of facing the people of this community. Gina was well aware that everyone knew she'd unexpectedly given birth, and she knew that Janine's real mother was likely to know the truth—that Janine was *not* Gina's daughter by blood. She still had a suspicion that Bernice, the new maid who had been hired a few months earlier, might be Janine's mother, but she had yet to meet Bernice, and she firmly believed that Janine's mother—whether it was Bernice or not—would want to keep the secret as desperately as Gina did. So, she did her best not to worry while she prepared to attend church for the first time since Dwight's death. Ruby and Emerald both agreed that her anxiousness about going was likely due more to how long it had been, rather than any concern about how people might perceive her unexpectedly becoming a mother. The story was plausible, and everyone had accepted it. Gina found comfort in their logic and was glad for their soothing encouragement as they helped her get ready while Elaine fed the baby and dressed her in a lovely pale-blue gown and bonnet. Elaine would be attending church with them in case Janine needed her; it wasn't at all uncommon for a nanny to accompany the baby in her care wherever the baby went; therefore, her presence would be completely natural. Gina concluded it was only her guilty conscience that made her uneasy, and she needed to push that away and become accustomed to the fact that Janine was *her* daughter, and she always would be. She'd grown comfortable with accepting that fact within the parameters of her life at Stonebridge Manor, and now it was time to show herself in public as a mother, and to do so with confidence.

Attending church with Radcliffe and her father, Gina wondered why she had felt any nervousness whatsoever. Both men were so kind and gracious toward everyone with whom they spoke, and they were also sensitive to Gina's every need or concern, as if they could practically read her mind. Before and after the service, people gathered around to admire the baby and offer their congratulations, and Gina and Radcliffe spoke with the vicar about arranging an official christening for Janine. Gina had to stifle more guilt as she considered the sacredness of such an event, and that it would officially declare Janine as her daughter—not only in the eyes of the public, but in the eyes of God. But in her heart, she honestly believed that God had brought this precious little girl into her life, and that He was with her in her need to keep Janine safe and cared for. Therefore, she found the idea of a christening to be more comforting than worrisome, since it would surely bind Janine to her more fully.

Janine slept through much of the service—which Gina enjoyed very much—and when she did awake, she remained contentedly quiet in her mother's arms, seeming eager to be admired afterward as many people commented on what a beautiful child she was, and there were several mentions of how she surely resembled her deceased father. Gina wondered if by some miracle, that was somehow the case—even though she couldn't see it herself—or if people only saw what they believed to be true.

In the carriage on the way home, with Elaine sitting next to Gina, and the men sitting across from them, Janine became suddenly very fussy, and with Gina's assistance, Elaine was able to feed the baby discreetly beneath a little blanket thrown over her shoulder, which Gina helped hold in place. The men were often in the same room at home while Elaine fed the baby, and the situation was all very matter-of-fact and completely lacking in any awkwardness, for which Gina was glad. She knew that in some households, people considered it entirely inappropriate for men—or sometimes even women who were not closely related—to be present when a baby was breastfed, but she also knew that in some households, nannies took care of babies and young children almost entirely, and they were hardly ever seen—even by members of the family. Gina couldn't even imagine such attitudes when she wanted to be a part of Janine's life every possible minute, and she was glad that her father and Radcliffe felt the same way. And Elaine was simply so easy to be around, and so comfortable and adept at doing whatever needed to be done, that she made the entire situation feel relaxed and appropriate.

The following day brought an excessively cold rainstorm that completely contradicted the warm October sun that had accompanied them to church the previous morning. Fires blazed in every fireplace where anyone in the house might be going about their business, and Gina stayed close to the fire in her sitting room, not feeling any incentive to even venture out into the cold hallway to go anywhere else in the house. She knew that Radcliffe had a day filled with meetings, which was something that happened regularly. He was required to remain apprised of every estate matter through his solicitors and overseers, and there were times when he needed to personally see to certain challenges. Knowing she wouldn't see Radcliffe until dinner, Gina settled in to spend the day with Janine, certain she would have the company of Ruby and Emerald at some point during the day, and of course Elaine was always pleasant to visit with while she fed the baby. Gina also felt certain her father would find his way here, since he would never go very long without visiting his granddaughter. Gina had taken to teasing Milton about how it was a good thing Gina was always near the baby; otherwise, she would hardly see her father at all. They both knew it wasn't true, and they both always laughed over such comments, but still there was no denying how smitten Milton was with little Janine, and the baby clearly liked her grandfather's company. He was gifted at being able to get the baby to smile and coo in response to his comical expressions and attempts at silly conversation with an infant.

Milton joined Gina in her sitting room not long after she'd finished getting dressed and having her hair put up. Elaine had just fed the baby and had left to spend some time with Tommy. Milton sat down on a little sofa with Gina, which had been moved closer to the fire and farther from the windows where the wind thrashed the rain against the glass with ferocity. They exchanged the usual greetings as Milton took Janine from Gina, then as always, her focus turned to the unique and entertaining exchange between Janine and her grandfather. The adults laughed a great deal as Janine proved to be in an especially bright mood and kept laughing over the most insignificant things. After Janine finally became bored of this game, Milton put her on the carpet where one of her little blankets had been spread. She loved to lay on her back and wave her arms and legs about wildly, which Elaine had declared was a baby's form of exercise, strengthening her limbs for the inevitable forthcoming ability to turn over on her own and to crawl. Gina loved observing every new stage that Janine entered, and each piece of evidence of her progress. She also loved having a small baby to hold in her arms, and a part of her dreaded having her little Janine become too wiggly and restless to want to be held. But she was glad that Elaine had prepared her for what to expect; and Elaine had also taught her to enjoy each day and each stage of her baby's progress.

When Janine was happily engaged, with a little toy in each hand, Milton turned more toward Gina and said, "There's something I've been wanting to talk to you about, daughter, but we don't often get time to ourselves—at least not long enough to have a serious conversation."

Gina felt a little surprised, and also noticed the way her father glanced toward the doors of the room, as if to make certain they were closed in order to ensure privacy—which they were; when the house was cold it was more practical to keep doors closed to hold the heat in the room. She felt compelled to clarify, "Dear Papa, you know that if you need to talk to me about something, you only need to ask for some time alone and I would be only too happy to comply. I don't ever want you to feel like you can't—"

"I know that's true, Gina, I really do; you mustn't worry. If this had been an urgent matter, I would have made certain we discussed it before now. But it's not urgent, and I've just been waiting for a good time. Today Radcliffe is busy, and the maids are about their business elsewhere and we have every reason to stay indoors and close to the fire."

"Yes, of course," Gina said, feeling nervous even though her father seemed completely relaxed. She didn't sense anything from him to indicate that what he had to say might be upsetting for any reason, but she also couldn't imagine what he might want to talk to her about that would require time and privacy.

"First of all," Milton said, "I want you to know how happy I am living here with you. I'd never imagined it as a possibility, but now that I've settled in here, I find myself anticipating each day with gladness instead of waking up and feeling dread over what kind of drama I might have to face. I've thanked Sir Radcliffe enough to bore him to death." He chuckled. "But I wanted to thank you again for helping make it possible, and for your warmth and love toward me, and for allowing me to enjoy the company of this beautiful child." He glanced toward Janine with overt adoration glowing on his face, then he turned back toward Gina, his expression turning completely serious.

Gina didn't know what he was working toward saying, but she responded easily to what he'd said so far. "It is more than my pleasure, Papa. I'm so glad you're here. My life is all the better for having you here, and I'm grateful Janine will grow up with her grandfather in *her* life."

"I'm grateful for that too," he said.

"And I know that little Tommy very much enjoys your company, and Elaine is grateful for the time and attention you give him."

"That is entirely selfish on my behalf." Milton chuckled. "He's a delightful boy, and his mother is a good woman. You are very blessed to have her assistance in caring for our precious Janine."

"Yes," Gina said, "I am *very* blessed."

Gina appreciated all the gratitude and sentiment being expressed, but she knew her father was trying to get to a point that was more serious, and she was growing increasingly nervous about what it might be. She saw his expression become even more somber, and she steeled herself to hear something difficult. Did he have a serious illness or disease? Despite all the good things he'd said about being here, was there an underlying problem of which she was unaware?

"You and Sir Radcliffe enjoy each other's company very much." Milton stated it as a fact, with no inflection in his voice whatsoever that might give her any indication of how he felt about what he'd just said, but he clearly had a reason for saying it.

"Yes, we do," she replied in the same matter-of-fact tone of voice. She already knew from discussing the matter with Radcliffe that they agreed that there was no problem with her father or the servants who worked closely with them—and were considered trusted friends—knowing about their quiet courting relationship. They'd both quickly realized that making any kind of formal announcement at this point didn't seem necessary, and so they'd agreed that if anyone asked either of them about it they would be forthright and honest, but otherwise the matter would be left unsaid for the time being—at least until they passed the one-year anniversary of Dwight's death, at which time Radcliffe felt that he could come forward and make a formal request to court her with the intention of marriage. Gina was prepared to answer any question her father had regarding her relationship with Dwight and felt relieved that his sober approach to this conversation was not so serious after all.

"And since I've spent a great deal of time with the both of you," Milton went on, "and I do consider myself a perceptive man, I am not fool enough to believe that your feelings for each other are limited to friendship, or even to the familial connection you share due to your having been married to his cousin."

"Neither of us would ever consider you a fool, Papa," Gina said, "and we haven't been trying to hide anything from you, or to keep secrets. We've simply felt it might be best to wait until the proper period of mourning has passed before we officially began courting. We both suspected you might figure it out without being told, and Radcliffe's only concern was that he wishes to be able to formally ask for your blessing in our courting, and I'm certain he will hope that you are not unhappy with him in any way for not coming to you before now. He would never want you to feel disrespected in your place as my father, but as you well know, the situation here is unique and therefore a bit awkward, and despite how much the two of us have discussed the matter, we are still left uncertain as to exactly how to handle it. We're both relatively certain that his valet and my maids have likely figured out the truth about our feelings, but as of yet, nothing has actually been said, and we're glad we can trust them to not spread gossip throughout the household."

"I daresay most of those who work in the household simply take for granted that the two of you sharing time together is natural given your circumstances; some might speculate, but I doubt there's any evidence to support anything beyond a natural camaraderie." Milton put his hand over Gina's on the sofa and leaned a little closer. "And I am not at all unhappy with you *or* Radcliffe for not speaking with me about it. I understand, truly. When he's ready to speak to me, I will be glad to do so, and of course I will offer my blessing on whatever the two of you decide is the right course for your lives. He's a good man, Gina. I've seen how well he cares for you and Janine; how kind and generous he is to all of us, and how well he treats those who work in the household. You can tell a lot about a person by the way they treat those who serve them, and I've rarely seen an employer as kind and respectful as Radcliffe. I can't think of any better option for your future than to be able to remain here with your daughter, and to find happiness with Sir Radcliffe." He smiled. "I just wanted you to know that I'm not blind." He chuckled and kissed her cheek. "And there's no reason for the two of you to have to pretend with me."

"Well, that's settled then," Gina said. "I will tell Radcliffe what you've said, and we will continue to go forward and see what happens. I believe by the time it's been a year since Dwight's death, Radcliffe and I will have a better sense of where exactly we want to go with our relationship."

"One year and one day," Milton said, lifting a finger and winking. "That's the actual social expectation, you know. Although I can hardly think of anything sillier." He chuckled. "Actually, I can think of a great many things sillier among the social expectations in our society. Nevertheless, I've never understood the reason for adding a day to the year before it's considered appropriate for a widow—or widower—to marry again. The important thing is that the two of you do what's best for *you*, and not worry too much over such things. You're both wise and insightful; I am not at all concerned about the two of you being able to make good decisions for your lives."

"Thank you, Papa," Gina said, feeling great relief to know that he was aware of the situation, and his expressions of confidence in her and Radcliffe helped eased some of her own misgivings. "He's such a good man; sometimes I can hardly believe that he has such affection and admiration for me."

"And why would that be a problem?" Milton asked, sounding concerned. "You are a good woman, Gina; you always have been. Radcliffe is fortunate to have found such affection and admiration from *you*."

Gina's habitual guilt rose inside and she quickly acted on the habit of pushing it away, which was aided by the distraction of hearing her father say, "Is this because of the way that Dwight treated you? I was always concerned that his attitude toward you would wear down your belief in yourself as a woman of value."

Gina had been surprised when Radcliffe had told her about his observations of Dwight's ill treatment of her, but she'd never imagined that her father would have noticed. Radcliffe had attended almost all the same social events with her and Dwight, and they'd all lived under the same roof for years. In truth, Milton's interactions with Dwight had been minimal. He'd consented to their courtship and marriage because Gina had vehemently declared that they loved each other, and she believed Dwight to be a good man. But she knew now that she had been terribly naive, and perhaps more in love with the idea of love and marriage, and likely a mistaken belief that the challenges she'd observed in Dwight would get better with marriage—when in actuality the opposite had happened.

Gina allowed herself a long moment to take in what her father had just said before she answered simply, "Perhaps. I can look back now and see considerable evidence of problems right from the beginning; problems that became worse following the marriage. But it was too late by then. I've actually felt relief that he died, Papa, and I feel guilty for feeling relieved." Gina was a little surprised to realize how easily she'd just admitted to some of her deepest, most guarded feelings, but then she knew how perfectly she trusted her father, and how completely comfortable she felt with him.

"I believe such feelings are understandable," Milton said, but he surprised her when he added, "because I certainly felt the same. I knew you weren't happy and that he didn't deserve a woman as loving and good as you. I too was relieved to hear of his death, and truthfully I felt no guilt over my relief, because I wanted to know that my little girl was safe and happy."

They shared a long, knowing gaze before Gina wrapped her arms around her father's neck and he hugged her tightly, the same way he had ever since she was a little girl, whenever she needed a parent's comfort. Following their embrace, she placed her head comfortably on his shoulder, and a minute or two of silence allowed her to catch up with all that had been said. Only Janine's happy noises filled the room before Milton said, "I assume you have talked with Radcliffe about such feelings?" He said it as if the answer to the question was a kind of test regarding the nature of their relationship.

"A great deal," Gina said, knowing her father would be pleased with the answer. "He observed much in Dwight's behavior that concerned him, and he too felt relief when I no longer had to contend with such things."

"I'm extremely glad to hear that the two of you are able to honestly talk about sensitive matters. That is a good thing—and mandatory to a happy marriage, I think." He paused and asked, "Do you sincerely believe this will eventually lead to marriage?"

Gina lifted her head to look at her father. "I truly hope so," she said. "We are well aware that there is still much we need to learn about each other, but our intention is marriage unless something comes up in the meantime that indicates a potential problem." Again, Gina had to force down her guilt, certain that if Radcliffe knew the truth about Janine, their relationship would be shattered.

"I can't imagine such a thing happening," Milton said, "at least not from what I've observed."

"I do hope that's the case," Gina said, looking down, "because I genuinely hope to become his wife." She looked up and smiled, feeling nothing but confidence as she added, "And then we could all live happily ever after here together as a family."

"And how lovely that would be!" Milton said with a smile, but there was a troubled expression in his eyes that let Gina know there was something else on his mind, and she wondered if he would talk to her about it, or if she might be left to speculate over what it might be. He answered that question immediately when he added, "There's something else we need to discuss."

"Very well," she said, wondering again if her father might be ill, or perhaps there was a problem regarding her siblings that she was not aware of and it held some threat to her father's happiness—or her own. Even though she couldn't imagine what that might be, she had no idea whatsoever of her father's concerns; therefore, her imagination had no choice but to run wild until Milton shared what was on his mind.

"Something's wrong, Gina," he said, and while she was waiting for him to tell her what it was, he added with confidence, "and I need you to tell me what it is."

"What?" she asked, completely taken off guard.

"Ever since I've come to live here, I have seen a continual contradiction in you, child. By all obvious accounts, you are happy and content, and yet I see something in your eyes—or at times your expression—that leads me to believe you are carrying a very heavy burden that you don't want anyone to see. You are very careful about trying to hide it, but I'm your father, dear girl, and there have been a great many times when you have believed no one was watching and I have been able to see what I can only describe as . . . well . . . I'm not certain what, exactly; a combination of things perhaps. Guilt. Confusion. *Terror.*" Milton paused and took Gina's hand which she was appalled to realize was trembling; that alone would let her father know that he was right. He was absolutely right. But she had no idea how she could handle answering his questions. Should she simply tell him that there was something in her life that was a problem that was private, and she couldn't talk about it and he needed to trust her? Or did she have no choice but to tell him the truth? A part of her would be greatly relieved to be able to share this burden with her father. Unlike Radcliffe, he was her father; he had proven to her time and time again throughout her life that he would love her no matter what—even if he disagreed with her choices. He would never abandon her, never treat her with disdain, no matter what she told him. She didn't have to wonder if she could trust him with the truth; he was above reproach when it came to integrity and keeping a confidence. But she quickly recognized within herself her biggest reason for not wanting to tell him; she didn't want him to be disappointed in her. She'd constructed a terrible lie, she was relying on her friends to help her protect that lie, and she was on the path to being betrothed to a man who had no idea whatsoever of the truth of the matter surrounding Janine's presence in their home.

Tense silence followed the declarations of her father's suspicions, while Gina felt horrified to realize she didn't have the strength or ability to behave in a way that might prove him wrong. He was a perceptive man and she knew it; he always had been. He'd discovered that his daughter was keeping a heavy secret. But what was she to do now? Could she honestly trust him enough to take him into her confidence regarding Janine? Did she have any choice?

While Gina was desperately trying to consider her options and the best path to take in this conversation, Milton added with far more compassion than criticism, "Whatever you are holding inside, my dear, is clearly very burdensome to you. My concern is that secrets cannot be kept forever; somehow, they are always discovered, and I don't want you to be caught off guard by the impact of such a thing coming to pass. I believe it's far better that we take courage in honesty and integrity. Of course, you are a grown woman, and I will trust you to make what you consider the best decision regarding whatever the matter might be; nevertheless, I am your father, and you can trust me. I'll not breathe a word to anyone without your approval, and I think you need my help in carrying this burden—whatever it may be."

Gina couldn't argue with that, and a part of her felt some relief to hear his promise that he would never betray her confidence should she choose to share her secret with him. And he wasn't going to force her to tell him anything; he was simply concerned for her—and she could never deny that he had good cause to be. Her secret was a heavy burden indeed, and she had a great many fears associated with the very idea of anyone discovering the truth about Janine, and what the consequences might be. Now that she'd taken this beautiful child into her life and her heart, the very idea of having to let her go—or being forced to leave Stonebridge due to the discovery of her deceit—were both devastating and unthinkable possibilities. Still, she didn't know what to say, and the silence stretched out painfully while she mostly looked at the floor and attempted to catch up with the storm of thoughts and fears swirling in her mind.

"It's all right, my dear," Milton said gently, brushing back a stray lock of hair from her brow the way he'd done a thousand times throughout her life. "There is nothing you can tell me that will make me think any less of you, and I could never—ever—love you less than I do now. Do you understand?"

"Yes, Papa," Gina said, still looking at the floor. "And I'm more grateful for that than I can say, however . . ." she paused and let out a weighted sigh, "I'm not entirely confident that you wouldn't think less of me. You haven't yet heard what I've done, so how can you say that wouldn't be the case?"

"Because I know you, Regina," he said. "I don't believe it's in you to do *anything* without the best of intentions in your heart. I also know that the circumstances of life are rarely something that can be marked off into parameters that are clearly defined and managed. We live in a gray world, daughter, where life is filled with shades and shadows. Relationships are never perfect, people make mistakes, and surely God understands all of that. And I know from a lifetime of experience that he surely understands the deepest desires of our hearts, and our unique limitations and circumstances. I'm not going to judge you for any choice you've made, Gina, and again I tell you that you can trust me to never repeat whatever you tell me, but I beg you to share your burdens with me. It's such a remarkable blessing that we are now able to share our lives in the same home, so let me *truly* share your life, Gina. Talk to your father."

Gina managed to nod, unable to dispute his logic in any way. But she still couldn't lift her eyes from their focus on the carpet, perhaps because she knew the shame in them would be readily evident. While she was still frantically searching for the right words to tell him, he said gently, "Sometimes it's difficult to speak about certain challenges in our lives." Gina nodded again; he certainly had that right. "Is it all right if I ask you some questions and you can just nod or shake your head to let me know if it's true or not?"

Gina glanced at her father only for a second and nodded before she looked again at the floor. She was relieved by this idea, wanting to share her burden and knowing she could trust him, but feeling utterly dumbstruck over the very idea of being able to come up with the words.

"It has something to do with Janine," Milton said with firm confidence; it was in no way a question. Gina looked abruptly at her father, no longer able to look away. He quickly added, "It's common when Janine is being talked about that you get a fearful look in your eyes, and you sometimes hold her as if you're afraid you might lose her. I cannot see any logical reason—when you live in such a secure environment—for you to have such fears regarding your daughter. I've been trying to make sense of it, and the only thing I can think of is . . . I know it sounds crazy, and I know you'll straighten me out if I'm wrong but . . . *is* she your daughter, Gina?"

Gina shot to her feet and hurried to the window where she could look out, even though she could see nothing but rain drizzling down the glass. The words that came to mind were a temptation to angrily tell him that the very idea *was* crazy, to insist that it was ludicrous to think that Janine was not her daughter. But her response to his supposition had already implied her guilt. He'd figured it out; somehow her father with his keen perception and watchful eye had figured it out, and she would be a fool to try and pretend otherwise now that he knew the truth—or at least he suspected it strongly enough to initiate this difficult conversation.

Still unable to put words to her thoughts, she was glad to hear her father continue, even though her heart was pounding over the very idea that he had figured out the truth, and she wondered what else he might have concluded from his observations. "Gina darling," he said with all the love in his voice that he'd always possessed, "I know how much you wanted a baby, and that you and Dwight were married enough years to make it evident that your desire was not likely going to come to pass."

Gina found it surprisingly easy to say, "Everyone in the household—and even the village—considers her birth a miracle." She realized as she said it that the words came out easily because they supported the lie she'd constructed; it was telling the truth about Janine that she found difficult, if not impossible.

"I don't doubt that her arrival is a miracle," Milton said. "She brings joy to everyone who has the privilege of being a part of her life. But I'm not at all interested in what people in general might believe; I'm interested in the truth of what happened." He paused long enough to give her time to respond but she didn't. He then asked, "Why do have such fear related to your daughter, Gina?" Again he paused, but she couldn't speak. "*Is* she your daughter, Gina? Or is that the secret you're trying to hide? The secret you're terrified will be discovered? And if that's the case, does Radcliffe know the truth? I suspect he doesn't, given my observations." Still another pause, and still Gina couldn't get a sound out of her mouth. "We need to talk, daughter, and I need you to be honest with me— for your own sake if not that of your daughter." She liked the way he still called Janine *her daughter* even though he'd figured out the truth. If he still saw Janine as her daughter, then perhaps he could help her contend with the dilemma she faced every day as her guilt battled with her joy, and both emotions were always mingled with the fear of being discovered. Well, she *had* been discovered. And if Milton had figured it out, who was to say that Radcliffe hadn't? Or that he wouldn't, eventually? He too was a perceptive man, and Gina had just been forced to face the undeniable fact that her father was right: secrets cannot be kept forever; somehow, they are always discovered.

CHAPTER EIGHT
the truth about dishonesty

THE VERY FEAR THAT MILTON was describing suddenly rushed through Gina's entire being with such force that the racing of her heart felt as if it might threaten to kill her, and she became so light-headed she had to grab hold of the windowsill to keep from falling over. A second later she felt her father's hands on her shoulders and heard his soothing words near her ear. "Come and sit down, my dear. Everything will be all right."

"Will it?" Gina asked, hearing anger in her voice, although she knew it was only a feeble attempt to disguise the stark fear consuming her.

"Whatever has happened," Milton said, sitting beside her and taking her hand, "and whatever happens from here forward, I will do everything in my power to help you. And you must believe that I meant what I said. I love you and I always will. There is nothing that will ever change the way I feel about you. But I do believe you must relieve yourself of this burden you're carrying. You clearly cannot carry it alone. Is there anyone else who knows the truth?"

Gina forced herself to breathe in and out slowly in preparation for being able to tell her father the story of how Janine had come into her life, and he waited patiently, as if he sensed that she was now determined to tell him everything. "Emerald and Ruby and Garn all know," she said, "but no one else . . . well . . . except the woman who gave birth to Janine . . . whoever she is . . . wherever she is." Gina heard her father gasp slightly, but he didn't speak, and he only tightened his grip on her hand as if to encourage her to keep talking. Gina considered the possibility that Janine's mother might be a maid working in this house, but she couldn't think about such a likelihood right now. She needed to focus on simply getting through this conversation. She took a deep breath and went on. "But . . . my dear friends were all with me when . . . we found Janine." Another deep breath. "We went into town . . . ironically for the first

time in months . . . the first time since Dwight's death. They were insistent
that I needed to get out, and they had conspired that they were not going to
take any excuses." Now that she'd gained some momentum, it was becoming
easier for her to keep going. "There was a big town meeting at one of the pubs
that day and they knew it; I believe they thought that a lack of crowds would
be easier for me. But because of that, there were very few shops open, and no
one was on the street. Garn parked the carriage in front of the bookshop we
had intended to visit, and . . . we heard the cries of a baby. She'd been left in an
alley between two shops . . . with a note. Clearly, she'd been abandoned, and
clearly the mother wanted someone to find her and care for her. Since I'd not
left my rooms for months, and I had put on extra weight due to far too much
eating in order to soothe my conflicted emotions, the plan fell into place easily
enough. Emerald and Ruby learned some midwifery skills from their mother
when they were younger, and they sent Garn into the bookshop to seek just
enough assistance from the shopkeeper's daughter for us to carry out the ruse
that I was giving birth in the carriage. So . . ." Gina put a hand over her eyes as
hot tears suddenly threatened to overtake her, ". . . I came home with a baby,
and we all managed to make the story completely believable that I had been
hiding my pregnancy due to my mourning and melancholy, and Janine was a
miracle that Dwight had left behind."

Her tears overtook her and flooded down her face, but Gina ignored them
and turned to look directly at her father. "When it was all happening . . . while
my mind was attempting to take in the situation and . . . attempt to foresee
the outcome . . . all I could think of was the story of Moses, hidden by the
woman who gave birth to him in order to protect him. I can't explain it, Papa,
but something inside of me believed from the very first moment I looked at
Janine's precious little face that I was meant to be her mother. There were
so many little factors that had come together to make it happen; so many
elements of the situation that made the story feasible and believable. Janine
is *my* daughter, Papa. The poor woman who gave birth to her was clearly not
in a situation to care for her and she left her abandoned in that alley with the
hope that someone would take on the role of being her mother; otherwise, she
wouldn't have left a note."

"I agree with you, daughter," Milton said, much to Gina's relief. "It makes
perfect sense that you took Janine into your life. She is very much loved and
will have everything a girl could ever hope for. I can understand why it's better
that the situation should not be common knowledge. For your sake, as well
as the woman who abandoned her baby, it's best to keep the truth within a

small and trusted circle." Milton leaned toward Gina a little and tightened his hand around hers. "However, I firmly believe that Radcliffe must be included in that circle. You are considering marriage. You absolutely cannot keep such a secret from a potential husband."

Gina couldn't hold back her deepest fear. "And what if he never trusts me again? I've lied to him in such an enormous way! If the situation were reversed, I wonder how I would handle such information regarding trust in a future relationship. This is his home; he would have every right to turn us all out. What would we do? How would we—"

"Listen to me, child," Milton said, taking Gina's face into his strong hands. "Your integrity must be stronger than your fear. In my opinion, you are denying Radcliffe the opportunity to prove his character; I personally find it difficult to imagine that he would go so far as to turn us out. But, Regina, even if he did, we would be all right. It would be sad for all of us, yes; it would be disappointing and difficult. But we are far from destitute. We could rent or buy a nice home and have plenty of money to live a comfortable life for ourselves, and to provide the same for Emerald, Ruby, and Garn. And Elaine and Tommy, for that matter. Of course we need them. And we would still have plenty to leave Janine a fine inheritance. I know it's not simply about the money; we have no fear of not being able to survive or live in comfort, and for that reason we are very blessed. We have found a home here; you much more than I because you've been here so much longer. It would be difficult to leave; I understand that. Nevertheless, remaining here with this deceit hovering over you continually will not do! You must tell Radcliffe the truth! You must! Or you cannot possibly pursue a relationship with him. If you care for him . . . respect him . . . which I know you do, then you owe him the truth! And I sincerely believe that even if it takes him some time to come to terms with it, he will understand."

Gina closed her eyes against the very idea of having a conversation such as this one with Radcliffe. She felt nothing short of terrified, certain he would want nothing more to do with her. She was aware of her continual flow of tears, and of the way her father kept her face in his hands, as if he didn't want her to leave or even turn away. She felt him wiping her tears with his thumbs as he said in a voice that was gentler. "Gina, if you believe that God brought Janine into your life, that she is meant to be your daughter, then you must trust that God will provide the way for both of you to live a safe and happy life. I believe that Radcliffe plays a large role in both of you being genuinely happy, but only if the two of you can be united in the knowledge of Janine's true origins."

Gina finally eased away from her father and stood up to look out the window, pulling her handkerchief out of her sleeve to dry her tears now that they were finally ceasing. Given a long moment's thought she had to admit, "I know you're right, Papa. I'm just . . . terrified. I've become so dependent upon him . . . and I love him; I do. I never felt this way about Dwight. I don't want to lose him."

"I can understand why you would feel that way, precious, but do you genuinely want to spend your life with such a secret between the two of you? I meant it when I said earlier that secrets don't last forever; I suppose it's possible that some secrets are never discovered, but as a rule, I don't believe that's the case. What happens, if years down the road, when you're long since married to Radcliffe, he discovers the truth and finds out that you kept this from him all along? Which prospect is more frightening, my dear? And again, I tell you that you cannot allow fear to compromise your integrity. And what of Janine's real mother? If the entire community knows that you supposedly gave birth to a baby girl on the very same day that she left her daughter in an alley, how can she not be relatively certain that you're raising her child? I would assume she would want to remain anonymous, given that she abandoned her baby, but how can you be absolutely certain she won't come forward one day, and—"

"I've had exactly the same thoughts," Gina admitted, still watching the rain run down the windows. "And Ruby and Emerald and I have discussed the possibility extensively. There is absolutely no way of knowing what this woman is thinking, or how she feels about the situation. It must have been impossibly difficult for her to do what she did; she must have felt nothing short of desperate or she surely couldn't have done it. And the truth is she likely *does* know that the baby I'm claiming as mine is likely hers. That's one of the detriments of being part of *this* family; the entire village seems to know everything about us. But the worst of it is that . . ." Gina stopped and cleared her throat, knowing she needed to tell her father everything, but this part was especially difficult to say aloud, ". . . there's a possibility that Janine's mother works here in the house."

"What?" Milton bellowed in a quiet shout. "How?" Gina heard her own fear in his voice; he had grown to love Janine as his granddaughter, and he clearly wanted to help protect Gina's secret, but he also had the insight and wisdom to realize what a precarious situation they were in.

Keeping her back turned to her father, Gina explained that a new maid had been hired not long after Janine's birth, and she had shown an excessive amount of curiosity about the baby. Gina had never encountered Bernice, and she'd not heard anything through her maids about the situation for weeks; whether Bernice was the baby's mother who had sought out work here in order to be close to her daughter, or it was simply coincidence that she had been curious about the baby, was anybody's guess. But Milton once again managed to express Gina's own feelings when he said, "The timing seems a little too coincidental to me. Of course, we can't know for certain, and we don't want to go asking her, but I daresay it's more likely than not that this Bernice is the woman who abandoned Janine. Do you know anything about her?"

"She's from the village," Gina said. "I've heard that she's kind and humble and a hard worker. Perhaps it's as simple as her wanting to be close to her daughter so she can be assured that she's all right, and I can certainly understand that. But there's no way of knowing whether she has ulterior motives; perhaps her coming across as kind and humble is a ruse to get people to like and trust her. I have no idea, Papa, and I can't deny that it frightens me."

"There is a great deal about Janine's existence that frightens you," Milton observed with compassion. "I would very much like to help you be free of all this fear. Everything you've told me will stay between me and you, although I think we should discuss how to go about steps you can take to alleviate all this fear so that you can live in peace and have nothing but joy in raising your daughter."

Gina liked the way he still referred to Janine as *her* daughter. She was glad that Milton knew the truth; it did help ease the burden she'd been carrying. She could see the wisdom in what he was saying, but she couldn't deny the fear that overwhelmed her. While she was lost in thought, her father stood beside her, turned her to face him and took both her hands into his.

"My dearest daughter," he said, "You don't need to tell me for me to understand why having this child come into your life has been a blessing . . . even a miracle."

"I was so unhappy, Papa; so melancholy and lost. Janine changed everything. She gave purpose to my life; she brings me such joy. How could I ever let her go? I was in such a terrible place in the months following Dwight's death, so confused and lost in guilt and regret and self-loathing. Janine is a light in my life; a light in this house; a light to everyone who knows her. I think I'm most terrified to consider the possibility of going back to that dark and horrible place if I lost her. No," she reconsidered, "I would spend the rest of my life wondering what was happening to her. Would she be happy? Cared for? I feel entirely responsible for her. I cannot lose her, Papa; I can't."

"And I don't see any reason why you would," Milton said. "I feel strongly about the need for you to tell Radcliffe; I'm not suggesting you tell the world.

As for the woman who gave birth to Janine, we must have faith that her greatest desire is to remain anonymous, and that she is as kind and humble as she seems. But I cannot stress how strongly I feel that you should tell Radcliffe. I honestly believe he will support you, but you must be patient with him. It may very well be a shock, and it takes time to adjust to shock. I know you have the wisdom and strength to do this. You are a remarkable woman. Just tell him the truth and you can stop being afraid of how he might react. If the worst happens, we will leave here with your friends who take such good care of you, and we will start a new life. There will be a period of grieving, but we will get through it—together. Do you hear what I'm saying?"

"Yes." She nodded. "I know you're right; I've been avoiding it and justifying it in my mind, but I know deep inside that I can't live this way; it would surely drive me mad." Gina impulsively wrapped her arms around her father and settled her head against his shoulder. "Thank you. I'm glad I no longer need to carry this burden alone; Emerald and Ruby have been incredibly supportive, and although I rarely see Garn because he's so busy, I know he is supportive as well. But you have such discernment and perspective—and I know I need both. I *do* need your help and support, Papa. I need you to help me know what to do so that I can protect Janine—and myself."

"I'm so glad that you trust me, Regina. And again, I swear to you that I'll not tell a soul. Right now, first and foremost, I believe you need to tell Radcliffe and be done with it. I know it will be a difficult conversation, and I think you need to be prepared for the possibility that he might not take it well—although I believe that given some time to think about it, he would choose to have you and Janine in his life rather than lose you, and I believe he will respect you more if you tell him the truth."

"It all sounds very logical and appropriate," Gina admitted, still allowing herself to be comforted by her father's embrace. "But the reality is not so easy to face."

"I know, my precious," he said, rubbing a hand gently over her back. "But you are far braver and stronger than you recognize. You can do this." He drew back to look at her. "Do you want me to be with you when you tell him? It's entirely up to you."

"It's tempting," she said, "and I appreciate the offer, but I believe I need to do this alone. I don't want to appear as though I need my papa to help me face a very adult problem that I brought upon myself."

"You see, my dear," he said, "you are much stronger and more mature than you likely give yourself credit for being. I'm certain you can handle the situation well, but still . . . I am here for you if you need me, and . . . well . . . may I offer one more thought?"

"Of course," she said, looking up at him.

"I've come to learn that when we are up against something especially difficult, it helps to consider the absolute worst outcome." Gina didn't like this thought at all and knew he could tell by the expression on her face.

"Hear me out," he said quickly. "I believe if you are prepared for the worst possible scenario, any outcome that is less than that is easier; and if the worst *does* happen, you already have a plan of how to handle it. Hence, even though what lies ahead may be extremely difficult, being prepared for the worst removes a great deal of the fear. I know you fear losing the relationship you've found with Radcliffe, and that is entirely in his hands; there is nothing that any of us can do about that. However, there is no need to fear the possibility of his expelling us from the house. If he does that—which I do *not* believe he will—but *if* he does, we will start a new life; we have the means to do so, we will be together, and we will be all right. Remember that. I will make certain that you and Janine have everything you need, and that you have a good life. We are blessed to have Ruby and Emerald and Garn who came here with you when you married; they will go with us if we leave. And we will take Elaine and Tommy; I very much like the idea of keeping them with our family indefinitely. Again, I don't think it will happen, but I want you to remember as you approach talking to Radcliffe about this, that we will be all right no matter how he responds. Do you understand?"

"Yes, Papa," she said. "Thank you. I *will* be devastated if he wants nothing more to do with me; I cannot deny it. I've grown to love him so much, and I've become invested in the possibility of having a life with him. Nevertheless, I agree that I can't enter into such a life with a lie at its core. I must talk to him, tell him the truth, take the risk. And you're right, we are very blessed to have all we need to start a life elsewhere and live in comfort; we need have no fear of being without shelter or necessities, and I need to keep my perspective and not let fear over one thing cross over into fear of another." She sighed deeply. "I need some time to prepare myself to speak with him, but I will do it soon, Papa; I promise."

"That's my girl," he said and hugged her tightly.

"Thank you," she said, still absorbing comfort from his embrace. "Now that we've been able to talk, I'm glad that you figured it out; I'm glad to know that I don't have to try and hide the truth from you, and that you love me and Janine just the same."

"Always!" he said emphatically. He drew back and took her shoulders again. "I've known of adopted children who were loved no less than those who came by natural means into a family. And though the circumstances here are entirely unique, there is no reason this cannot be the recipe for a happy family—as long as you are honest with the people who are directly involved."

Gina nodded and felt the temptation to start crying again, which she very much did *not* want to do. She was relieved to hear Janine starting to fuss, which meant that it was nearing time for her to be fed again. The baby's timing was perfect, since Gina believed there was nothing more to be said between herself and her father for now; she simply had to summon the courage to tell Radcliffe the truth, and until she had that conversation, they couldn't know what their future might hold. Radcliffe's response to the news would determine whether she and Janine remained here at Stonebridge; but the future of her father and the three siblings who worked for them were also a part of the situation. And Elaine as well; they were completely dependent upon Elaine to help with Janine's care. Gina hated the idea that her dishonesty regarding Janine affected so many lives; but it couldn't be undone now. She simply had to tell Radcliffe the truth, even though she had no idea how she could ever find the strength to admit her treachery to a man who set such a high priority on integrity. It would take a great deal of prayer and every bit of courage she possessed to follow through on her father's wise admonition, but now that she'd realized this conversation needed to happen, she knew she could never feel relaxed until it was over. And what might occur beyond then was entirely up to Radcliffe; she could only hope and pray that he would be compassionate, that he would understand, and that he would not abandon her—or their growing relationship—once he knew the terrible truth.

In the hours following her conversation with her father, Gina felt progressively more ill over the reality of what Milton had discovered—and even worse— what she had committed to telling Radcliffe. Concluding that she'd been right when she'd told her father she needed time, she took advantage of feeling ill— even though her illness was only the result of her own inner turmoil—and kept close to her bed, having her meals brought to her there, and requesting that Radcliffe be informed that she was not up to receiving company and she would see him when she was feeling better. She had to insist her illness was nothing that needed a doctor's attention. Thankfully, she was able to discuss honestly the reasons for her malady with Ruby and Emerald, and they were able to help mediate between herself and anyone else in the household who might be concerned. Gina didn't even feel up to sharing conversation with Elaine while she was feeding the baby—according to their habit—and Ruby or Emerald intervened there as well and brought Gina the baby after her stomach was full following each feeding.

Gina was more grateful than ever for the support and understanding of Ruby and Emerald, although she couldn't admit to her present dilemma without also telling them the full truth about her relationship with Radcliffe. Of course, they were both bound to know sooner or later, and they each confessed they had strongly suspected there was a blossoming romance between Gina and Sir Radcliffe. But their pleasure regarding this was overshadowed by the impending need for Radcliffe to know the truth about Janine. Still, Ruby and Emerald were as loving and supportive as Gina's father had been. Gina was able to discuss in-depth the conversation she'd shared with her father, and they were both relieved that he'd figured it out—although they both agreed that meant Radcliffe might have figured it out as well.

"Or," Ruby suggested one evening right after Gina had finished her supper, "perhaps your father simply knows you in a way that Radcliffe doesn't, because your father raised you. It's highly possible that Radcliffe has no intuition that anything is other than what it appears to be, because he simply can't comprehend otherwise."

"I do hope that's the case," Gina said. "At least I think I do. I can't decide which will be worse: telling him something that will completely shock him because he has no idea, or telling him something that he's suspected, and he's been waiting for me to come clean."

"Either way it will be fine," Emerald said. "He's a good man; I really believe he will understand."

"Oh, I do hope so!" Gina said. "I can't hide away in bed forever. I must speak with him; it can't be delayed because I don't think I have the strength to be in his presence any further and behave as if everything is all right. Now that I've come to terms fully with the fact that I can't in good conscience keep the truth from him, I don't believe I'm capable of putting forth any acting skills for his benefit." She sighed deeply, almost feeling tangible pain in her heart over the conundrum she'd created. "I can see now that there is a price to be paid for being dishonest." She sighed again, grateful that she could speak her thoughts and feelings in such a forthright manner with Ruby and Emerald. "I'm willing to pay that price on Janine's behalf—and my own as her mother—when it comes to what people believe when I barely know them. But I can see now the price is too high when it comes to those with whom I share close relationships. What was I thinking to believe that I could keep up this ruse with Radcliffe for a lifetime? How can a marriage be a *good* marriage if I would always have to be on guard about what I say or how I behave regarding any reference to Janine's birth or origin?"

After Gina had said nothing more for a minute or two, Ruby said gently, "Yes, it seems that there is a natural consequence to not being truthful; something that none of us took into account when we hatched this plan."

"We hatched this plan very impulsively in order to keep Janine in our care," Emerald said, "which is where she's meant to be. It would have been impossible to predict *any* consequences at that point. But I still believe we did the right thing."

"As do I!" Ruby insisted. "I would not have done any differently. I don't believe that going to the police would have been in Janine's best interest, and that could have ultimately gotten Janine's mother into trouble, when she was surely just desperate and afraid."

"I agree that we did the right thing," Gina said. "We did the best we could under the circumstances, and for the most part I believe we've done rather well at managing the situation—with the exception that I need to be truthful with Radcliffe, and I'm utterly terrified to say what needs to be said. What if he's angry? What if he *does* toss us out and—"

"We've talked about all of this," Ruby said, "many times, actually. And we all agree with your father. If the worst happens, we'll be all right. I daresay your greatest fear is likely rooted in the possibility that he may choose to end his relationship with you, because we all know that you love him."

Gina couldn't hold back tears as Ruby spoke an absolute truth, and Emerald added tenderly, "There's no denying that such a possibility is horrible to consider, although I truly believe that he loves you enough to accept you and Janine despite the truth. Nevertheless, as we've discussed, he may need some time to come to terms with it; he may be angry initially, but hopefully he will decide that his love for you is stronger than his disappointment, and he will understand why you felt the need to do what you did. And in the grand scheme of a lifetime, you will be glad you were honest with him; it will relieve such a great burden from your shoulders if Radcliffe knows—however he may choose to handle the situation."

"I do hope you're right," Gina said. "And I suppose I should just pull myself together and get this over with. I think I'm growing weary of hiding here in my bed and dreading the conversation."

"Then it would seem your time hiding has served its purpose," Ruby said. "You needed time to think and plan and adjust, and now you're ready."

"I'm not certain I could ever be *ready* for something like this," Gina insisted, "although I'm likely as ready as I could ever be." She sighed loudly, then sighed again. "I wonder if this is how soldiers feel when they're going into battle and they don't know whether they'll be killed, or injured terribly."

"I daresay the comparison is a bit dramatic," Emerald said, "but I suppose that for emotional reasons, you could feel that way—to some degree. Given that none of us are soldiers, we can't possibly make such a comparison."

"Might I suggest," Ruby said, "that you not wait another minute, and simply get it over with."

"What . . . now?" Gina asked, her heart suddenly pounding over the very idea.

"I happen to know that Sir Radcliffe is in the library reading," Ruby went on. "He requested a fire be lit there, and not in any other rooms; therefore, it's highly likely he's there. We can help you get dressed quickly, and we only need to brush your hair and tie it back with a ribbon. You can find him alone and say what you need to say, and then you no longer need to dread doing so."

"I wholeheartedly agree," Emerald said. "Every day—indeed every minute— that you put this off will only bring on internal torment for no good reason. Once you've told him the truth—even if the results are negative—every day will be moving us all toward a resolution, whatever that might be."

"Oh my!" Gina muttered breathlessly, putting a hand over her wildly beating heart as if she could calm it down by doing so. "I can't argue with any of that. I just . . . feel so unprepared."

"And yet you just said that you were as prepared as you could possibly be—or words to that effect." Emerald made the statement while she tugged on Gina's hand to urge her out of bed.

Gina felt so overcome with terror that she could barely move as Emerald and Ruby helped guide her arms out of her nightgown and into a simple dress of pale pink with darker pink flowers scattered over the fabric. Ruby brushed through her hair and tied it back with a pink ribbon, and Emerald handed her a gray shawl, reminding her that the hallways were cold because winter was coming on.

"Go along now," Ruby insisted. "Get it over with and you'll feel better."

"Or we will all be packing our belongings tomorrow," Gina said, certain it was a distinct possibility.

"Not likely," Emerald said, "but if that's what happens, so be it. And better that we know and can move forward with our lives than to just wait and wonder and always be filled with fear."

It occurred to Gina from the way Emerald had said the last that she'd perhaps been inconsiderate about the way this lie had affected those involved; their place with her and their positions in this household were also deeply impacted. She needed to not be so self-absorbed and remember that her friends had put a great deal at risk to support her in claiming Janine as her own child.

"Forgive me," Gina said with a sincerity that forced heated tears into her eyes.

"For what?" Emerald demanded.

"For . . . bringing both of you and your brother into this; for not even thinking about how it might affect *your* lives. You've been nothing but supportive, and I have very much only worried about myself. If you—"

"Nonsense," Ruby interrupted. "We love you, dear Gina. And we know you love us, and you would always be certain we're cared for. We know it!"

"Indeed we do!" Emerald said. "Which is one of many reasons that it is so easy for us to *care* for you, and little Janine. We are as good as family, and we know that will never change. You have no need to apologize."

"I'm not so sure about that," Gina said. "So . . . just let me say that I'm sorry and . . . I promise that I will do everything I can to work out this problem with Sir Radcliffe as soon as possible."

"Which would be *now!*" Emerald announced and opened the door, practically shoving Gina into the hallway. "We will pray for you."

"Thank you," Gina said while she just stood there, attempting to gather her courage. A thought occurred to her and she had to say it before she ventured forth on this terrifying endeavor. "You realize I have no control whatsoever regarding his response. This could go very badly, and our lives could change very quickly as a result."

"I think we have already discussed that," Ruby said from where both sisters hovered in the doorway, as if they were determined to prevent Gina from going back into the safety of her room. "Now, go!"

"Yes, go and be done with it," Emerald added.

Gina took a deep breath, squared her shoulders, lifted her chin, and tightened her shawl around her arms to help ward off the chill in the hallway. It was difficult to take that first step, but once she started walking, she quickly gained momentum and hoped that Radcliffe was in the library as predicted; if she had to go searching for him, her initiative would surely dwindle. And if she were unable to find him at all, she wasn't certain she could gather her courage all over again on another day. Now that she'd come to this decision—with all the encouragement and goading from Ruby and Emerald—she *did* want to have it over with and done.

Gina found herself at the closed doors of the library more quickly than she'd expected, and she had to take a good minute to steady her breathing, utter a silent prayer, and summon her courage all over again. If Radcliffe could accept her and Janine once he knew the truth, she believed their relationship could survive anything. But at the moment she felt as if she were more on the verge of preparing herself to see the growing love between them come to a horrible and abrupt halt, where all her hopes for a bright future with him would be dashed. As she reached for the elegant door handle, she imagined herself leaving this room following their conversation, with everything changed between them forever. She could hardly bear the thought, so she pushed it away and focused simply on the need to tell him the truth and be done with it. She would face the consequences after she'd taken the necessary steps to be certain that there were no more secrets between her and Radcliffe.

Gina took a deep breath and opened the door, both relieved and terrified to immediately see Radcliffe sitting near a blazing fire with a great many candles lit in the room to make reading possible. He looked up from the book cradled in his hand when he heard the door, and his face immediately broke into a loving smile.

"Gina, my dear!" he said with enthusiasm as he set his book aside and came to his feet, stepping around the sofa to greet her with a kiss on the cheek. "I've been missing you terribly! You're feeling better?"

Gina smiled up at him, hoping he wouldn't see the evidence of how she was forcing her smile past a great deal of anxiety. "I'm feeling . . . ready," she said, and he looked confused. She hurried to add, "I've missed you, as well—so very much." Seeing that his brow was creased with concern, she quickly clarified, "I've been needing to talk to you about something . . . and I confess that it's difficult . . . and it's the biggest reason I've been hiding away; I've needed time to consider all the implications and . . . well . . . I . . ." She heard herself starting to stammer as her words suddenly became jumbled in her mind.

Radcliffe took Gina's hand and guided her to the sofa where he'd been sitting near the fire. They both sat down but he kept hold of her hand, saying with his typical kindness, "There's nothing you can't tell me, G. I will never stop loving you." He chuckled without humor. "I can't begin to imagine what you would believe to be so serious. I can assure you that there's nothing we can't take on together."

"I daresay you might be wise to hold back on that sentiment until you hear what I have to say," Gina said, and the creases in his brow deepened while one eyebrow raised into a distinct arch. Unable to look into his eyes, Gina looked down at her hand in his, wondering how she would ever cope with losing him now that she'd become so accustomed to being a part of his life. They loved each other; there was no doubt about that. But would love be enough to overcome the challenge before them?

"I love you, G," he said as if he'd read her mind. "Surely the love we have for each other is strong enough to weather any storm. I think we both know it's only a matter of time before we can be together officially—and forever."

"I do hope so," Gina said. "In fact, it is my greatest hope, Rad." She briefly lifted her eyes to meet his, if only to echo the statement so that he knew she meant what she was saying. Looking down again she added, "Nevertheless, is trust not as vital as love in creating a good relationship? Love is something people feel for each other, but trust and respect are surely necessary in creating and maintaining a solid foundation in *any* relationship."

"Yes, I agree," Radcliffe said, which caused Gina's stomach to tighten, but that only made her more determined to have this over and done.

"I've kept a secret from you, Radcliffe, and it is not a small secret by any means. I've been terrified to tell you the truth, because I don't want to lose you, and a part of me can't imagine your ever being able to trust me once you hear what I have to say . . . and I don't know if you could ever forgive me, even though I do believe my motives were pure and—"

"Do you have so little faith in me?" he asked, and the question startled her, forcing her to look at him. This was not at all what she'd expected to hear, and it completely halted her momentum. "Do you honestly believe that I couldn't love you, accept you, forgive you if you tell me that you're imperfect? That you've made a mistake? Is life not full of human error? I am certainly far from perfect; I would be a hypocrite to expect *you* to be perfect."

"You're a good man, Radcliffe," Gina said firmly. "I don't doubt your ability to be gracious about anything I tell you. Again, however, I think you should reserve judgment until you hear what I have to say. This is by no means any small error, Rad, and I—"

"Wait!" he said and erupted to his feet, startling Gina. "Before you go any further, I must tell you that I too have been burdened with secrets that have troubled me for a very long time, and I have been engaged in an internal battle over whether you should know the truth. If you're telling me that complete honesty is vital to our sharing a good and meaningful relationship, then it must apply to both of us."

Gina watched Radcliffe pacing in front of the fire, and he was more agitated than she'd ever seen him. Her frustration over being halted in getting the truth out into the open was overshadowed by the distraction of wondering what kind of secret *he* had been keeping that would upset him so much. Did it have something to do with another woman in his life? She didn't at all like the idea of him having been intimately involved with someone else, even though she knew it wasn't uncommon for men to sow their wild oats, as her father had put it to her when he'd taught her about the ways of the world. But as long as it was in the past and over and done with, she could absolutely believe that he would remain faithful to her from this time forward. While Radcliffe paced, she tried to imagine what other secrets he might have been keeping from her, and she couldn't begin to think of a thing. But then, she seriously doubted that he could imagine the secret she needed to tell *him*.

Gina waited for Radcliffe to speak, even though it became obvious he was having difficulty coming up with the words he needed, and the minutes dragged by while Gina wished to go back to the original path of the conversation so that she could free herself of the burden she'd been carrying for so long.

Radcliffe finally stopped pacing and picked up a chair, moving it so that he could sit and face Gina directly. He leaned forward and took both her hands into his, looking firmly into her eyes with a determination that barely masked a measure of fear. Gina's heart quickened with dread just before he muttered, "Dwight was not at all the man you believed him to be, Gina."

"What?" Gina blurted before she could even think of a more articulate response. "Does this have to do with Dwight or you? From what you said, I was expecting to hear that *you* had been keeping a deep secret from me about yourself. Is there anything about you or your past that you've kept from me?"

"No!" he insisted in a way that filled Gina with deep relief, but also left her confused as to why he would be so concerned over things he knew about his cousin; things that Gina obviously *didn't* know.

"Dwight is dead and gone from our lives, Rad," Gina said, feeling as if she were stating the obvious. "What difference does it make now what he did or did not do?"

"What matters to me is the fact that I helped keep his ugly secrets, and when I think about the life he was living—a life completely separate from the man you knew—I often feel sick about it, and I have so many regrets. I don't know if it's right to go forward in pursuing marriage with you when I'm carrying this burden regarding the actions of your first husband . . . who is also my cousin. As you said, we should not live with secrets between us; we need trust and respect as well as love if we hope to have a good marriage. Therefore, I believe you need to know the truth, and I can only hope that you will forgive me for keeping it from you all this time."

Gina was a little startled to hear Radcliffe voicing her very thoughts regarding the secret *she* had been keeping, and her reasoning about feeling the need to tell him the truth. But that thought was quickly smothered by her curiosity over what kind of separate life Dwight could have been living about which she'd had no knowledge, and why it would still be so upsetting for Radcliffe since Dwight had been dead for several months. Then suddenly she was overcome with a debilitating wave of panic. She stood and took over the role of pacing in front of the fire while Radcliffe remained seated. All her own deceit—which she had been prepared to share with him in this conversation—swirled in her mind with the possibilities of what Radcliffe had been keeping from her regarding her deceased husband. And all at once it became too much.

"What is it, G?" Radcliffe asked with his typical concern. "Talk to me. There is clearly a great deal we need to say to each other if we wish to go forward in our relationship. I can only speak for myself, but I can't imagine any path except going forward with you—therefore we must talk about these things that have been weighing on us. We must!"

"No!" she insisted, still pacing, now wringing her hands. "I'm not certain I want to know whatever it is you know about Dwight. I've worked hard to put my life with him behind me. Must I contend with learning horrible things about him *now*?"

"Are you saying you prefer to spend your life pretending that everything was as it appeared?" he asked, and she wanted to blurt out a strong and determined *yes*! But he quickly added, "Would you have me carry that burden alone for the rest of *my* life, always feeling the need to measure my words with you so as not to say something relating to these secrets? That's one of the problems with being dishonest, G, is that I'm not certain the human mind can keep an accurate tally on what's true and what isn't. If two people spend decades of life together, will the secrets not slip out over time and cause distress in some way? Is it not better to have them out in the open, to contend with them now before we make a formal commitment to one another?"

Gina felt flustered and agitated by everything he'd said, but she didn't know if it was truly that she didn't want to know the truth about Dwight's dealings while he'd been alive, or if she had become so distracted from her original purpose of this conversation—to tell Radcliffe the truth about Janine—that she could hardly think straight. All she could manage to say was, "I . . . don't know, Rad. I sincerely don't know. I need time . . . to think about it."

Gina stopped pacing only so she could move hastily toward the door, desperately wanting to be alone.

"Wait!" Radcliffe stood and moved quickly to block her way. "You came here to tell me something—something important, something that's kept you hiding away in your rooms for days. I should have just let you speak and saved the confession of my own guilt for another time. Come sit down, G. Tell me what you were going to tell me."

Gina looked up at his pleading eyes, unable to miss the love for her that still glowed there brilliantly. She quickly weighed and measured all that had been said and all that she felt, and the only words she could manage to speak were a succinct, "I can't. Forgive me."

Leaving Radcliffe stunned, she hurried from the library and practically ran up the stairs and to her room where she could find solitude. She needed to review so many things in a new light, and she hardly knew where to begin. Perhaps she would end up spending *more* days confined to her room, like a prisoner bound by the lies she'd told—and apparently the lies that had been told to her—and so weighed down by them that she felt trapped and unable to function normally. At the moment she wasn't certain how to keep going, and for reasons she couldn't even discern, she wondered if it would ever truly be possible to get past all this mayhem that had arisen between her and Radcliffe and be able to resume the hopeful relationship they had shared. Presently, it felt impossible. But she had to believe that the situation was not nearly as bad as it seemed right then, and surely, they both had the strength and maturity to get past this. She could only hope.

CHAPTER NINE
extortion

GINA DIDN'T GET THE SOLITUDE she'd been seeking, since Ruby and Emerald were both waiting in her bedroom—as usual—to make certain she had all she needed to get ready for bed, but they were also both anxious to hear how the conversation with Sir Radcliffe had gone.

"It was a complete disaster!" Gina muttered hotly as she slumped into the chair in front of her dressing table so that Ruby could brush her hair and weave it into a long braid. "I'm not even certain what happened. I was working up to telling him the truth, and the next thing I know, he's telling me that he too has kept secrets—things about Dwight that he believes I should know—and they've been weighing heavily on him. He said that he feels a great deal of guilt for deceiving me, and he needed to tell me the truth—or words to that effect."

Ruby stopped working, and Emerald gasped before she said, "What in the world could that be about? I hope you're going to tell us!"

"I can't tell you because I don't know," Gina said. "I told him I didn't want to know, and then I just felt so overwhelmed that I . . . I ran away like a frightened puppy. He said that we shouldn't have to always be on guard about the secrets we've kept; that things will inevitably slip out over the years. And I know he's right. But I needed time to think. He doesn't know what I was trying to tell him, but I don't see how anything that Dwight may have done or not done is relevant anymore; he's dead and gone. His influence on our lives is over. The situation regarding Janine is very real and present; it will always be the truth of her existence."

"That's all true," Emerald said, "although I am not so sure that the influence Dwight has had on your life—or that of his cousin—is no longer relevant. You don't know what Sir Radcliffe was trying to tell you; perhaps it's particularly important."

"If it's weighed so heavily on him," Ruby interjected, having returned to her work on Gina's hair, "it *must* be important; or at least it feels important to him. Surely he has a right to be heard. If Dwight's actions in life are no longer relevant, given that he's now dead, then whatever Radcliffe needs to tell you should not be a problem—whatever it might be. Perhaps what is important is the fact that you allow Radcliffe to tell you."

"I agree," Emerald added, "and perhaps your willingness to accept and forgive Radcliffe for whatever he believes he did to deceive you will help him be more willing to do the same in return regarding the situation with Janine."

Gina thought about that and sighed before she said, "You both make particularly good points. "I think I always knew that Dwight was keeping secrets from me, and I worked awfully hard to pretend that I didn't notice the evidence, because I didn't want to believe it could be possible. Perhaps whatever Dwight did or did not do, it's important that I allow Radcliffe to tell me whatever he feels the need to tell me." She delved back into deep thought while Ruby plaited her hair to keep it from tangling while she slept, and both of the maids allowed her the silence necessary to sort through the chaos in her mind. "I can see now that . . . perhaps I need to separate the secret *I've* been keeping from whatever he needs to tell me. Even though I believe we've both made the point to each other over the need to be honest, it's not as if it's some kind of game where I tell him my secrets so he'll tell me his—or the other way around."

Gina sighed and moved to a more comfortable chair now that her hair was taken care of for the night. Ruby and Emerald sat down where they could face her, there for her in every way as they always were, brimming with wisdom and insight, as well as compassion and concern.

"Now I feel like such a fool for running away like I did," Gina said. "I told him I needed time to think about it. Hopefully, he will have accepted that explanation and I will be able to speak with him more reasonably tomorrow."

"I'm certain everything will be fine," Ruby said as if she fully believed it.

Gina declared that she was very tired, and her maids hurried to help her get ready for bed before leaving her alone in the dark to recount once again the bizarre conversation she'd shared with Radcliffe in the library. She prayed that they could get past whatever it was he needed to tell her, and the secret she'd finally accepted that she needed to share with him. She'd grown so accustomed to having him in her life—and believing that he always would be—that the very idea of anything coming between them threatened to crack her heart right in two. Oh, how she hoped and prayed that they could get beyond all of this and simply share a good life together! Was that too much to ask?

Despite Janine waking up to be cared for a couple of times in the night, Gina was deeply grateful for the distraction of caring for her daughter, which made it easier to not think about the inevitable difficult conversations she needed to share with Radcliffe. The natural exhaustion of caring for a baby during the night made it easier to go back to sleep, which also helped her to not think too much about what she could do nothing about until she actually had the opportunity to speak with Rad. She knew now that she *did* need to hear him out, and that she needed to tell him everything regarding Janine. But that was all she knew. She couldn't predict what he was going to tell her or how it would make her feel, any more than she could guess how he might respond to the truth about Janine. She didn't know if all their secrets would be disclosed in one conversation, or if it might require more time in order to fully address all that they both needed to reveal. The only truly good thing she could see in all of this was that she'd grown a great deal more confident over her need to tell Radcliffe the truth, and she didn't feel nearly as nervous to do so as she had previously felt. Perhaps the very fact that he'd admitted to having his own secrets and carrying his own guilt had helped her believe he might be more empathetic concerning her reasons for doing what she had done. Either way, she wouldn't know the outcome until they had a chance to talk; therefore, she hoped that it could be arranged as soon as possible.

Gina was relieved to have Elaine ask if she could take Janine to the playroom so that Elaine could care for the baby and be with Tommy, since he wanted to spend time playing with the numerous toys there. When a maid brought Gina's breakfast to her sitting room as usual, she already had a sealed note prepared for Radcliffe, which she turned over to the maid with the request that she have it delivered to him as soon as possible. In it, Gina had simply apologized for her hasty retreat the previous evening and asked that they talk at his earliest convenience, assuring him that she would make herself available whenever he had the time. Before she even finished eating, his reply was delivered, and her anxiety over the whole matter returned as she broke the seal and unfolded the page, conflicted by the hope that they could talk soon, yet also dreading it with her entire being. Clearly, despite the progress she'd made in knowing it was right to tell Radcliffe the truth—and her belief that he would be more accepting than she'd previously believed—she still had a great deal of anxiety over actually carrying out her objective. Regardless of how she might be feeling about this complicated mess she'd gotten herself into, she now had an appointment scheduled at half past ten to speak with Radcliffe in his study. She'd visited with him many times in the room where he conducted estate business; it was a lovely room, but it had been designed for business matters and not for personal confessions. She found the idea of talking with him there to be somewhat intimidating, but in her mind she resolved that problem with the determination to make certain the two of them sat in the chairs located near the windows, instead of him sitting behind the enormous desk and her sitting across from him. She didn't want any barriers—literal or figurative—between them as they shared what were obviously some serious matters. And she could only think of getting through the conversation; the consequences would have to be faced beyond that, but she had no way of predicting what they might be; therefore, she tried not to think that far ahead.

Hearing her thoughts repeating themselves over and over in her mind, Gina tried to force the entire matter out of her head. However, not long after she'd finished her breakfast and settled herself comfortably in her sitting room with a book, a maid brought her *another* sealed note with no explanation. Since Ruby and Emerald were both in the room with Gina—one of them mending a nightgown and the other knitting a muffler for her brother—it was evident from their expressions that they had no idea what this might be about. The sisters set aside their work as Gina set aside her book in order to break the seal and unfold the page. Before she had even had a chance to read the brief message, Emerald asked, "What does it say?"

"Oh, good heavens!" Gina muttered weakly and put a hand over her suddenly pounding heart.

"What does it say?" Ruby repeated more emphatically as both sisters moved to the edge of their chairs, seemingly ready to jump forward and rescue Gina from whatever was clearly upsetting.

Gina cleared her throat and tried to read the note aloud, but she couldn't. She abruptly shoved it toward Ruby who was sitting closest to her, and Ruby immediately read what was written there so that her sister could hear it as well. *"Forgive me for intruding upon your privacy, m'lady, but I very much need to speak with you privately right away. It is a matter of great urgency! Bernice Bott'"*

Ruby and Emerald both repeated Gina's reaction in nearly perfect synchronicity by putting their hands over their hearts and muttering in raspy voices, "Oh, good heavens!"

Emerald added quickly, "It is highly inappropriate for a maid of her station to request to speak to you in such a direct manner. I doubt the maid who delivered the note had any idea that it wasn't a communication from the baronet or the housekeeper."

Gina looked at the seal, and even though it was now broken, she could see it was the housekeeper's seal, which she used for official household matters. "Did Bernice sneak into Mrs. Darby's office and use her stationery in order to get the note into my hands?"

"It would appear that way," Ruby said, and Gina realized that both maids had suddenly become afflicted with shallow breathing, just as she was.

"Does this mean that Bernice *is* Janine's mother?" Gina asked, her voice beginning to tremble. "It would seem so! But what on earth could she want to speak to me about? And why the urgency? Why now?"

"Those are all very valid questions," Ruby said, "and only Bernice can answer them."

Emerald stood up and declared, "There's no need to write a response. I will go and find her and bring her to speak with you right away, assuming she can get away from her work without any trouble."

"I don't want any suspicion aroused regarding any connection between us," Gina said. "How is that possible if she's—"

Ruby interrupted to say, "The answer to that is in her postscript; we failed to read the entire message. It says: *"I will be working alone today cleaning the east summer parlor. My absence for a short while will not be noticed."*"

Gina jumped to her feet. "No need for her to come here and attempt to not be seen by anyone. Let's go and talk to her now and be done with it. I cannot bear the suspense for another minute. And I need the two of you to come with me. If nothing else, that will prevent me from having to repeat the conversation to you, and I also need you both to be especially alert and observant; I know you are both very discerning. I need to know if you think she's telling the truth given *whatever* she has to say."

Gina took a deep breath and brushed her hands down the front of her dress as if that might put some kind of protection in place. She then headed out of the room with the sisters following directly behind her. The east summer parlor was very rarely used, and Ruby informed Gina that Mrs. Darby had a list of every room in the house, and even those that were hardly ever occupied were assigned to be cleaned by the maids in a kind of rotation so that none of the rooms ever became too dusty to be used should the need arise. Given the lack of social engagements that took place in this house, guest rooms and superfluous parlors were rarely if ever used—not to mention the ballroom and the grand dining room, which accommodated a number of people beyond anything

Gina had ever bothered to count. She'd only eaten in there twice when parties had been held here years earlier, and she'd felt nothing but overwhelmed. Gina knew there were many rooms in the house where Radcliffe enjoyed having tea or relaxing, and he appreciated the variety; but there were also some that he simply didn't care for due to the window view or the decor. And the east summer parlor was one of those rooms. How fortunate that Bernice had been assigned to work in *that* room, or perhaps she'd sent her message at a time when she knew she'd be in a room where no one would notice whether or not she left, or if she received visitors there.

Gina was glad that the sisters knew exactly where to find the room, since Gina couldn't recall ever going there for any reason. The three women paused outside the door and simultaneously took in deep breaths before Emerald knocked lightly, then opened the door without waiting for a response. Gina entered with the sisters coming behind her and closing the door. Bernice was standing near the fireplace where there was no fire, wringing a dusting rag in her hands. She was average height for a woman and appeared far too thin, judging by the way the typical maid's uniform hung loosely on her. She was younger than Gina had expected; she looked barely old enough to be called a woman, which might explain her reasons for not being able to care for Janine— if indeed she was the baby's mother. The white cap on her head covered most of her brown hair, and her eyes were wide with fear. While Gina didn't like the idea of this woman being so afraid, she preferred that over having her look smug or prideful, which would be an indication that she wanted to cause trouble for Gina.

"M'lady," Bernice said and curtsied quickly but much deeper than necessary or typical.

"Bernice?" Gina asked, needing to be certain she hadn't accidently happened upon some other maid; she didn't want to open a secretive conversation with the wrong person.

"Yes," the maid said, her voice quivering.

Gina saw Bernice glance skeptically toward Ruby and Emerald, and Gina said, "It's all right. There is nothing in my life they don't know about, and I trust them completely. They will keep anything we say in absolute confidence."

Bernice nodded, but the rag in her hands looked as if it were being tormented brutally. Attempting to lighten the mood, if only a little, Gina said, "Shall we sit down and—"

"No!" Bernice insisted in a loud whisper. "We must be quick. Did anyone see you come here?"

"No," Gina said.

"We're certain of it," Emerald added.

"Very well," Gina said, "please tell me what it is you need to say. You look utterly terrified, my dear girl. I hope you know that you have no need to fear me for any reason."

"You're truly kind, m'lady, although . . . you don't yet know what I need to say. And . . . it's not you I fear . . . except that . . . even though I am only the messenger of bad tidings, I am the cause of the problem, and . . . I would understand why you might be angry with me. Still, I beg you to not dismiss me from working here. I need the job so badly, you see. I have nowhere else to go and—"

"As long as you are honest and fair," Gina said, "your employment is not at risk. I have no power over such things anyway."

"And yet you are close to Sir Radcliffe; you have influence on his decisions, and—"

"Please, Bernice," Gina said, unable to bear the suspense. "You said that you needed to be brief. Please tell me what the problem is so that we can—"

"Your little Janine is my baby," Bernice said, and tears rolled down her face as the confession spilled out on a quavering sigh. Gina took a deep breath, and despite hearing the sisters both gasp, she reminded herself that she wasn't surprised to hear this; she only needed to know what Bernice intended to do with this information. So she just listened as Bernice went on. "I was able to hide my pregnancy. Her father made many promises to me, which he did not keep, and he is long gone and far away now. I gave birth alone, and—"

"With no one to help you?" Ruby asked with overt compassion. "You poor, dear girl!"

Ruby's kindness seemed to give Bernice more courage as she continued. "I knew I couldn't care for her, and I knew my mother would toss me out on the streets if she discovered the truth. I had no choice but to leave her . . . praying that the right person would find her. And my prayers were answered." Her tears increased and she wiped her sleeves over her face while still holding to the rag with both hands. "I hid in an alley across the road to see what happened. I didn't let her out of my sight until I saw her taken into your carriage; I recognized the markings of the carriage as being from the manor, and then word spread that you'd had a baby girl." Bernice choked back a sob while Gina wanted to just embrace the young woman and offer some comfort. She couldn't imagine the heartache involved in giving up a child in such a way. Bernice hurried on, as if she knew what she wanted to say and needed to be done with it. "I want you to know that I'm nothing but grateful to you for taking her in. I know you've led people to believe you gave birth to her, and I'm glad for it, because I want her to have the best life possible, but I never imagined she would be able to grow up in such a fine home with such good people to love her. I'm nothing but grateful," she repeated, "and I would never personally do anything to interfere with her happiness. I confess that when I heard there was a position available for a maid here, I very much wanted the job just so I could feel closer to her, and perhaps get a glimpse now and then as she grew, but I did not come here to cause any trouble, m'lady. I swear it. I only want what's best for Janine, and it's evident you want the same."

"I do," Gina said, "and I swear to you that I will always do everything I can to give her the best life possible, and not just in monetary things; I promise you she will be loved and safe."

"I know," Bernice said and wiped away more tears.

Gina wondered if the purpose of this meeting had simply been for Bernice to announce her existence in the house and the facts about her place in Janine's life, but then she noticed the fear in the maid's eyes returning with more intensity, and she recalled the mention of urgency in her note, and how she'd said that she was the messenger of bad tidings. *What did that mean?* They had just exchanged words of kindness; Bernice had to know now that she had nothing to fear from Gina. So, what was the source of the fear? The question made Gina's heart begin to thud as if it had the power to burst right out of her.

"What is it?" Gina asked when Bernice seemed unable to speak.

"Oh, m'lady!" Bernice said. "I realized after I found myself pregnant and abandoned that I was terribly gullible and naive, and I swore I would never be that way again. But . . . it's clear to me now I learned nothing." She drew in a ragged breath and blew it out slowly. "There is a young man who works in the stables here; he was so kind to me when I arrived . . . and I knew no one . . . and I confess my heart was aching at having to give up my baby, and . . . we became friends, and then he . . . told me that he loved me . . . he said all the right things, and . . ." Gina nearly expected to hear that Bernice was pregnant again, but Bernice quickly put that theory to rest. "I was careful this time about not letting him have anything more than a kiss; I've learned my lesson about that. But I honestly believed I could trust him, given the way we talked so openly about so many things and . . ." Bernice hung her head and began to sob.

The inkling of a suspicion over the possible problem sank into Gina with a sickening dread that tightened her stomach and slowed her heart in a way that made the room seem unsteady. Realizing it was *she* who had become unsteady, she moved carefully to a chair, trying not to appear alarmed, but not wanting her weakening legs to fail her. A quick glance at Ruby and Emerald showed equal alarm in their expressions, but they each stood firm like sentinels at her side.

"What's happened, Bernice?" Gina asked with the strongest voice she could muster. "You must tell me everything; no secrets or lies. Is there some reason I should be concerned about being able to keep Janine safe?"

Bernice visibly mustered her courage and composure, if only barely. She looked directly at Gina and said, "I'm so deeply sorry, m'lady. I believe you love my daughter as if she were your own, and you will always keep her safe—which is why I needed to warn you. It's my fault; it's all my fault. The situation here was perfect as far as it seemed to me, and then I was fool enough to tell him the truth about Janine and . . ."

"What?" Gina muttered breathlessly. "Who?"

"His name is Lyle; he works in the stables." Bernice sniffed and again wiped her sleeves over her face to clear away her tears. "I thought I could trust him; I only wanted to talk to someone about my feelings on the matter. I believed he would understand, that he would keep my secret, but . . . now he's full of talk about all we could gain from this . . . how our knowledge of the truth about Janine could earn us a great deal of money in order to keep us quiet." Bernice went to her knees and dropped the rag before she clasped her hands together as if in fervent prayer. "I swear to you, m'lady, that I want nothing from you or anyone else in this house except for the employment I already have. I beg you not to send me away! I so want to be close to my . . . your little girl, even if I never see her; I just want to be nearby. I swear to you I'll not cause any trouble or harm; that's not my intention; it's never been my intention. But . . . Lyle seems intent on causing trouble. I've begged him to leave it alone, to keep my confidence, to let it go, but he won't listen. I've wanted very much to stop seeing him completely, but if I did that, I wouldn't know what he's thinking . . . what he's planning . . . and I have to know . . . and I had to warn you! You've risked so much to make Janine your own, to give her everything I could never give her. I owe you nothing but gratitude. Please forgive me, m'lady. Please . . . please . . . know I want nothing from you, and—"

Gina had to interrupt, fearing Bernice could go on with her pleadings and gratitude indefinitely. While Gina appreciated her sentiments more than she could say, and she absolutely believed Bernice was telling her the truth, the problem at hand had to be addressed. Despite how tangibly ill she felt over what she was hearing, Gina managed to ask in a calm voice, "What exactly is this Lyle planning to do, Bernice? If you know, you need to tell me."

"He is going to ask you for money in order to keep your secret, m'lady, and if you don't give it to him, he intends to tell Sir Radcliffe the truth, assuming he doesn't already know." Bernice said it as if the very thought horrified her. "Then he will ask the baronet for a large sum of money in order to guarantee Lyle's silence on the matter."

Gina certainly felt horrified over the idea that this villain Lyle knew the truth about Janine, but if his plan was to get gain by telling Radcliffe, he had very little leverage on that count—since Gina had already made the decision to tell him the truth regardless. She simply needed to do so as soon as possible so that he heard it from her first, and not some scoundrel who was out to damage the lives of other people in order to benefit financially.

"Bernice," Gina said, marveling at how calm her voice sounded when her inner turmoil was becoming physically painful, "I have every intention of telling Sir Radcliffe the truth, and I will do it right away before Lyle has the chance."

"Oh, m'lady!" Bernice exclaimed on the wave of a sigh so loud and long Gina thought the girl might fall over from its force. With her hands still clasped she muttered, "I never imagined such a solution! I do hope he is not angry with you; surely he will see you did right by Janine, and—"

"I have no idea how he will respond," Gina said, "and that is between me and him."

"Of course," Bernice said humbly. "Forgive me. I don't wish to be intrusive; I only wish to know that my little . . . *your* daughter . . . is all right."

"She will be," Gina said, resisting the urge to tell Bernice that if Radcliffe rejected her once he knew the truth, she intended to leave here with her father, her servants, and her daughter. That was a personal matter as well, and for all Bernice's sincerity and humility, she had still been gullible enough to tell an evil man secrets she never should have shared. Gina had no intention of giving Bernice any further information. "I can tell Sir Radcliffe the truth, which will prevent Lyle from being able to get money out of me *or* him in return for his silence." Gina didn't want to admit to the fear circling in her mind that was far worse than Radcliffe being told the truth, but she had only this brief time to speak with Bernice and it had to be addressed. "And if Lyle doesn't get money for his silence, does this mean he intends to spread gossip about the situation until the entire community knows the truth? Does he intend to bring shame upon our household? Upon you?"

Bernice began to cry again and whimpered, "I don't know. I'm so sorry, m'lady."

Gina thought about her questions and Bernice's response for a long, tense moment of silence before she concluded that she needed her father's advice, and she needed to speak with Radcliffe right away. She was glad to know she already had an appointment to do so because it couldn't be put off any longer, and if he didn't take the news well, she would have to suffer the consequences, whatever they might be. She was horrified to realize that the very fact of someone like Lyle now knowing the truth would surely put the entire situation in a less favorable light. This terrible man *did* have the power to bring shame upon their household, and perhaps Radcliffe would see that the only way to remove that shame would be to send Gina and the child she'd taken from an alley away from here forever. But Gina couldn't think of that now. She felt an urgency to do all she could do to minimize the potential damage.

Gina summoned all her strength and came to her feet, saying with compassion, "Come, Bernice. You must calm yourself." She took hold of the girl's shoulders and helped her to her feet. Looking briefly into her tear-filled eyes, she saw only the woman who had given life to Janine, and she felt a sudden and deep affinity with Bernice. There was no malice in this young woman, and they were united in wanting the best for Janine. "Listen to me carefully. I will do everything I can to handle the situation. Thank you for being honest with me. From now on we will keep this secret among those we trust completely. I swear to you that I will always take good care of Janine, and you have no need to worry about her welfare. If I need to communicate with you, Ruby or Emerald will find you." Gina nodded slightly toward her maids. "For now, I want you to do your best to appease Lyle and not give him any indication that you've talked to me."

"Oh, he'd beat the life out of me if he knew I'd done such a thing!" Bernice blurted, and Gina felt a new level of sickness rise inside of her.

"Has he hurt you before?" Gina asked.

"A little," Bernice muttered, looking down with shame, "but only a time or two."

"But you have reason to fear for your safety?" Gina asked.

Bernice looked back up. "I'll be all right, m'lady. Just take care of our little Janine."

"I will," Gina said, "and . . . if you need help . . . if you feel threatened . . . tell Mrs. Darby or anyone else in the household; they don't need to know anything except that he hurts you. I assure you it won't be tolerated. Not here."

Bernice nodded, seeming perhaps skeptical that anyone could protect her. Gina simply hurried to say, "Thank you for warning me. Please be careful."

"And you, m'lady," Bernice said before Gina hurried out of the room, Ruby and Emerald close on her heels. She could well imagine Bernice closing the door and crying long and hard while she attempted to continue with her work of cleaning the parlor. Gina walked briskly with the hope of releasing some of her fears and concerns. She wanted to be angry with Bernice for trusting someone like Lyle with such a volatile secret, but she could only feel compassion for the young woman. She clearly had no self-confidence, and her own insecurities had put her into these deplorable situations. How could Gina judge a woman for being naive and gullible when she had married Dwight for the very same reasons? Her circumstances were dramatically different from those of Bernice, but the tenderness of their hearts was likely very much the same, and Gina needed to keep that perspective as she attempted to hold back the storm that was threatening their secrets—and subsequently their security—in this home and this community.

With the exception of Gina asking Emerald to tell her the time, reminding herself that she needed to be punctual in meeting with Radcliffe, not a word was said between Gina and her maids until they were walking through the open doorway of Gina's sitting room and she said, "Emerald, will you find my father and tell him I need to speak to him right away, and that it's urgent?"

Before Emerald could answer, Milton said from where he was sitting with Janine in his arms, "No need for that. I'm right here. What is so urgent, my dear?"

Gina turned toward Ruby and Emerald, who needed no instruction to graciously leave the room and close the door behind them. Gina glanced at the clock on the mantel, noting before she sat close to her father and took a deep breath, that it was a few minutes past ten. She knew she just had to dive into this directly and not waste time trying to be delicate about the situation.

"I'm so glad you're here," she said. "I've just spoken with Bernice . . . the maid . . . who is indeed Janine's mother."

Milton looked surprised but his voice was even as he said, "I see. And is she causing trouble for you?"

"Not her," Gina said. "She was nothing but humble and grateful regarding the situation; however . . . she put her trust in a man who works in the stables . . . and he has turned out to be entirely untrustworthy. He intends to demand money from me to keep my secret, and if I don't give it to him, he will demand it of Sir Radcliffe."

"Extortion?" Milton muttered in an angry whisper. "Well, that cannot be tolerated!"

"I agree," Gina said, "and yet . . . how much can we control what this man does or does not do? Even if he's given the money he asks for, how are we to be certain he won't divulge the secret anyway? I already know that you would advise me to tell Radcliffe everything, because if he knows the truth, then this secret has no power over him or me."

"You're right," Milton said, "that's exactly what I would tell you. I see you've been paying attention to your old father all these years."

"He's a very wise man," Gina said, giving him a wan smile. "But oh, Papa! I've gotten myself into such a terrible mess, and now . . . now . . ."

"If you had it to do over again, would you have not brought Janine home with you?"

"I would have! Yes! But perhaps I should have been honest with Radcliffe right from the beginning. And perhaps I should have informed the police so that it was not a public secret. I don't know. I sincerely don't know. But there's no good in regret. I can only do my best to manage the situation as it is now. I need to speak with Radcliffe right away . . . before anything else can happen to make the situation worse. And God willing, the solution to the problem won't necessitate our leaving here."

"We pray such is not the case," Milton said, "but if it comes to that, we know we will be all right."

Gina nodded in agreement, but the very idea of leaving Stonebridge broke her heart; it was difficult to imagine life being all right without having Radcliffe by her side, and without being here in this beautiful home she'd come to love so dearly.

⚜

Gina left her father to play with the baby, knowing that Elaine was nearby to assist. She hurried to freshen up and check her appearance in the mirror, both wishing she had more time to gather her courage, and grateful that she didn't have even a minute to think about what she now had to face. She hurried to Radcliffe's study, mentally trying to plan what she might say exactly, but the words in her head only swirled around in chaos, and she focused instead on simply trying to muster every bit of courage she had inside of her, reminding herself that she could not control his reaction; she simply had to be entirely honest with him and hope for a positive outcome.

Gina found the door to the study open, and from the hallway she could see Radcliffe seated behind the enormous, ornate desk where she imagined generations of men before him must have sat to attend to estate business. While he was oblivious to her standing in the doorway, taking in deep breaths hoping to remain calm, she uttered a silent prayer that God would soften Radcliffe's heart, and that all would be well for everyone involved—most especially little Janine.

Hearing the clock in the study chime half past ten, Gina knocked on the open door to alert Radcliffe to her presence. He looked up as she stepped into the room, and his smile helped ease her nerves—if only a little.

"Right on time," he said, moving from behind the desk—much to her relief. Knowing they needed complete privacy, Gina closed the door as Radcliffe came toward her, both of his hands outstretched. She slipped her hands into his and he pressed a kiss to her cheek. "You must forgive me," he said, looking into her eyes. "I know you came to tell me something that was very important to you, and I selfishly turned the conversation to my own issues."

"Of course, I forgive you," she said earnestly. "I only hope that *you* can forgive *me* once you've heard what I have to say, and . . . since we last spoke, something terrible has happened regarding the matter I need to discuss, and . . . I . . . well . . ."

As Gina's words turned into helpless stammering, Radcliffe escorted her to a chair and sat down beside her after he'd moved his chair slightly so that he could face her more directly. Gina was relieved by this, since it prevented her from having to insist that they not converse with the intimidating desk between them.

"You're clearly very upset," Radcliffe observed, his brow furrowing. Gina wasn't at all surprised by his observation, since she was making no attempt to hide how her conversation with Bernice had affected her—and that on top of her need to now disclose *everything* to Radcliffe, having no idea what his response would be.

"Yes," she admitted, "I'm upset." She took a deep breath. "I've been dishonest with you, Rad, and the secret I've been keeping is not small by any means. I've been weighed down by guilt and wondering for months if it would be better to keep the matter to myself, or if I should tell you the truth. I can see now that if you and I have any hope of sharing a future together we need to have absolute trust and honesty between us. I've spoken with my father about it, and he told me what I think I've known all along in my heart: I need to tell you the truth, even if doing so might risk losing everything we've come to share."

Radcliffe leaned back more fully into his chair, and that one eyebrow went up as it often did; he clearly couldn't fathom anything possibly being so severe, and he echoed this sentiment when he said, "Do you not believe we have the ability together to overcome the challenges of life?"

Gina took in a long, quavering breath. "What I'm about to tell you could never fall into the category of the normal challenges of life. I wouldn't blame you in the least if you wanted nothing more to do with me, and I hope you know that losing you—and the hope of a future with you—would utterly break my heart. But I cannot live with this secret between us any longer. When I came to speak with you about it, I was determined to tell you everything, but the conversation did not go as planned, and—"

"Which was *my* fault," he insisted.

"Nevertheless, I couldn't have predicted that just this morning something regarding the secret I've kept has come to light and now . . . well . . . now I'm in a great deal of trouble, Radcliffe, and I fear that the trouble brewing may very well cause trouble for *you*, and there is nothing fair or right about that. Perhaps if I had told you sooner this could have been avoided; I don't know, but . . . now I *must* tell you, and I pray that you will not think too badly of me, even if you decide that you can never trust me enough to continue our courtship, and—"

"Gina!" he interrupted. "I love you; you know I do. There's nothing you can tell me that will ever change how I feel about you, and—"

"But is love enough, Rad? Is trust not vital to a good marriage?"

"I cannot dispute that," he said. "I also cannot dispute that forgiveness is also vital, and as I admitted to you recently, I too have kept a secret and—"

Not wanting to have their conversation veer off course as it did last time, Gina hurried to say, "Please . . . just . . . let me say what I need to say . . . so that we can address the problem at hand . . . then we will determine the impact on our relationship—even if that may very well take some time." Gina added the last with the realization that it was likely not realistic to expect Radcliffe to hear what she had to say and immediately be capable of accepting and understanding it; whether or not he could ever forgive her or trust her would likely take a good deal longer.

"Go on," Radcliffe said, motioning with his hand. She hated the skepticism in his eyes and the doubt in his expression, especially knowing they were about to become far worse.

CHAPTER TEN
the secret

GINA ONCE AGAIN TOOK A deep breath before she ventured to tell him the story he needed to hear; she wanted her explanation to remain as brief as possible, but she also knew there were important details he had to know. "I don't need to tell you—but perhaps I need to remind you—that following Dwight's death I became . . . lost. I believe now that the way I isolated myself—eating too much and remaining far too sedentary—was far more about my confusion and disappointment regarding my marriage to Dwight than it was about having any real sorrow over his death, which in turn left me feeling guilty, which only added to my confusion."

"Yes, I know all of this," he said, not impatiently but perhaps with obvious confusion over what it could possibly have to do with the secret she'd kept from him.

"A day came when Ruby and Emerald and Garn had conspired to get me out of the house, no matter what it took. When we arrived in town, many shops were closed down and the high street was devoid of any people because of a town meeting taking place; they had known this would be the case and had believed it would cause less duress for me. Our intention was to go into the bookshop to find something new for me to read."

"You're talking about the day Janine was born," Radcliffe said.

"Yes," Gina clarified, her heart suddenly beginning to pound. "But . . . what you need to know is that . . ." She hung her head in shame, unable to look at him, and she couldn't keep her voice from trembling as the truth finally spilled out. "I was never pregnant, Rad." She heard him gasp but ignored it and forged ahead before she lost momentum. "We had barely arrived at our destination when we heard a baby crying and Garn went to investigate." She sighed, then sobbed softly. "He found Janine in an alley . . . left there . . . with a note that made it evident the mother wanted her to be taken and cared for. I have to say that all the shame I had felt over not being able to conceive vanished in that moment. When I held her in my arms, I recalled the story of Moses, and how he had been found and raised by the Pharaoh's daughter, because the mother who had given birth to him could not keep him safe. I felt with all my heart and soul that she was meant to be mine." Gina sighed and forced herself to look up at Radcliffe, not surprised by the unadulterated shock in his expression. But she pressed on and stated matter-of-factly, "And that's when we constructed a feasible story to make it appear that Janine was my baby. Ruby and Emerald both have some midwifery experience they had gotten from their mother, and they helped make certain that everything appeared exactly as it should in order to make the story believable." Gina sighed, relieved to have the truth in the open, but hardly able to breathe as she waited for some kind of response. She concluded firmly, despite the way her entire body felt as if it were trembling, "You likely know the rest, but you are more than welcome to ask me any questions you might have, and I swear to you that I will answer honestly, and I will never, ever lie to you again. I only want to add that when I constructed this lie—to protect Janine from any social stigma or legal consequences and to be able to care for her—I had no idea that the relationship between you and me would change as it has. Still, I brought Janine into *your* home, and I likely should have told you the truth from the beginning. I wondered initially if I should have gone to the police about finding an abandoned baby, but I didn't want to risk losing her when I felt so strongly that she needed to be in my care." Gina looked down again, unable to bear staring into Radcliffe's astonished eyes another moment. "That's all."

Gina could suddenly hear nothing but the ticking of a clock in the room as she waited for some kind of response from Radcliffe. She couldn't dispute that it was only right that she allow him some time to take in all that she'd said. If he'd just told her something equivalently absurd, she would surely need to weigh and measure her reaction. Still, the seconds ticking away felt eternal, and she began to fear she might scream or burst into tears simply out of the need to fill the silence.

Radcliffe finally spoke in a voice that did not express any disdain or disgust, but it was certainly lacking its usual warmth. "That is *not* all," he said. "You told me that you're in trouble; you told me that something regarding your secret has come to light, and you fear that it will cause trouble for *me*. Isn't that what you said?"

"Yes," she answered, unable to look at him.

"Then I believe you need to tell me exactly what has happened," he stated, his voice tight and strained, as if he were trying very hard not to sound angry, but it was taking every bit of self-restraint he possessed. Gina could feel the potential love between them slipping away, dissolving around her, but she had to focus on getting through this conversation or she would completely fall apart, and at the very least she needed to maintain her dignity—what little might be left of it.

"The young woman who gave birth to Janine works here in the household," Gina said.

"What?" Radcliffe countered in a quiet shout, clearly not wanting to be overheard but so astonished he couldn't hold back. "How in the name of all that is holy did *that* happen?"

Gina explained as briefly as she could manage all that she knew about Bernice's history and how she'd come to work at the manor, then she repeated the conversation that had taken place between her and Bernice just this morning. At the mention of Lyle and his malicious intentions, Radcliffe erupted from his chair and began to pace frantically, as if holding still might cause him to explode and either start shouting or breaking things—or both. When Gina knew she had told Radcliffe all there was to tell, she took in a deep breath and let it out slowly, relieved at least to know that she no longer had anything to hide from him. He knew every detail of the secret she'd been keeping. There was nothing more to be done except wait to see how Radcliffe might respond to the knowledge she'd shared with him. Wondering how long she might have to wait to know his true sentiments regarding her deception, or if the worst might happen, she felt compelled to simply state the possibilities aloud rather than allowing her own understanding of the situation to go unspoken.

While Radcliffe continued to pace, his expression betraying that his thoughts were going wild, Gina spoke in a voice that she wished sounded less timid. "I would completely understand if you no longer wish for me to remain in your home. I've deceived you terribly, and if word of this gets out among the community—as it very well might—it's clear that the only way to truly preserve your reputation would be to expel us from the house. My father and I between us have more than enough funds to support ourselves, so you have no need to be concerned about our welfare. I just want you to know that I would harbor no ill feelings toward you if that's what you feel is the best course, and—"

"What?" Radcliffe suddenly stopped walking and stood to face her, his fists planted firmly on his hips. As if he'd been snapped out of a daze enough to fully hear what she'd been saying, he demanded in a voice angrier than she'd ever heard, "What on earth are you talking about? I don't care a *whit* about my reputation! *What* reputation? What exactly might I lose by people gossiping about what might be going on in my household? I can assure you, Regina, that this has *nothing* to do with my reputation and I should hope you know me well enough to be certain that I would never place the opinions of others above the welfare of the people I care about."

"Forgive me," she said. "You're right. I *do* know that. I confess that all of this has muddled my thinking. Allow me to clarify. It's surely more accurate to say that if you can no longer trust me—and I completely understand why that would be the case—and you prefer that we leave, then we will do so. Perhaps that is the easiest solution to the problem. This Lyle villain would have no leverage if we just left here right away and—"

"And again I ask," Radcliffe interrupted, sounding even more angry, although he kept his voice quiet enough to not be overheard by any servants who might be eavesdropping for the sake of gathering gossip, "what *are* you talking about? I would *never* expel you or Janine or your father—or the servants who are your friends—from this house! This is your *home*! Merciful heaven, G! This is complicated and ugly, no doubt! But don't think for a moment that I'm the kind of man who would solve such a problem by displacing you and the people you love. And how could you possibly believe that I would want Janine to grow up anywhere else? Wherever she came from, she has become a part of this family and she always will be! Don't you *dare* think that the solution to this problem is to take away from me the only real joy I've ever known and leave this house hollow and empty like a blasted . . . mausoleum."

Gina heard his voice quiver the same moment he turned his face away, then he hurried toward one of the room's many windows and planted his hands on the sill, hanging his head as if it had suddenly become too heavy to hold up. She heard him sniffle and realized he was likely crying and attempting to hide it from her. Despite her distinct fear that he could very well reject her efforts, Gina moved instinctively to his side and put a hand on his arm, attempting to offer some measure of comfort. Yesterday such a gesture would have been completely natural and comfortable between them, but clearly that was no longer the case.

"Don't!" he snapped and shrugged off her hand, moving abruptly away, turning his back to her.

Gina hurriedly recounted all the mental preparation she'd endured regarding the strong possibility that Radcliffe would never be able to trust her again, and that their personal relationship would be shattered. But in that moment, she realized that no amount of rehearsal could have prepared her for the shock of his total rebuff. Hot tears rushed into her eyes before she could even try to hold them back, and her throat burned with the need to scream or sob or howl like a wounded animal. So deep and piercing was the pain of his rejection that she wondered how it was possible that she'd managed to remain standing. In her mind she saw herself melting onto the carpet in a quivering heap. By some miracle she was able to stay upright and swallow the heat in her throat, but tears fell in abundance down her cheeks, thankfully unseen by Radcliffe who was still turned away from her.

Gina was surprised and relieved to hear him say in a gentle tone that was more like himself, "Forgive me, G, but I need some time to . . . take all of this in. I don't . . . even know what I feel. As I see it . . . what we feel . . . and how we proceed . . . regarding our personal lives will have to wait. There are only two things that matter right now." He turned so abruptly to face her that she gasped, but even as he looked at her directly he seemed oblivious to her ongoing flow of tears, and there was a sharpness in his eyes that led her to believe he truly would never trust her again. "First of all," he raised a threatening finger in front of her face, "you will *not* leave this house! Not you, nor your servants, nor your father. This is your home! Do you hear me?" Gina could only nod, certain that it was likely his love for Janine—and for her father—that surely motivated such an edict, far more than having anything to do with her. He didn't want to lose the close relationship he'd gained with her daughter, nor the evolving friendship with her father. Gina would have to accept that her place in this house was likely dependent upon her relationship to her family members that Radcliffe had grown to love and didn't want to lose. But she felt certain that her own relationship with Radcliffe would never be anything more than his tolerance of her presence because of her connection to Janine and Milton—and perhaps a sense of duty in providing a home for his cousin's widow.

While she felt as if her heart were literally crumbling into millions of unfixable pieces, Radcliffe spoke again, his finger still held threateningly in front of her face. "The only other thing that matters right now is making certain this Lyle monster does not get away with whatever it is he thinks he's going to accomplish. I won't stand for it! I will have him forcibly bound and gagged and transported extremely far away before I will ever allow him to blackmail me or my family!"

Gina appreciated the way he referred to *family*, but still she felt certain his affections were focused on her daughter and her father, and simply defending the honor of those who bore his surname—even if Janine only bore it out of deception. Still, Janine was innocent in all this, and Gina felt certain Radcliffe was fully aware of *that*. She could easily imagine years into the future, with Radcliffe and Janine sharing a treasured closeness, while Gina remained on the outer perimeter of their relationship as uncle and niece. She'd made the decision to bring Janine into Radcliffe's home—and his life—and she could see now that it would be terrible of her to even think of ever taking her away from here for any reason. Allowing him to be a part of Janine's life was likely the only thing she could do to offer any kind of recompense for the way she'd deceived him. But that would mean never marrying again; if she didn't marry Radcliffe—and her hopes of that had already completely dissolved—marrying anyone else would mean leaving Stonebridge, and she didn't believe she ever could, simply because Radcliffe had grown to love Janine so dearly. Gina reminded herself that this meant they would always have a home, and that Janine would have a good life. She no longer had to entertain the fear that Radcliffe might expel them from the house, but that didn't mean her heart wasn't broken on other counts.

After taking a long moment to absorb all that Radcliffe had said, Gina pulled her handkerchief out from where it was tucked beneath the cuff of her sleeve and hurried to press it beneath her nose before she embarrassed herself even worse. Radcliffe still seemed oblivious to her tears, which only bothered Gina because he had always been so tender and sensitive toward her and any display of emotion she'd exhibited. Now he was cold and seemingly shrouded in a mixture of anger and determination, which was clearly meant to keep her at a distance. She forced herself to focus on her gratitude that he was determined to deal with Lyle's threats. She felt certain he would not literally do as he'd threatened; nevertheless, there was relief in knowing that a man with the power and confidence Radcliffe possessed was now aware of the situation and he would surely know how to handle it far better than Gina ever could.

The silence beyond her own sniffling became unnerving and Gina felt the need to ask, "What will we do? You must know my deepest concern is for Janine's safety. Perhaps I should have taken her to the police to begin with and—"

"I thank God you did not!" he said, sounding angry again. "They likely would have planted her in some horrible orphanage, and if anyone else had found her, that would have surely been the most probable outcome." Gina was glad to hear in his voice some validation of her decision, even though he had spoken it with anger. It was impossible to tell if he was angry with her, or just the situation; likely both.

"I never wanted to bring any trouble upon you, Radcliffe," Gina said, hoping to appease his anger, if only a little. "You must believe me. I acted impulsively, but I acted on my deepest instincts. And then it all just . . . became too big to manage, I suppose. But . . . I never anticipated something like this. Please believe me when I tell you that second only to my concern over Janine's well-being is my concern for how this is affecting *you*!"

"There's no need to worry about me," he said, but his tone implied that he might very well search out this Lyle and physically take out every bit of his current turmoil and frustration on the man. "And there's no need to worry about what *we* will do. *I* will take care of this, Gina."

"What will you do?" she asked, her concerns over him doing something rash escalating dramatically. "Surely you must not act while you are so . . . upset!"

"I can assure you I will think everything through carefully and I will take time to calm down. For now, that's all I can promise. Although it seems reasonable that we should wait for him to act and see if these threats actually come to pass, and then we will deal with them accordingly. Promise me that you will tell me anything and everything that might arise so that I will know exactly what's taking place. And then *I* will handle it."

"Of course," she said firmly, hating the way his tone implied that she might continue to withhold information from him. She wished he could understand how difficult it had been to keep her secret, and now that he knew everything, she never wanted to keep back even the tiniest thought from him in the future. She felt compelled to add, "You must promise me you'll do the same. If anything at all happens, you must tell me immediately."

"Of course," he insisted, his manner entirely businesslike, and his mood clearly very foul. "Then for now that's all we can do," he concluded. "Unless you have something else to tell me that you've been keeping from me, I think this conversation is over."

Gina felt as if she were a kitchen maid being dismissed because she had no right to be in the same room with the master of the house. She swallowed her hurt and said with forced calm, "No, that's all."

"Then go," he said, waving his arm dramatically toward the door. His gesture came across with a finality of his dismissal of her, as if he were banishing her from his life. Gina could do nothing but hurry from the room as quickly as she could manage, without stumbling over her own unsteady feet. She resisted the temptation to stop on the stairs or in one of the many hallways she needed to traverse and just give in to the storm of grief and horror threatening to devour her. But she kept herself together with the incentive that she didn't want *anyone* to see her disintegrate into a puddle of helpless sobbing.

Relieved to finally arrive at her bedroom—and to find no one there— Gina locked both doors, kicked off her shoes, and crawled into the bed. Her head barely made contact with the pillow before she began to sob with such a heaving force that she had to press the pillow over her face to make certain no one overheard her.

While trying to calm herself, Gina made a concentrated effort to focus on her relief over having finally shared her secrets with Radcliffe. She no longer had to carry that burden, and she no longer had to fear his finding out. But her relief was smothered by the distinct likelihood that his knowledge of her deception had created a barrier between them that could never be overcome. She didn't doubt Radcliffe's love for her, but she wondered if he would ever again trust or respect her—and she felt certain he could never forgive her—and if that was the case, her hope of becoming his wife had now become utterly foolish and ridiculous. She felt certain she had lost him. And while she felt grateful beyond words that he had been so insistent about Gina and her loved ones remaining here at Stonebridge, she wondered how it would be to live out her life here with Radcliffe under the same roof, while denying the love they shared and always remaining at a distance.

Gina cried long and hard, until a severe headache clamped down on her and she had to force herself to be calm, knowing that the more she cried, the more her head was likely to hurt. She settled into a dazed shock that reminded her of how she'd felt upon learning about Dwight's death. Her emotions then had been complicated and confusing—just as they were now—even if the reasons for her feelings had been entirely different.

Gina wrapped her arms tightly around one of her pillows and stared blankly at nothing until a light knock at the door startled her, but she recognized its unique rhythm as belonging to Ruby so she called with a raspy voice, "Come in." She heard the doorknob rattle and recalled that she'd locked it. "Just a moment," she added and hurried to open the door.

Both Ruby and Emerald entered timidly, closing the door behind them, while Gina returned to the safety of her bed. The maids had known she'd spoken with Radcliffe, and they had likely suspected that she would have been upset following such a conversation, so they'd left her alone for a reasonable amount of time. But it wasn't like them to leave her unattended for long when they knew she was struggling for any reason. They took particularly good care of her in every respect, and she was grateful to have such devoted maids, but perhaps now—even more so more than ever before—she was especially grateful that these women were her trusted friends. They each sat down near the bed as Ruby inquired gently, "May we ask what happened? Was he upset?"

Gina leaned back against the headboard. "*Very* upset," Gina said and went on to tell them exactly what had happened and what had been said. They were both completely kind and compassionate—as always—and agreed that surely Sir Radcliffe only needed time to adjust to the shock of the situation, then he would come around to a place where he would forgive her and their relationship would be as it had been before.

"I'm not so sure that will be possible," Gina said, resigned to facing a life without Radcliffe's love. She sighed and attempted to focus on the positive, for the sake of Ruby and Emerald if not herself. "At least we know he will allow us to stay here, and we also know he will help handle the situation with Lyle—although I still feel afraid, as I'm sure Radcliffe does, of what kind of trouble this man might be capable of causing."

Ruby and Emerald both attempted to offer reassurance that surely Lyle couldn't cause too much damage, but their efforts were unconvincing when it quickly became evident that they too were afraid the situation could be utterly disastrous.

Gina was glad to have their grim conversation interrupted by a knock at the door. Then when the maid that entered gave her a sealed note from Sir Radcliffe, Gina's hands began to tremble as she held it and wondered what kind of terrible news it might contain. Once the maid had left the room and closed the door, Emerald insisted, "Please open the thing! It surely can't be as filled with doom as you are clearly imagining."

Gina realized the sisters had observed her trembling hands, and her expression likely revealed her trepidation. She wasn't so sure that the note *didn't* contain terrible doom, but she broke the seal and unfolded the page, trying to ignore the pounding of her heart as she read Radcliffe's cordial explanation that he would be very busy the remainder of the day with a great deal of business and he wouldn't be able to join her for lunch, tea, or dinner. He made no mention of whether this would only be for today, or if they would no longer be sharing their meals and tea. Perhaps he would now only see her in the playroom when he came to spend time with Janine, and they would settle into a state of minimal tolerance of each other's presence. Gina felt sick at the thought as she read the note again to be certain she'd perceived the message correctly. She knew that Radcliffe rarely had a day when he didn't have business to attend to, and he'd always managed to work his obligations around their scheduled time together. The sisters insisted that he simply needed some time to take in and come to terms with all she'd told him, and that he would come around, but

Gina didn't feel convinced. She would be a fool to not allow herself to seriously consider the possibility that she had lost Radcliffe forever.

❦

Gina spent the remainder of the day in her rooms, sharing her meals and tea with the women who helped care for her and Janine. She felt comfortable and at ease with them, and their company helped keep her mind off all her present turmoil and the uncertainty taking place in her life. Of course, Elaine knew nothing of the specific challenges related to Janine's birth and the lies Gina had told, nor did she have any idea of the current upset that had been caused by Gina having finally told Radcliffe the truth. And she certainly didn't know anything about Bernice or Lyle or the impending threat hovering over them. But it was the very fact of Elaine's ignorance that kept their conversations steered away from the things that Gina wanted to avoid thinking about. Still, she found it difficult to not wonder what Radcliffe was doing, or more importantly, how he was feeling and what he was thinking regarding all she had told him.

When the day was coming to a close and Janine had been put to bed for the night—even though that meant at least two feedings before morning—Gina realized she'd not yet received any communication from this villain Lyle, and she wondered if Bernice had given her an accurate rendering of the situation. Gina didn't doubt Bernice's sincerity or the fact that her fears were genuine, but perhaps she'd misunderstood Lyle's intentions, or perhaps—God willing—Lyle had changed his mind; perhaps Bernice had been able to talk some sense into him and this would all just go away. Gina managed to convince herself that this might be the case, which allowed her to get *some* sleep; her worries were more focused on the damage that had been done to her relationship with Radcliffe, and her fear that it could never be repaired.

The following morning at breakfast, a note was delivered on one of the trays of food that came up from the kitchens. The moment Gina noticed it, she was glad that Elaine had just fed Janine and had left her playing contentedly nearby while Elaine had gone to the playroom to have breakfast there with Tommy. She was also glad that Emerald and Ruby were there to have breakfast with her, so that she wouldn't be alone when she read whatever the note might say. She knew from a glance that it wasn't from Radcliffe. The paper was not the quality parchment he used, and there was nothing written on the outside of the folded note; Radcliffe always scribed an elegant letter G on the front of his correspondence to her.

"Oh, my," Gina said as she reached for the paper with a suddenly trembling hand, bringing Ruby and Emerald to an awareness of what they hadn't noticed until now. "Do you suppose this is what we've been waiting for . . . and hoping wouldn't come?"

Following a long moment of strained silence while Gina picked up the note, Emerald finally said, "We'll never know until you read it."

Gina turned the folded note over to see that it was sealed with wax but it had not been stamped; she couldn't recall ever receiving any written correspondence in her life where the wax had not been stamped by the sender with their own uniquely created symbol. This led her to believe it was likely from Bernice's beau-turned-blackguard, and her heart thudded painfully as she broke the seal and unfolded the page, becoming even more aware of the trembling in her hands as it became difficult to hold the page still enough to read what it said. The handwriting was overly large and sloppy, almost like that of a child who was barely beginning to learn to write; Lyle was clearly not very educated; the grammar and spelling were also terrible. Her eyes scanned the brief message quickly, which made her insides quake with pure fear. Ruby and Emerald both cleared their throats impatiently and then Gina cleared her throat, forcing herself to read it again, and this time aloud, despite the quiver in her voice.

"*I knows the truth abouts yer baby. If yous wants me to keep quit meet mes behind the carrug house at ten tonit and comes by yersef. Bring ten thousund pounds or ill be tellin every wun.*"

"Good heavens!" Ruby blurted, her voice much louder than her generally soft-spoken manner.

"It's beyond belief!" Emerald spouted even more loudly.

Despite the fact that Gina felt the urge to scream and was keenly aware of an irrepressible trembling consuming her, she was able to say with remarkable calmness, "He's truly a fool if he thinks I have that much money just tucked away in a drawer. I could get it from the bank, of course, but not without some trouble. And withdrawing such an amount would surely arouse suspicion. What on earth am I supposed to do, exactly?"

"You told us that you and Sir Radcliffe agreed to tell each other if something happened," Ruby reminded her. "You need to go to him immediately and follow his advice."

"Yes, I agree," Emerald said firmly, but it was evident they both shared Gina's fears. This was all too horrible to comprehend.

"However, I think you should first eat your breakfast," Ruby said in a motherly tone of concern. "I believe you're going to need your strength."

"I can't eat," Gina said, putting a hand over her quivering stomach as if that might verify how impossible it would be to try and force down even a morsel of food. She rose to her feet, clutching the diabolical note tightly in her hand. "I must speak to him before I will even be able to think clearly. I trust the two of you will see that all is well with Janine and—"

"Of course," Ruby said.

"Go," Emerald added. "We'll take care of everything for as long as you need."

"Thank you," Gina said and hurried from the room, desperate for Radcliffe's help with this. She didn't even care that he would likely be angry, or even that he had rejected their personal relationship. She only felt grateful that he had pledged to protect Janine—and the secret surrounding her birth. With Radcliffe as her ally, she felt hopeful that they might actually get through this nightmare. Even if he now considered himself nothing more to Gina than a cohort in the cause of protecting Janine, she was thoroughly thankful to know that he would help her.

Gina hurried to Radcliffe's study, realizing as she approached the door that he wouldn't necessarily be here at this time of day. He could very well still be eating his breakfast, or he could have gone riding. Or for all she knew, he was still in bed, given the early hour. She knocked at the door, almost certain she'd have to go searching for him elsewhere; thankfully the servants generally kept fairly good track of him and she hoped to find one of them who might let her know where he could be found without her having to personally search the entire house and grounds.

Gina was startled to hear Radcliffe call, "Come in," and it took her a long moment and the conscious drawing of a deep breath to prepare herself to face him. But in that moment, she had to acknowledge there was no amount of mental preparation that could help her get through this; she simply had to face him and turn over the crude correspondence she'd received. How glad she was to know that Radcliffe possessed good common sense and a level head; she could surely count on him to think more clearly—and handle the situation more to their advantage—than Gina would ever be able to manage.

Gina took hold of the doorknob with a sweaty palm and forced a semblance of courage into her visage as she turned the knob and pushed open the door, stepping into the room. She immediately saw Radcliffe seated at his desk, his head bowed over a ledger, which he was reading intently. Gina hated the way her stomach fluttered and her heart quickened at the sight of him, and she wished desperately that she could make herself stop loving him, since she was relatively certain that his lack of trust and respect toward her had surely made him stop loving *her*. Or perhaps he still loved her, but he knew that could never be enough now that he knew the truth.

Gina closed the door, and Radcliffe looked up abruptly. When he saw her, he came to his feet, saying, "Forgive me. I assumed it was one of the servants."

"It's only me," she said, unable to keep from sounding sad. Before she had spilled her secrets to him, she believed he would have been happier to see her than any other person; now she felt certain it was exactly the opposite.

"Do you have news?" he asked, getting straight to the point, his countenance all business.

"I do," she said and hurried to a chair, noting that her legs suddenly felt less than steady. She was glad when Radcliffe came out from behind the desk and sat beside her. She held the now-crumpled note out toward him and added, "This was on my breakfast tray." She gave him a minute to read it while she could almost literally feel heat rising from him as his anger was triggered. When he stared at the note longer than necessary and didn't speak—as if he were trying to fully take it in—Gina finally added, "What kind of fool is he to think that I have that much money simply tucked away somewhere in the house? Do I need to go to the bank and withdraw the amount? If so, will that not draw attention to us and—"

"You will do no such thing!" he growled. Gina wanted to believe his anger was entirely directed toward Lyle, but she couldn't dismiss the possibility that at least a portion of it was aimed at her. And she couldn't blame him. "Neither you nor I are going to give this . . . this . . . *imbecile* . . . what he's asking for, when his motives are so clearly evil."

"And what if not getting what he wants presses him to follow through on his threats?" Gina asked, expressing her deepest fear.

Radcliffe's hesitation to answer made her nervous. He was clearly trying to think the matter through, but the fact that he *didn't* have an immediate solution only heightened her awareness of the horror of the situation. When he finally turned to look at her with cold, steady eyes, his voice held those same qualities. "Did you not tell me that Garn is aware of the situation?"

"Yes, that's right," Gina said, wondering what on earth that might mean in solving this problem.

"I want someone to go in your place tonight . . . to deliver a message," Radcliffe said. "And I would never want you or the women who assist you to be put into such a vulnerable position when we have no idea to what lengths this Lyle would go to in order to get what he wants. Tell Garn to take a weapon with him and—"

"What?" Gina practically shrieked, alarmed at how dangerous this was becoming, but even before Radcliffe explained, it took her only a moment to be able to easily understand his reasoning.

"He needs to be able to protect himself," Radcliffe stated. "If he doesn't own a pistol, tell him he can use one of mine. Even though I suspect his delivering a message shouldn't go awry, he should still be prepared for any possibility."

"I'll tell him," Gina said. "And then what? Exactly what is this message going to say?"

"That Lyle needs to come and talk to *me*!" Radcliffe declared, his anger betraying itself even more.

"And what will you say to him?" Gina demanded, not necessarily feeling confident over this plan, especially when Radcliffe was clearly so angry. "If the result of this is having the entire county learn the truth about Janine, then Lyle will have won—even if he gets no financial benefit from his threats. The most important thing is protecting Janine. Do we want her to grow up surrounded by people who will always treat her differently because her origin is tainted by scandal?"

"Oh, I will make certain this deplorable man never utters a word," Radcliffe said with complete confidence.

"And how exactly will you do that?" Gina demanded.

"Why don't you join us for our conversation," Radcliffe said, "and then you'll know exactly what's going on. Tell Garn to bring Lyle *here*, and we'll be waiting for him. And I'd like that foolish girl who blabbered all of this to him in the first place to be here as well."

Gina jumped to defend Bernice. "She is certainly young and naive," Gina said, "but she is Janine's mother, and she is a sweet and humble soul. Lyle is the villain here; Bernice is a victim to his villainy, just as we are. I know you're angry, and you have good reason to be, but don't go throwing your anger around at every person who has made mistakes. I'm the one who created this disaster; be angry with me if you must, but don't you dare take it out on *her*! She's already terrified and filled with regret. She does *not* need to face the master of the house while he's in such a tyrannical state of mind!"

The shock on Radcliffe's face made Gina's own words echo back to her and she could hardly believe she'd been so bold. But she couldn't regret what she'd said, because it was true. She was sick to death of lies and secrets, and of holding back the truth to *any* degree. If there was no hope left for their personal relationship, she had to put her focus entirely on getting past this debacle.

After staring at Gina for what felt like minutes, Radcliffe stood as if something unseen had shoved him out of his chair. He walked abruptly toward the windows as if he needed distance between himself and Gina and put his hands behind his back as he looked outside where the sky was overcast but refusing to rain. After what felt like *more* minutes, he finally asked, "Is that how you see me, G? Tyrannical?"

Gina was quick to answer truthfully, "Never before this conversation."

More silence ensued, and Gina tried to be patient while fear and frustration roiled inside of her.

"I admit I've not been myself," he stated, sounding *more* like himself than he had since she'd told him the truth about Janine.

Attempting to offer some perspective that was equally applicable to both herself and Radcliffe, Gina said, "This is a deplorable situation, and you did nothing to warrant ending up in the middle of it. For that I could never apologize enough. But until we can get *past* this situation, I'm not certain it's possible to even attempt feeling like ourselves."

"You are very wise, as always," he said, still keeping his back turned to her.

Gina appreciated the compliment, but given the present context, she didn't allow herself to read any kind of deeper meaning into it.

"I would like to ask you to join me for our meals and tea today," he added, much to Gina's surprise, "according to our usual habits. Yesterday I did feel the need to have some time alone, but having given the matter some thought, I don't believe we should change our routine; we don't want anyone in the household suspicious enough to start wondering what might be wrong."

Gina sighed her disappointment. She had hoped to hear that he'd missed her company, but his motives were based in appearances. Still, perhaps if they shared their meals, they might be more likely to talk through some of their feelings. She could only hope.

"Of course," was all Gina said, realizing at the same moment that she very much just wanted to leave the room. She came to her feet and added, "I will give your instructions to Garn, and have him come to speak with you if he needs anything in order to carry out his assignment. And I will bring Bernice here at the same time Garn will be meeting our . . . nemesis."

Gina waited a long moment for a potential response, but he didn't give one, so she just hurried out of the room, closing the door behind her, wishing with all her heart that she didn't love him so deeply and thoroughly. When this debacle *was* over—assuming it *could* be resolved—she would have to face the reality that her heart had been utterly broken.

CHAPTER ELEVEN
the threat

Despite the cold, Gina went directly outside where she walked briskly through the gardens, attempting to dilute the tumultuous emotions consuming her. She paused for only a moment on the little stone bridge, recalling fondly her time there with Radcliffe, but the memories became painful considering the present situation, and she hurried to the carriage house in search of Garn. He wasn't there, but another man politely told her where she could find him. He was actually having his breakfast in the manor house with other members of the staff who ate on the same shift, so Gina went back into the house, then paced quietly in the hall outside of the servants' dining room, not wanting to interrupt Garn's meal. She also felt she needed a bit of time to consider how to talk to him about all of this without sounding upset. Garn knew all there was to know about the present situation, since his sisters saw him every day and kept him apprised. Thankfully, Gina wouldn't need to tell him the entire story; it was only Sir Radcliffe's request that she needed to communicate.

When people began leaving the dining room, having finished their breakfast, Gina leaned back against a wall in the hallway where she wouldn't be seen easily, waiting for Garn to emerge. He was among the first few to leave and she softly called his name the moment she saw him.

"M'lady," he said with a pleasant smile as he turned to see her there.

"We need to speak privately," she said in a low voice that no one could overhear.

"At your service," he said, his smile disintegrating into a grim scowl as they went in the direction opposite to where everyone else was going.

Gina realized then that she had left the note from Lyle in Radcliffe's study; she would have preferred to just show it to Garn, but she had no choice now but to simply try and explain the situation. She did so as briefly as possible while Garn's scowl steadily deepened.

"What will you do?" he asked in a tone as soft as the one she'd been using; there was not a soul in sight, but neither of them wanted to risk being overheard.

"Sir Radcliffe wishes for you to meet him in my place, since you are the only other man beyond my father who knows the truth about what's taking place. And he wants you to escort this . . . thug . . . to the baronet's study."

"I can do that," he said without a moment's hesitation, and Gina felt inexplicably grateful for his devotion and ever-present willingness to help her.

"You are so very good to me!" she declared, and his scowl softened again into a smile.

"Always a pleasure, m'lady," he said as if it were nothing and he would willingly lay down his life for her in that very moment if she were to ask it of him.

Gina hurried to add Radcliffe's other stipulation. "And the baronet asks that you carry a pistol. He said if you don't have one you are welcome to use one of his and—"

"Oh, I have one," he said. "'Twas my father's, and he taught me how to use it well. Don't you worry, m'lady. I'm more than capable of carrying out the baronet's request."

Gina thanked him profusely, and they discussed the details for another minute or two before he hurried off to get back to work. Gina went upstairs to find Ruby and Emerald right where they'd been sitting when she'd left, and her breakfast still on the tray. With the hope that eating might soothe her rumbling stomach, Gina sat down and ate a cold sausage and some scones with jam while she reported everything to her maids, all of them hoping fervently that this evening's escapades would be carried out without any mishaps or unforeseen challenges. Ruby and Emerald agreed to inform Bernice that she would be expected at the strange meeting in the baronet's study, and to make certain that she arrived there at the right time. And Gina decided that she was going to ask her father to accompany her; she didn't really care whether or not Radcliffe wanted him there—although she couldn't think of any reason he wouldn't—but Gina knew she would feel more confident with her father present, and perhaps Radcliffe might be less likely to show his recently revealed tyrannical side if Milton was there.

Because the morning had been so busy, Gina was startled to realize that lunchtime was not so far off. She made a point of seeing Janine, unable to go very long without holding her daughter close and absorbing her sweetness. This morning had been highly unusual, given that she had hardly seen her daughter, and while she was grateful as always for Elaine's help in caring for Janine, Gina missed her baby when she couldn't spend as much time with her as possible. Remaining carefully cryptic, Gina informed Elaine that there was a problem in the household with which Sir Radcliffe had requested her assistance, and that of Ruby and Emerald and Milton, as well. "A family matter," was the only explanation Gina gave her. "Therefore, we won't be available late this evening, but I know Janine is always in good hands with you."

"Of course, m'lady," Elaine said, seeming mildly curious but not questioning Gina's reasoning. "I'm here for you whenever you might need me. There is no need to be concerned."

"Thank you," Gina said and forced a smile toward this kind and gracious woman who was such a blessing to her and everyone else who loved Janine.

Gina reluctantly put Janine back into Elaine's capable hands before she hurried to freshen up and meet Radcliffe for lunch. Arriving to find Radcliffe already seated, reading a newspaper while he waited, she was disappointed to find her father absent.

"Ah," Radcliffe said when he saw that she'd arrived. He folded the paper and set it aside as he came respectfully to his feet. "Your father informed me he would not be joining us. You know how he enjoys lounging about and reading this time of day."

"Yes," was all Gina could think to say while she wished she would have implored her father to join them for their meals today. She intended to seek him out right after lunch to request his presence for the grand meeting this evening, and to plead with him to join her and Radcliffe for tea and dinner. She wasn't certain she could bear so much time alone in the baronet's presence, given the undeniable tension in the air between them.

Radcliffe helped Gina with her chair—as he always did—and then sat back down himself without speaking another word to her. She hated the way he had become so aloof, and it was so unlike him to not be forthcoming about his feelings. She felt relatively certain he was wrestling with the emotional impact of all she'd told him and the quandaries that lay ahead of them as a result. She didn't know if Lyle's threat was worse for Radcliffe than her betrayal, or vice versa. She only wished he would talk to her about it; she would even prefer hearing him tell her how angry he felt toward her—anything except this grueling silence.

Gina was desperately trying to think of something to say when servants entered the room to serve the first course and she didn't want any of their conversation to be overheard, even if it was trivial in nature. After the servants had left, closing the doors behind them as they always did, Gina cleared her throat and asked, "May I ask how you are doing, all things considered?"

"You may ask," Radcliffe said, placing an excessive amount of focus on his soup, "but I don't know that I have any kind of appropriate response to give you."

"You could simply be honest," Gina said, then took a deep breath, hoping she wouldn't regret it when she added, "Surely we can still share our feelings honestly with each other."

"Can we?" he asked, sounding only mildly bitter.

Hating his bitterness and the guilt it triggered in her, Gina simply said, "Then perhaps it's best that we just eat our meal in silence."

"Perhaps it is," he agreed all too quickly.

"Although you should know I've spoken with Garn, and he is willing and well prepared to do what you've asked of him."

"Excellent," Radcliffe said.

She wondered whether or not to tell him that she intended to invite her father to accompany her this evening, then realized that Milton would be joining them for tea and dinner—or at least she hoped he would—and therefore he was not likely to refrain from talking about the situation. She felt the need to say, "My father will be coming with me this evening." She didn't bother telling him that she'd not yet spoken to Milton about it; she preferred to imply that he already knew so that Radcliffe couldn't insist that she come without her father.

Gina was both disappointed and relieved when Radcliffe said, "Fine." She might have preferred an argument, which in her opinion would be preferable to all this taut silence.

The silence continued throughout the remainder of the meal. Gina forced herself to pretend she was alone, which made it easier to get through this ridiculous ritual for the sake of attempting to make everything between them seem normal to the rest of the household. Hating this ruse for more reasons than she could count, Gina was inexplicably grateful when the meal ended, and she quickly excused herself. Radcliffe stood when she came to her feet, but he said nothing to her as she left the room, and she had to forcibly swallow the threat of tears as she hurried to her father's rooms, wishing instead to go and spend some time with her daughter, but knowing she couldn't even hope to relax until she'd spoken with Milton. Janine was in good hands, and Gina would be able to enjoy some time with her later.

Gina found Milton in his sitting room, just as she'd suspected, with his feet up, engaged in a book. He looked up when she knocked on the open door, then broke into a smile as he stood to greet her.

"There's my beautiful daughter!" he said, holding out both of his hands to take hers as she crossed the room to greet him, pressing a kiss to his cheek. "I came looking for you earlier, but Ruby told me you had gone to speak with Sir Radcliffe." He paused to study her expression. "Is something wrong?" he asked, furrowing his brow.

Gina realized that both doors were open, and she hurried to close them, which increased the concern on her father's face before they sat down on the same sofa and he took her hand. "You know that you can tell me anything," he said.

"I know," she replied and took a deep breath before she hurried as quickly as possible to just get the words out. She caught him up on everything that had happened since they'd last spoken about the situation with Janine. He was as compassionate as he was astonished, but he readily agreed to accompany her to the meeting late this evening in Radcliffe's study, when he would be confronting this brute.

"I don't think any of us know what to expect," Gina said. "I pray that the outcome is positive. I honestly believe I will go mad if I have to live with this always hanging over us like a dark cloud."

"I'm certain Radcliffe will be wise and reasonable in the way he handles the situation," Milton said.

Gina sighed. "I wish I could share your confidence. Normally I would agree, but he's clearly been angry since I shared all of this with him; he's not the same man, and I don't know what to say to him that might make any difference. I fear his anger will overpower his wisdom and reason."

"I'm sure you'll agree that his anger is understandable," Milton said, and Gina nodded. "And perhaps his anger is directed more at this blackmailer than at you. When all this drama has settled, I believe he will come to himself, and the two of you will be able to talk about the situation with more honesty."

"I do hope you're right," Gina said and hung her head, hoping to hide the sudden spilling of tears down her face. But her father was a perceptive man and he touched her chin, lifting her face to his view before he took a clean handkerchief out of his pocket and wiped away her tears. "I fear he will never forgive me, and that I've lost him forever."

"I don't see Sir Radcliffe as an unforgiving kind of man," Milton pointed out.

"Perhaps he will forgive me," Gina said, "but I doubt that he will ever trust me again."

"I believe you both need some time, and you need to get this other matter out of the way. You may be right, or you may be wrong. Until you can talk with him—minus any anger—you will never know for certain. Let's worry about one problem at a time."

Gina nodded again, then implored her father to join her and Radcliffe for tea and dinner, declaring that she couldn't bear the tension between herself and the baronet, and his company would surely help ease that. Milton agreed with enthusiasm and Gina felt better on that count. She just dreaded having to face whatever might happen in Radcliffe's study later this evening. But she followed her father's suggestion to just do her best to remain distracted and try not to think about it, since they could do nothing in the meantime.

Gina thanked her father for his time and his perfect love and support before she returned to her own rooms, delighted to find Janine freshly bathed and fed and wide awake. She played with her daughter for a good, long time—until the baby became fussy due to her need for another feeding and a nap. Gina turned the baby over to Elaine and decided to attempt a nap herself before tea. She didn't know whether she could fall asleep, but she felt utterly drained of energy and longed to just curl up in her bed and close her eyes.

Gina was awakened by Ruby's gentle nudge, letting her know it was time she freshened up in order to arrive downstairs in time for tea. Gina was relieved that she'd been able to get some rest, especially since she'd found a complete reprieve in sleep from any of the problems weighing on her. The rest was also welcome since she knew the meeting in the study would take place late in the evening, and there was no telling how long it would go on—although she couldn't imagine any lengthy conversations taking place.

Gina found it difficult to come fully awake, given how deeply she'd been sleeping, but with Ruby's encouragement she was able to get out of bed, make herself presentable, and arrive the very same moment a maid brought the tea cart into the room where her father and Radcliffe were already seated. They stood to greet Gina, who couldn't help noticing that Radcliffe seemed more cordial toward her, even though she sensed that it was a forced effort, surely for the benefit of her father. Still, as they were seated and began to enjoy their tea and its delicious accompaniments, she felt deeply relieved over the way that Radcliffe and her father were sharing comfortable and trivial conversation, as if nothing in the world was wrong or out of the ordinary. Gina mostly just listened, basking in her gratitude for the lack of tense silence between her and Radcliffe. Once she'd had her fill of warm tea and satisfying cakes and sandwiches, Gina excused herself, explaining that Janine needed her, and she left the two men to talk. Grateful to make her escape, Gina easily acknowledged that it was she who needed Janine, and once again she was glad to find her daughter awake and in a happy mood once Elaine finished feeding her. There was no better distraction from the troubles of life than this sweet, innocent child whose smiles and precious charm melted away everything except the joy of just cuddling and playing together.

Dinner with Radcliffe and Milton was also much more relaxed for Gina, given the way the men dominated the conversation she was able to mostly just listen and enjoy her meal. Gina felt certain her father knew how tense she was feeling regarding every complicated facet of the situation, and that he was purposely keeping the conversation afloat while she felt certain his absence would have surely caused it to sink like a stone.

Just as she'd done at tea, Gina excused herself while the men were still engaged in eating and conversing. They stood when she did and the mood became suddenly very somber as Radcliffe said to her, "I will see the both of you in my study at the appointed time. I want to make certain we're all there before Garn arrives with his charge."

Gina was grateful when her father answered for her. "We'll be there," he said, "and I'm certain everything will be fine."

"I hope you're right," Radcliffe said in a voice that implied he didn't at all believe everything would be fine. Gina just nodded at each of the men and hurried out of the room, longing for tomorrow when all this would be behind them. Or at least she *hoped* it would be behind them. Oh, how she prayed it would be resolved this evening, and the threat that Lyle had created would no longer be hanging over them.

⁂

When the time came for the dreaded meeting in the study, Gina was indescribably grateful to be able to hold onto her father's arm as they walked down the stairs and toward Radcliffe's study. Her heart was thudding painfully, and she was finding it difficult to fill her lungs with air. She felt relatively certain her father could feel the way she was holding to him far more tightly than necessary, but he didn't comment other than reassuring her gently, "I'm certain everything will be fine."

Gina couldn't answer. She didn't share her father's confidence, and she was more focused on making certain she didn't become light-headed. She needed to keep herself together and exhibit an aura of courage. She had created this disaster, and she had to maintain her dignity as they did all they could to resolve it. She would not take responsibility for Lyle's villainous role in all of this, but still, she had constructed the lie at the heart of the situation, and she prayed that—above all else—Janine would remain in her care, safe and secure.

The door to the study was open and Gina entered, still holding tightly to her father's arm. The room was well lit with far more candles and lanterns than that which would normally be used, and Gina wondered if Radcliffe wanted to be able to clearly see everything that was going on as he faced Lyle; even the man's expressions would surely be very telling, and Gina could well imagine Radcliffe not wanting a dim room to leave him at a disadvantage. Radcliffe was standing near his desk, as if he'd just paused amid vigorous pacing when they'd entered the room. They all exchanged a simple nod, but none of them spoke before Radcliffe resumed his nervous pacing.

Gina then noticed that the furniture had been rearranged so that the small sofa and comfortable chairs had been situated to form somewhat of a circle. Gina was relieved when her father guided her to the sofa and she was able to sit down, which left her feeling less unsteady. But as her father sat beside her, she was glad to be able to continue holding to his strong arm and the support it represented.

Only a moment later, Bernice appeared in the open doorway, wringing her hands and looking as terrified as if she were about to face the guillotine.

"Come in and sit down, my dear," Gina said in the most comforting voice she could manage, knowing the poor girl needed some kindness. At the sound of Gina's voice, Radcliffe stopped pacing and turned to glare at Bernice. The young woman visibly shrunk from his silent accusations and she slithered into the chair that was closest to the door, as if she might want to be prepared to make a hasty escape. As Radcliffe resumed his pacing, Bernice looked at Gina in what seemed an attempt to seek out an ally. Gina could well imagine how terrified Bernice had been ever since she'd been informed that this meeting would be taking place, and that she was expected to be present. Gina attempted to offer a smile, however feeble her efforts might have been, and Bernice nodded in return before she hung her head to focus on her hands in her lap. She was wringing them so hard it appeared almost painful.

Milton exchanged a silent glance with Gina, which required no explanation. He knew this was the young woman who had given birth to Janine, and they were wordlessly agreeing how very strange all of this had become. They'd become comfortable with behaving as if Janine had come into their family through the normal means by which babies generally came. Bernice's presence was a tangible—and perhaps difficult—reminder that the situation was—and always would be—anything but normal.

Gina was startled by the sound of heavy footsteps approaching, and an indiscernible exchange of male voices. She knew it could only be Garn escorting

Lyle to the study, and her already thudding heart threatened to leap out of her throat. Radcliffe stopped pacing and moved closer to the door, taking a firm stance that she knew he fully intended to be intimidating. Milton rose to his feet as if he were determined to do his part to defend his daughter's honor and Janine's safety. Gina and Bernice exchanged a concerned glance before Bernice looked fearfully toward the door. Gina wondered if Bernice was afraid that Lyle might blame her for this and punish her later; if there was even the slightest possibility that Bernice had reason to fear for her safety, Gina knew that she had to find a way to protect her.

When Garn and Lyle came through the open doorway, Gina had to hurry and contend with her surprise over what she was seeing. She was first struck with how handsome Lyle was. His sleek, dark hair and fine features were more what she might have expected to see at a fancy social event. She had to quickly reprimand herself for thinking that a person could be judged by their appearance. After taking a quick second to set her mind straight on that count, her eyes were drawn to the way that Garn was holding tightly to Lyle's arm, and he had a pistol pressed to Lyle's side. Was this the only way he'd been able to get Lyle to come here? Gina's nerves increased but she was determined not to let them show.

"Delivered as requested, m'lord," Garn said with a mild smirk and a nod toward Radcliffe.

"Thank you," Radcliffe said. "Please close the door, Garn."

Garn nodded again and kicked the door closed since both of his hands were occupied. Gina saw Lyle's eyes quickly scan the room, as if he were taking in the situation while planning his escape. She found it strange that she could actually see the scheming in his eyes and the malice in his expression. He showed surprise at seeing Bernice, who exhibited great courage in the way she met Lyle's angry glare. But her courage was short-lived, and she visibly shrank farther into her chair, lowering her head and wrapping her arms around herself, as if a cloud of shame and terror had enveloped her. Gina took a quick glance at Radcliffe, just long enough to see that he had noticed Bernice's reaction, and Gina hoped that he would have assessed for himself that Bernice was being intimidated and manipulated by Lyle, and despite the evidence that she had not handled the situation well, she had no malice or ill-intent.

Once Lyle had silently put Bernice in her place, he faced Radcliffe directly. While it was well-known etiquette that a servant should not speak to their titled employer until asked to do so, Lyle showed his disregard of any etiquette or respect for the baronet when he spoke to Radcliffe with a sour smirk. "Do ye think all this is gonna keep me from gettin' what I come for?" He let out a brief but malicious chuckle, and Gina felt astonished that he could be so casual—not to mention arrogant—given the fact that he had a pistol pressed to his side and he was facing the most wealthy and powerful man for miles around. "Just give me whats I want, and I'll be on m' way, and you high and mighty folks can keep yer secrets. Makes no difference t' me so long as I gets what I come for."

"Oh, you'll be on your way, for certain," Radcliffe said, putting his hands on his hips, showing no evidence of being intimidated or concerned. Gina wondered if he was simply putting on an air of confidence in order to handle the situation, or if he sincerely didn't feel threatened. She prayed it was the latter, but she felt so nervous herself that she hardly dared breathe for fear of letting on how absolutely terrified she was of this awful man and what he was capable of doing to them with the knowledge he possessed. "As soon as this little meeting is finished, you will be escorted to a waiting carriage and Garn is going to drive you very far away from here, and you will never, ever, *ever* show your face here again. And if you so much as breathe a word to any soul about what you know—if gossip begins to spread—I will know who is responsible, and I will use my every resource to have you hunted down and punished, and you will regret ever having crossed me. Do I make myself clear?"

"Clear enough, Mr. High and Mighty," Lyle snarled, his evil smirk growing larger. "I'm all for leavin' here, the sooner the better. But don't think I'll be leavin' without what I comes for. Just give me th' money an' I'll—"

"I'll not be paying you a single farthing," Radcliffe said, growing visibly angry—but it was a controlled and threatening kind of anger, and certainly something Gina had never before seen in him. "You will *not* be rewarded for threatening my family! And certainly not for taking advantage of this young woman." He motioned toward Bernice, and Gina felt some measure of relief at seeing that Radcliffe was defending her.

Lyle looked confused, then frustrated, then angry, all in the breadth of a long second. Then in the span of another very brief second, he somehow managed to grab Garn's arm and twist it so hard that Garn cried out in pain and the pistol fell to the floor. Lyle grabbed the gun, and before Gina could even grasp what had happened, she became completely unable to breathe. Lyle was pointing the pistol directly at *her* while he spoke malevolently to Radcliffe, "Give me the money *now*, or somebody's gonna die!"

Considering the threat Lyle posed to her life, Gina only took her eyes off him long enough to glance at Radcliffe and see that he had raised his hands in a gesture of surrender. "Fine," Radcliffe said as Gina looked again at Lyle who held the pistol aimed directly at her own heart. "The money is in a desk drawer," Radcliffe added, sounding more intimidated than Gina believed he was—and she wondered why. "I need to unlock it."

"Then do it!" Lyle barked.

Gina forced her eyes away from the threat Lyle posed to her and looked instead at Radcliffe as he went behind the desk and opened the center drawer from where he lifted a key and showed Lyle both his hands to indicate that he was holding the key and nothing else. A great many questions swirled in Gina's mind. Did Radcliffe always have such a large amount of money hidden in a desk drawer? Or had he moved the money from the safe she knew existed somewhere in the house on the chance that this would become necessary? She also wondered if his willingness to pay the price of Lyle's extortion was some indication of his personal concern for her—considering that it was *her* life being threatened—or if he would have paid the price no matter whose life was being threatened; of course he would never put any amount of money over the value of a human life.

Gina saw Radcliffe unlock another drawer in the desk, which he reached into while keeping his eyes riveted on Lyle. She gasped as Radcliffe drew out a pistol and aimed it at Lyle so quickly that the motion was almost a blur. Gina looked back and forth between Radcliffe and Lyle, the latter looking momentarily taken off guard, but he recovered his evil visage all too quickly and growled, "Now that's not th' the way this is gonna go. I'm leavin' here with that money. If I leave somebody dead, it don't make no difference t' me."

"You will leave here with nothing!" Radcliffe declared firmly. "No one threatens me or my family! No one! You may leave right now as I suggested previously, or I assure you this will not end well for you."

"I don't think ye know who ye're dealin' with," Lyle said to Radcliffe, his eyes narrowing.

"I think it's the other way around," Radcliffe said.

Only a second later, Gina heard the hammer of a pistol being cocked. It was coming from the direction where Lyle was standing. Her father had taught her many years ago how to shoot, and she knew the workings of a gun well enough, which meant she had no doubt what that sound meant. Only a second after that, the same sound came from where Radcliffe was standing. Given the fact that one of those pistols was aimed at her, Gina suddenly felt so light-headed she sincerely feared she might faint.

"First this lady," Lyle said, pointing at Gina with his free hand, "and then this one." He pointed at Bernice. "Or just give me th' money and we'll be done with this." Gina wondered exactly how Lyle meant to carry out the threat of shooting *two* people when she knew the pistol had only one shot; but regardless of whether or not he could carry out the entirety of his threats, he still had the obvious capability of killing Gina if he pulled the trigger.

"Put the gun down," Radcliffe ordered as if he'd not heard Lyle's threats.

"That's not gonna happen," Lyle said, and Gina's next awareness was the horrible crack of two pistols firing so close together that it was impossible to know which man had pulled the trigger first. But it was evident that Bernice had seen something Gina had missed, because the young woman launched herself out of her chair and literally leapt in front of Gina. The loud thud of Lyle falling to the floor occurred in the same instant that Bernice fell across the laps of Gina and Milton, blood oozing across the front of her dress.

"Oh, no!" Gina cried. "No, no, no!"

Garn rushed out of the room, shouting that he was going to get the doctor. "And the police!" Radcliffe ordered, letting Gina know he was all right.

Milton was quick to lift Bernice into his arms and turn to lay her gently on the sofa. Gina knelt beside Bernice, frantically trying to assess the source of the bleeding, praying she would survive this. The wound appeared to be more toward her shoulder than her middle, which Gina hoped was a good sign.

"M'lady," Bernice said in a weak and raspy voice, reaching for Gina's hand.

"I'm here," Gina said, holding Bernice's hand tightly.

"I saw him . . . taking aim . . . and I knew . . . he was going . . . to shoot . . . and . . ." Her voice faded into a groan that was evidence of her pain.

Gina found Radcliffe on his knees next to her, assessing Bernice's condition. "I think she'll be all right," he said, but Gina didn't know if that was true or if he might simply be attempting to offer Bernice some reassurance and comfort. "But we should get her upstairs to a bed where the doctor can see to her properly."

"Take her to one of the rooms near mine," Gina insisted, "so that I can help care for her."

Radcliffe scooped Bernice into his arms and headed toward the door with Milton right behind him. Gina paused only a moment as a thought occurred to her. Neither Radcliffe nor her father were showing any concern about Lyle—or his threats. Gina looked down and sucked in a harsh, painful breath. Lyle was so obviously dead that Gina could only look at the body for the brief second it took to be reassured that it was true. Radcliffe had killed a man to save Gina's life, and Bernice had literally put herself between Gina and the bullet from Lyle's gun. Gina felt an overwhelming urge to just drop to her knees right there and sob. She'd come so close to dying, but all that had happened to save her was so horrible she couldn't even mentally process the implications.

Knowing that Bernice was seriously injured, Gina pulled herself together and hurried to catch up with her father and Radcliffe, who was carrying Bernice up the stairs. His strength and stamina in being able to do so—and with a fair amount of speed—left Gina a little in awe. But then, she was always in awe of Radcliffe. She loved him, and he had now saved her life. She was grateful beyond words, but she had to remind herself that his doing so didn't necessarily mean that anything had changed between them. The threat that had been hanging over them had come to an end—a horribly inexplicable end—but that didn't change the trust that had been broken between them. For now, she needed to focus her attention on Bernice, and she prayed the young woman would recover from this tragedy. And Gina would never forget that in order to save her, Bernice had been willing to give her life.

❦

Once they had settled Bernice into the bed of a guest room across the hall from Gina's rooms and near those of the women who helped care for Gina and Janine, Ruby and Emerald went to work, bustling around the patient, cutting away the blood-soaked clothing that surrounded the wound, and carefully cleaning it while Bernice was awake and aware, but clearly in a great deal of pain, especially when Emerald pressed a clean rag tightly over the wound in an attempt to stop the bleeding. Gina was grateful that Elaine had been made aware of the situation and she was caring for Janine so that Gina could remain close to Bernice's side, kneeling next to the bed opposite of where the maids were working to do all they could to care for the wound before the doctor arrived. Gina kept Bernice's hand firmly in hers and offered quiet reassurances and expressions of gratitude.

Bernice seemed only partly aware of all that Gina was saying, but she kept talking anyway. Gina was surprised when Bernice turned her head on the pillow and looked directly at Gina. "I'm so sorry to have brought you such trouble," she muttered in a strained voice.

"You mustn't concern yourself with any of that," Gina assured her. "It's all over now."

"Is he . . ." Gina didn't seem to want to say the word.

"Dead?" Gina provided. "Yes, he's dead. And his knowledge will be going to the grave with him."

"But what if . . ." Bernice began a question she couldn't finish as her focus suddenly shifted to her pain, and Gina could see sweat rising on her brow. She couldn't begin to imagine how painful such a terrible injury might be!

"I'm certain Sir Radcliffe will take care of everything properly," Gina said. "All you have to worry about now is getting better. The doctor is coming." Gina managed a dry chuckle. "I should warn you that he's not necessarily warm or kind, but he's very skilled when it comes to serious issues. I'm certain he will see that you're all right, and then my maids and I are going to take incredibly good care of you. I don't want you to worry about a thing, Bernice; just try to relax. We won't leave you alone; I promise."

"You're so . . . very . . . kind," Bernice said with a feeble smile.

"We share something very precious, you and I," Gina said in little more than a whisper, her voice cracking as she considered just how precious a bond she *did* share with Bernice.

"Promise me . . . you'll always . . . take care of her . . . you'll always . . . protect her . . ." Bernice seemed to use up all her energy in managing to say what she felt was important.

Gina tightened Bernice's hand in hers and said emphatically, "I promise. We will keep our secret between us, and Janine will have the best life I can give her. I promise!"

Bernice relaxed and let out a long breath, as if that were all she needed to know. She became so still and quiet that for a heart-thumping moment, Gina thought that Bernice might have died now that she'd been promised her daughter would be all right. But another squeeze of her hand prompted Bernice to shift slightly, and Gina knew she was alive.

A moment later, the doctor burst into the room in a flurry, as if he considered himself a miracle worker who should be treated as such. Following some quick communication regarding the problem, while Ruby and Emerald explained their experience and their desire to help, the doctor told the maids to wash their hands thoroughly so they could assist him, and he sent Gina out of the room. She reluctantly let go of Bernice's hand after reassuring her once more that she would get through this. Then she left the room, closing the door behind her before she leaned back against it and began to cry, fighting to keep her tears silent, given that she didn't want to be overheard.

"Are you all right?" she heard Radcliffe say out of the darkness of the hallway, and she gasped.

Gina attempted to adjust her eyes to the absence of light and recalled that the doctor had entered the room carrying a lantern. She suspected now that

Radcliffe had escorted him here personally. Gina was accepting that she simply couldn't see him when she heard a match strike and watched Radcliffe touch it to the wick of a candle that was on the little table next to the chair where he was sitting, his ankle crossed over his knee. The candle's glow was feeble, but Gina could still see that his eyes looked strained, and that his expression was a combination of exhaustion and shock. She doubted that he—or anyone else—had truly expected this evening to end so violently.

"Well?" he said, not unkindly, reminding her that he'd asked her a question which she hadn't yet answered.

"As well as could be expected," Gina said. "I'll be better once I know that Bernice is all right." She sighed, feeling suddenly so drained of strength that she wanted to just find her bed and crawl into it. "And you?" she asked.

"As well as could be expected," he said, repeating her words exactly, but there was no hint of mocking her or being unkind. It was simply the most honest answer either of them could manage. "I'm afraid the police will be here at any moment. Garn is with . . . the body; he has strict instructions not to let anyone into the room until the police arrive, but . . . perhaps you should wash up; I'm certain they'll want to speak with those of us who were in the room when it happened."

Gina looked down at her hands, noting even in the dim glow of the candle that they were covered with Bernice's blood. Despite her urge to go and scrub her hands vigorously, she asked Radcliffe, "And what will we tell them?" Her concern for Janine was foremost on her mind and she felt certain Radcliffe knew this and there was no need to explain.

"The truth," he said, "omitting any reference to how the situation was related to Janine. I've already spoken to Garn and your father and they know what to say. I'll not allow the police to speak with Bernice until she's recovered sufficiently. That will give you time to make certain she says what she needs to in order to protect Janine."

"I have no qualms about her desire to protect the baby," Gina said, wanting to make certain that point was clear.

"Nor do I," Radcliffe said, and Gina wondered if Bernice's courageous actions—and even her obvious fear of Lyle prior to that—had shown Radcliffe the kind of woman she was. "I simply want to be certain we all tell the police the same story so we can protect Janine and put this matter to rest. All they need to know is that Lyle was holding us hostage with the hope of getting a large sum of money for reasons I will share with the police, reasons that have nothing to do with Janine. I'll tell them that no one else had knowledge of Lyle's motives for trying to blackmail me. The story is that he held Garn at gunpoint and forced him to bring Lyle to my study where the rest of us were discussing the matter because Bernice was romantically involved with the man and had come to us with her concerns—which is true. The rest of the story is exactly as it happened. Telling the truth will keep everything consistent."

"That makes sense," Gina said. "Thank you . . . for thinking all of that through. Thank you for . . . for everything."

Radcliffe didn't respond except to say, "Go and get washed up. We'll go down together to speak with the police when they arrive."

"Of course," Gina said and hurried across the hall to her room, certain she couldn't get Bernice's blood off her hands fast enough.

CHAPTER TWELVE
truth reciprocated

GINA AND RADCLIFFE WALKED TOGETHER back down the stairs in silence. She was relieved when they went to the drawing room instead of the study, knowing that Lyle's dead body was likely still there on the floor. She wondered if she would ever be able to go back to that room again, given the memories of all that had taken place there this evening. How could such an event not haunt a person for the rest of their life? She wanted to believe she could forget about it, but for now, she kept seeing Lyle's pistol pointed at her, and his angry malevolence as he'd threatened her life. And the sound of the pistols firing echoed over and over in her mind in a strange rhythm that seemed to have synchronized itself with her heartbeat.

Hating the tense silence between herself and Radcliffe, Gina was relieved to enter the drawing room and find two police officers in uniform waiting for them. The officers came to their feet, and appropriate greetings and introductions were exchanged before they all sat back down, and the officers directed all their questions to Radcliffe. Normally, Gina would have felt a little miffed at being ignored simply because she was a woman, but in this case, she was more than happy to allow Radcliffe to repeat in detail the events that had led to one of the maids getting shot, and a stablehand ending up dead. Radcliffe told the story exactly as he'd said he would, except that he completely took Gina off guard when he said to the officers, "The truth is that this man claimed to have knowledge of some misdeeds of my late cousin, Dwight Everleigh, and he was attempting to blackmail me in order to buy his silence."

Gina was glad for the way she managed to keep her expression steady; she credited her ability to all the practice she'd gotten from lying about Janine's origin. But she was surprised by the way the two officers exchanged a quick but unmistakable glance, as if such news about Dwight didn't surprise them at all, and they might know something that she didn't.

Radcliffe continued with his report of all that had happened while both officers took notes, seeming entirely satisfied and not the least bit suspicious over what had taken place. The two men finally acknowledged Gina when they asked her if she had anything to add to the baronet's recollection of events, and she simply said, "No, as far as I can remember, that's exactly how it happened. I admit to having been terribly frightened and therefore perhaps not very observant . . . but I don't believe there's anything else."

"We're glad that you're all right, m'lady," one officer said with compassion.

The other one directed his comment to Radcliffe, "It's shameful the lengths some people will go to trying to get money that don't belong to them."

"Indeed," Radcliffe said.

The officers stood and so did Radcliffe, but Gina remained seated, not certain her legs would hold her as the fear she'd just acknowledged enveloped her freshly. Radcliffe went with the officers back to the study, and she heard them saying that the undertaker had likely arrived by now to take the body. Once the men had left the room, Gina suddenly found a burst of energy, fueled by her desire to not have to see Radcliffe again tonight. She had far too much turmoil taking place inside of her already without having to contend with the tension between her and the man she loved—and had lost.

Gina hurried up the stairs, anxious to check on Bernice, silently praying the maid would survive. Gina wondered how she would live with the reality that Bernice had died in her stead; all things considered, she doubted that she would ever be able to make peace with such a sacrifice. Gina was surprised to find the door to the room open, and when she stepped tentatively inside, she saw the doctor gathering his things into his bag, clearly getting ready to leave. Her heart pounded as she feared that this meant Bernice had died and therefore his services were no longer needed. Then she realized that he was giving Ruby and Emerald instructions on how to care for Bernice's wound, and what to do if she developed a fever. He then walked out of the room without paying any heed to Gina, but Ruby and Emerald saw her straightaway and they both rushed to embrace her at the same time, creating a tight, tiny circle.

Gina soaked in their comfort and strength before she eased back and asked what seemed obvious, "She's going to be all right?"

"It seems that way," Ruby said. "He was able to remove the bullet very quickly."

"Praise heaven for that, since it was very painful," Emerald added. "He disinfected the wound thoroughly and left us plenty of bandaging and disinfectant to keep it clean."

"His only concern is the possibility of infection," Ruby explained, "although he doesn't believe it's likely under the circumstances."

"Not that he explained what *the circumstances* meant exactly," Emerald said. "But I'm grateful he had the skill to do what he did. We will take exceptionally good care of her, and, God willing, she will be all right."

"We have no reason to believe otherwise," Ruby declared.

Gina moved tentatively to Bernice's bedside, a little shocked to see that her face was as pale as the white pillow on which she was lying, and her lips were equally white. She was asleep but breathing evenly, and Ruby whispered in Gina's ear, "The doctor gave her something for the pain before he started; he said it would make her sleep."

"Unfortunately," Emerald whispered in Gina's other ear, "it didn't take effect until he was nearly finished."

"At least she's resting peacefully now," Ruby said. "The worst is over."

"I will take the first shift sitting with her," Emerald offered.

"And I'll make certain you have what you need so you can get some sleep," Ruby said to Gina, taking her arm and practically dragging her from the room.

Gina couldn't deny her relief. She was so thoroughly exhausted that she felt unsteady on her feet. She wanted to help care for Bernice but was glad that Emerald offered to watch over her for now. After Gina was able to get some rest, she would be better equipped to assist in caring for the woman who had not only brought Janine into the world but had also saved Gina's life.

Gina was quickly ready for bed and never more relieved to crawl between the covers and feel her head settle into the pillow. The echo of gunshots was still firing in her head, and memories of Lyle's threats brought the fear tumbling over her as freshly as if she were once again sitting in the study with his pistol aimed at her. She reminded herself that Lyle was dead, and his threats had died with him. And moments later her exhaustion lulled her into a deep sleep.

❧

Over the next few days, Gina didn't leave the hallway where her own rooms and those of the women who helped care for her and Janine were located. And now Bernice had a room there as well, which felt strangely right and natural to Gina. Elaine had been given the same explanation as the police, and she had been eager to assist in offering the care that Bernice needed while she recovered. Gina appreciated the help of these fine women more than ever, and she was grateful for a viable excuse not to share her meals with Radcliffe. However, she was grateful that her father came to check on her at least twice a day and to be apprised of Bernice's well-being. Gina always felt better after talking with her father, and she was increasingly grateful to have him here in the same home. She knew he was sharing at least one meal a day with Radcliffe, but they didn't talk about him. Instead they talked about how much Milton enjoyed playing with Tommy and Janine, and what a delight they were to his life.

Bernice was in a great deal of pain the first few days, and they were all grateful for the medicine the doctor had left, which helped ease the pain and allowed Bernice to mostly sleep. On the fourth day after the shooting, she had more color to her face and expressed a desire to sit up in bed longer than to just barely consume the broth and gruel she'd been fed to sustain her. With an increase in her appetite and much lower doses of the medicine during the day—so that she wouldn't be so sleepy—she enjoyed the company of the women who were helping care for her. Gina had quickly come to realize that she very much liked Bernice, and the other women agreed. Ruby and Emerald told Gina privately that they sincerely believed Bernice to be a woman of integrity and kindness, and they too liked her a great deal.

On the fifth day, Gina sat at Bernice's bedside, enjoying their conversation as much as she was appreciating the evidence that Bernice was recovering very well. Gina was surprised when Elaine brought Janine into the room, saying, "She's fed and changed, and I thought it was about time that Bernice met our little miss."

"Oh, of course," Gina said, hoping she didn't reveal any of the nervousness she felt. She wasn't so much nervous for herself as she was for Bernice, who had been told that Elaine knew nothing about Janine except what everyone else believed, and it needed to remain that way. And Bernice had been adamant—more than once—about her dedication to keeping the secret, given the fact that she wanted her daughter to have a good life, and she would never do anything to compromise all that Janine had been blessed with. Knowing this was the first time Bernice had seen Janine since the day she'd left her in the alley with the hope of her being found by someone who would take her in and care for her, Gina hoped that Bernice would be careful in not showing too much emotion in Elaine's presence. Bernice's eyes widened and sparkled when she saw the baby, but not in a way that would arouse any suspicion.

"This is your daughter," Bernice said as Elaine placed Janine on Gina's lap.

"Yes, this is our precious Janine," Gina said.

"Oh, she's lovely!" Bernice said, leaning forward a little in order to see her better. Elaine slipped from the room and left them alone, but she didn't close the door, so Gina knew—as she felt certain Bernice did—that they still needed to be careful.

Gina laid the baby on the bed right next to Bernice, where she could use the hand not constrained to a sling to touch Janine's little hands. "Oh, m'lady!" Bernice declared with a cracking voice and the glisten of tears in her eyes, but her joyful smile was brilliant. "I never dared hope that I'd get to see her again; never so close, at least. I feel so very, very blessed."

"It is I who am blessed, Bernice," Gina said earnestly. "Having Janine come into my life is surely the greatest blessing that has ever happened to me, and I hope you have no doubts about my devotion to her, and that I will never cease to make sure that she is not only safe and well, but happy."

"Oh, I do know that, m'lady!" Bernice said, equally earnest, meeting Gina's eyes firmly. "And I hope you have no doubts about *my* devotion to making certain that our secret is kept safe so that she *will* be able to have a good life; the kind of life I never could have given her. I feel ever so certain that God gave me a miracle when my little one came into *your* life, and no one else's; it was surely meant to be. And I will never, never, never do or say anything ever again that might put her or you in danger. I swear it to you, as God is my witness. My only wish is for Janine to be safe and happy, and she is. *You* are her mother; you're the one who can give her what she needs. I only feel ever so privileged to have been able to see her." Bernice turned her attention back to the baby, her eyes wide with fascination.

"Given that you risked your own life to save mine, Bernice, I feel that—"

"Oh, m'lady!" Bernice said, looking again at Gina, her eyes showing alarm. "I knew with my whole soul that it was far more important for *you* to live. You're Janine's mother. She needs you!"

Seeing further evidence of Bernice's sincerity, Gina instinctively knew that this sweet young woman was absolutely a trusted ally, and there was no need to ever be concerned about Bernice's loyalty in the future, or her devotion to the baby's security and happiness. "What I'm trying to say, Bernice, is . . . well . . . I've grown to care very much for Elaine, and I want her and her son to remain here even after Janine no longer needs a wet nurse, so that she can help care for Janine and have a good home in which to raise her own son. Even though I always want to be involved with Janine's care, I've come to see that in such an enormous house, and with the way that details are managed, I simply can't do so alone, and Elaine cannot be responsible for her every minute that I'm not available, especially when Janine continues to grow and become more active. She will surely need to be shadowed constantly in order to keep her safe. What

I'm trying to say is that I want to have your position within the household promoted so that you might be one of those who helps care for Janine, and then you can see her for a little while every day." Gina had given the matter careful consideration, and she'd even prayed for guidance, knowing it was a serious situation. She'd come to believe that giving Bernice this opportunity would be best for two significant reasons. In all practicality, if Bernice—given her maternal instincts toward the child—were given the opportunity to be a part of Janine's life, she would be less likely to do anything impulsive or rash in order to see her daughter. And for reasons that were far more tender, Gina had deeply considered how she might feel if the situation were reversed. Bernice had been desperate, and if Gina had ever found herself in such a dire predicament, she would have wanted very much to just be close to her child in any way possible. Gina knew that Bernice would do anything to keep Janine safe; therefore, having her help care for the child was surely a good decision for many reasons, and Gina felt completely comfortable and confident about it.

Bernice's initial response was an abrupt rounding of her mouth, but no sound came out. Her eyes showed deep gratitude and amazement before tears spilled from them and she finally managed to close her mouth. "Why would you do this for me, m'lady? Surely, I am not worthy in any way to—

"We can talk more about the reasons another time," Gina said. "For now . . . I only need your promise that the secret between us will always remain a secret, and if I have your word on that, then I know that Janine will be safe with you. And Bernice . . . in order for our secret to remain completely safe, those of us who know the truth must vow to never speak of it again. I have spoken with my father and the servants who know the truth about this, and they agree; I only need to speak with Sir Radcliffe, but I'm certain he will agree, as well. From this day forward, we will all carry the truth in our hearts, and we will all love her in our own ways, but we will never speak of it. She must be my daughter in every way, and we can never risk making even the slightest comment that could be overheard. Do you understand?"

"Oh, I give you my word!" Bernice said as if she were ready to once again launch herself in front of a bullet.

"Then it's settled," Gina said. "We'll discuss more details after you've recovered sufficiently."

Bernice wiped her tears and focused on admiring the baby, something that Gina could do all day every day. It occurred to her that Janine was very blessed to have the love of two mothers in her life; even if she never knew the truth about which woman had actually given birth to her, she would grow up loved and blessed.

After knocking, Ruby entered the room to inform Gina that Sir Radcliffe had asked that she join him for tea. The very mention of it made her feel as if a rock had dropped from her throat into the pit of her stomach. She'd not seen him since they'd spoken with the police, and she wasn't certain she wanted to see him now. She missed him; but being with him while he was clearly angry with her—and recalling how it used to be between them—was little less than pure torture. But Gina swallowed her concerns and said evenly, "Of course. Tell him I'll be there."

Ruby left, and Gina stayed a little longer to visit with Bernice. Before Gina left, she made certain Bernice had everything she needed, then Gina took the baby to her own room to just enjoy some time alone with her daughter, trying to distract herself from her dread of seeing Radcliffe.

Gina walked slowly as she went to meet Radcliffe for tea. She considered all she wanted to say to him, feeling strongly there were some things that needed to be voiced between them, even if there was no longer any hope for a personal relationship. In fact, she wanted to know exactly where she stood in that regard, instead of just having to make assumptions, since he'd exhibited little but angry silence toward her ever since she'd told him the truth about Janine.

When Gina finally arrived at the specified room, she had to pause a long moment and take a deep breath before she felt ready to enter and face him. The moment she opened the door, Radcliffe stood from where he'd been waiting. Gina hated the way she felt herself reacting to his very presence. How could it be possible that he was taller than she'd remembered, when she'd become so accustomed to standing beside him and taking long walks? And even worse, he was even more handsome than she'd remembered, and it had only been a handful of days.

Gina turned to close the door, willing herself to remain steady and strong, whatever their conversation might entail. Perhaps he'd requested her presence so that he could formally end their relationship; the possibility seemed likely—and heartbreaking. But Gina reminded herself of her gratitude that he was willing to let her and her family and friends remain in his household. She needed to make certain he knew how grateful she was, and in fact considered that a good place to begin their conversation—before it wandered into other more formidable paths.

"Thank you for coming," Radcliffe said as she was seated, then he sat back down. "I wasn't certain you would."

"Why wouldn't I?" she asked. "Despite all that has happened, I would hope we can find our way to at least being friends; we are after all living under the same roof. It would be ridiculous to do so for years to come, while carrying any animosity between us." His expression was impossible to read, and Gina found herself unnerved by his gaze, so she looked down before she added, "I want to thank you—officially and with all my heart—for allowing us to stay here. It means more than I can say, and I'm grateful that you love Janine as you do. She will need you in her life, I'm certain."

"I need her too," he said. "And there's no need to thank me. No matter what, we are family. I would never want you or your loved ones to be anywhere else."

"For that I'm grateful," Gina said, still unable to look at him.

The silence grew uncomfortably long, which made Gina exuberantly grateful when a maid entered with the tea cart and carefully laid everything out on the table between Gina and Radcliffe. The baronet thanked her before she left the room, closing the door behind her. Gina put her full attention to pouring out tea for both herself and Radcliffe, since she knew exactly how he liked it. He spoke a quiet "Thank you" as she handed him a cup and saucer. She nodded politely and held her own cup close to her face, soothed by the warmth in her hands and the steam that rose into the air. Neither of them said anything, nor did they take advantage of serving themselves any of the little cakes and sandwiches and biscuits that had been left on a tiered serving dish in the center of the table.

Gina wondered if their tea would pass in unproductive silence; she wanted so desperately to just be able to talk to him about all that had happened. She wanted to stop wondering how he felt and just hear him say the words, even if they were a declaration that he could never trust her again and therefore any hope of a relationship was gone. She'd mostly accepted this was likely the case, but she needed to hear him say it, and she didn't want to leave the room with so much still unspoken between them.

Gina was nearly ready to just ask him to tell her his thoughts and feelings on the matter so they could be done with it when he abruptly set down his cup and saucer, clearing his throat at the same time in a way that seemed to announce he was preparing to speak. Gina too set down her cup and saucer when she realized her hands were beginning to shake and she didn't want to have the cup rattling against the saucer and give her away. She forced herself to look up at him and realized that he was nervous. She could well imagine how difficult it might be for him to tell her that despite the warm feelings they had for each other, circumstances made it impossible to pursue a relationship. She was entirely unprepared to hear him say, "I owe you an apology, G. I have been trying hard to think of what to say, and yet the words are still jumbled in my mind. I ask that you be patient and allow me to say what needs to be said."

"Of course," Gina said in an even voice that didn't betray the pounding of her heart.

Their eyes met, and for the first time since Gina had revealed her secret to him, she saw warmth and vulnerability there. "Forgive me," he began and cleared his throat again, "for responding so badly when you told me the truth about Janine. I was shocked, yes, but I want you to know that I understand why you did what you did, and now that I've had time to become accustomed to the situation, I must say that I truly believe you did the right thing."

"You do?" Gina squeaked. She'd become so accustomed to his silent anger that she'd never imagined him saying such a thing.

"Yes, G. I do. If you'd gone to the police, I'm not certain what would have happened to Janine; I don't know if we could have legally been able to take her in, and that makes me fear where she would have ended up. And even if they *had* allowed us to keep her, everyone would have known she was not born to you, and given the pretentious, snobbish, and narrow mindset of our social class, that would taint her for the rest of her life. We certainly don't want that."

"No, we don't want that," Gina said if only to fill the silence while he seemed to be gathering his words to go on.

"I also understand why you felt like you couldn't tell me," he said, and Gina had to put a great deal of effort into swallowing her tears so that she didn't disrupt this conversation with an emotional outburst. "I know I have been cold and distant from you, and that was entirely unfair. Now that all of this is behind us, I can look back and see that one of the most prominent reasons for my behavior was my anger toward Lyle, and my fear that the truth about Janine would come out and compromise our right to keep her with us. I became so consumed by my fear and anger that I didn't even stop to consider how my behavior was coming across to you, and how you might interpret my attitude. For that I am sorry."

"Thank you," was all Gina could think to say. She swallowed hard and fought to keep her voice steady as she added, "I very much appreciate your clarification."

His brow furrowed as he said, "So you *did* believe I was angry with you?"

Gina felt tears slide unheeded down her cheeks and knew there was no point now in trying to hide them. "How could I believe otherwise?" she admitted. "I had lied to you, therefore I could only assume that you would never be able to trust me again, and therefore . . ." Gina couldn't finish for fear of sobbing; as long as her tears remained silent she could maintain some measure of dignity.

"Oh, my dear Gina!" he said, sounding more like himself than he had since she'd told him the truth. He stood and moved to the chair directly next to hers and took her hand. "There are no words to express the horror I felt when I realized that . . . blackguard . . . might kill you. And that I might lose you. The very idea was unthinkable." He let out a harsh breath. "Forgive me. As I said, my dear, I understand why you did what you did. I've thought it all through a great deal, and it's not difficult to see that when I first became aware of your supposedly having given birth, you and I did not share the kind of relationship where we could know whether or not trust was present. If the situation were reversed, I would have surely kept my secret hidden in order to protect Janine. I understand; I truly do. And I don't believe your efforts to protect Janine make you untrustworthy. I *do* trust you, Gina."

"You do?" she said again, this time squeaking the words out in an even higher pitch.

"Of course I do!" he declared, but he hung his head in a way that implied he was holding something back, which made Gina decidedly nervous. "The truth is that . . . your confession incited my own guilt regarding a terrible secret that I've kept from *you*."

Gina took in a sharp breath, recalling the hints she'd heard of this, and realizing now how her concern over such a thing had been overshadowed by many other worries.

Radcliffe looked up again and said earnestly, "I want to make it clear that you are not required to forgive me simply because you have kept your own secrets, and if you realize you cannot trust me after what I have to tell you, I will understand."

Gina felt decidedly afraid of what she was about to hear, but at the same time relieved to know that he *would* tell her. She pointed out what he had stated already in this conversation. "As you said, until recently we have not shared the kind of relationship where we could know whether or not trust was present. I understand why you might have felt the need to keep something from me." She took a deep breath and blew it out slowly. "I assume it has to do with Dwight."

"It does," he said, his voice sounding mildly shaky. That combined with what she saw in his eyes made her realize he was terrified to tell her whatever secret he'd been keeping. "Again, I ask you to be patient with me; I've been trying to come up with the right words to tell you, and I don't know how to do so except to just . . . . tell you."

"Then just tell me," she said. "Dwight's gone now. I doubt that it matters nearly as much as you might think."

"I beg you to reserve judgment on that count until you've heard what I have to say."

This increased Gina's nervousness, but she simply nodded, focusing on the feeling of his hand in hers, realizing how much she'd missed something so simple as having him hold her hand. She prayed it was evidence that their love could still be salvaged, and that it was not just a friendly gesture during a difficult conversation.

Gina had barely entertained the thought before he withdrew his hand from hers and leaned back in his chair, as if he needed distance from her in order to say what he had to say. He looked away, seeming to stare at nothing as he proceeded. "Let me begin by saying that when I learned that Dwight was without family and I invited him to come and live here, I had no idea how much I would grow to dislike him. Our interactions prior to that time had shown me nothing negative that might have alerted me to potential problems. But once he was living under the same roof and we were attending many social events together, I began to see that he was a man lacking in integrity, and he often embarrassed himself—or me—with his less-than-dignified behavior."

Gina looked at her hands as she clasped them in her lap; she knew exactly how he felt.

"My first regret is that I did not warn you about his true nature when the two of you began courting, and certainly when you became engaged. I told myself that Dwight's life was his own business, and his living in my home did not give me the right to interfere. As I've told you, I observed his ill treatment of you, which deepened my regrets; but there was nothing to be done about it and so I continued to look the other way."

"I understand, Radcliffe; I do," Gina said. "What could you have said or done—either before we were married or after—that would have accomplished anything except creating a rift between you and your cousin? And truthfully, I was so naive, and so in love with him—or so I'd believed—that I doubt I would have listened to anything you might have told me. There's no reason for you to feel regret over this."

"You're very kind, as always," Radcliffe said, tossing her a wan smile before he again looked away with distant eyes. "But there is something else, and it is by no means a small thing." He took a deep breath. "I'm just going to say it as quickly as possible, and then you can decide whether you should be angry with me for keeping such a secret; I personally believe you *should* be angry with me. And I warn you . . . this will likely be very shocking to you."

Gina's breathing became increasingly shallow with his warning, but she braced herself to hear him out and hopefully maintain her dignity; she couldn't begin to imagine what might possibly be so grim.

Radcliffe turned to look at her, as if he knew she needed to see his eyes in order to know that he was telling her the truth. "Gina, my dear . . . before Dwight met you . . . quite some time before—in fact, this began before he came to live with me—he fell in love with a woman, and they had intended to marry." Gina was caught off guard; not only had she never heard anything of this, it was not where she might have expected Radcliffe's story to begin. She only nodded slightly, and he continued. "But her father disapproved of the match and intervened with the threat of cutting off his daughter completely; therefore, she married a man of her father's choosing, and Dwight was devastated. Ironically she married a man who lives not so many miles from here; I now look back and wonder if Dwight was eager to accept my invitation to come and live here because he knew that she lived in the area."

"But . . . she was married by then, and . . ."

"Indeed, she was . . . and had a child," Radcliffe said, sounding mildly angry, "and yet I discovered that Dwight was meeting her secretly; I might have never known except that he was not necessarily discreet." Gina felt literally sick as she considered the fact that her husband was the kind of man who would have done such a thing. She wasn't certain if Radcliffe was implying that Dwight and this married woman had been intimate—an idea that made her feel even more ill—but either way it was deplorable. "I warned him that such actions could lead to nothing but trouble, and his secrets would surely see him undone. He not only disregarded my warnings, he did so flippantly. When he met you, he assured me that you had won his heart and he no longer felt drawn to this woman. Of course, I was deeply relieved, and naturally encouraged the relationship, believing that you had the ability to bring out the best in him and change his less-than-admirable ways. I saw absolutely no evidence that he was seeing this woman any further, and I genuinely believed he had put the relationship in the past."

Radcliffe sighed and looked away again, but not before Gina saw shame in his eyes, and she wondered why might be coming. "Only a few months after you were married, I realized that Dwight had once again become involved with this woman, and indeed I wonder if it had ever stopped, or if he'd just been more discreet because he was courting and getting married. And he actually bragged to me about the nature of their relationship." He coughed. "I'm so sorry, Gina, but he was having an affair with her in every sense of the word."

Gina's entire body began to respond to what she was hearing, despite her mind feeling nothing but shock. Her heartbeat quickened painfully, her breathing became difficult, she trembled from head to toe, and her stomach rumbled. For all that she'd detested the way Dwight had treated her much of the time, never would she have imagined that he had been unfaithful to her. The very idea of him sharing with another woman all that he should have been sharing with her almost made her fear that she might burst out of her chair and start throwing things.

"I want to just . . . hurry and get to the end of this horrible tale," Radcliffe said. "Dwight continued to ignore my warnings, and I couldn't bring myself to tell you, knowing there was nothing you could to about it, and that such knowledge would only bring you grief. And then this woman's husband discovered the truth, and he challenged Dwight to a duel."

"What?" Gina practically shrieked, which startled Radcliffe. "A duel?"

Radcliffe looked directly at her as he said in a voice of compassion, "That's how he died, G. It was not a riding accident. He'd told me about the duel, and he had asked me to be his second, but I refused. I suggested it would be better for him to just leave the country and never come back, and I suspected that you wouldn't necessarily be heartbroken over his absence. And then the next day he left early in the morning and didn't come back. Of course, I suspected the reasons, but I didn't confide in anyone but the constable who was leading the search for him. I was with the constable—and no one else—when we found Dwight, and he had been shot through the heart. The constable could do nothing regarding the cause of his death, since dueling—for all its absurdity—does not fall outside the requirements of the law. But I asked if the reason for Dwight's death might be kept discreet, and he was kind enough to agree, although I'm not certain he would have been able to keep it a secret from some of his fellow officers; but I had to believe they would be discreet, as well. The two of us put Dwight's body over the back of a horse in a way that the bullet wound was not visible, and I confess that I bribed the undertaker to whom the body was taken. It was declared a riding accident in order to preserve *my* good name, and I had hoped that it would be more palatable for you to accept." Radcliffe sighed loudly. "There. That's all. I apologize with my whole soul for keeping such terrible secrets from you, G, and I can only hope that one day you will forgive me."

More than a few minutes of silence passed while Gina attempted to accept everything she'd just learned, and she was surprised at how easily it settled in once the shock subsided. She could look back now and see that she wasn't terribly surprised. Dwight had rarely shared a bed with her, which she had considered to be the main reason she hadn't been able to get pregnant—and yet he had blamed her for the problem. Somehow knowing what she now knew only validated how thoroughly she had disliked her husband, and how grateful she was to no longer have him in her life—even if the manner of his death had been so terrible. And yet he had brought it upon himself with his many poor choices.

Once Gina had settled everything in her mind—although she felt certain it would take time to fully come to terms with this news—she took Radcliffe's hand and said with deepest sincerity, "Thank you for telling me. I can't imagine how difficult it's been for you to carry such a burden. I'm glad to know the truth; but rest assured that it only makes me even more grateful that Dwight is gone, and all the more delighted to be here with you."

"Truly?" Radcliffe squeaked much as Gina had done earlier. His eyes showed complete disbelief, as if he'd expected her to be furious with him. "You're not . . . upset with me for . . ."

"Not at all," Gina said. She went on to share with him all that she'd been thinking, and they ended up talking a long while about how Dwight's deplorable behavior had impacted both of their lives, and how glad they were to now fully be able to put him behind them. Gina went on to initiate some conversation about all that had happened with Lyle, and she was relieved beyond measure to hear Radcliffe repeat his convictions about not being at all angry with her, and his understanding of why she'd felt the need to lie in order to protect Janine, and that her doing so was not an indication that she couldn't be trusted.

Grateful to her core that she and Radcliffe were talking openly and comfortably once again, and that everything between them seemed as it had been before she'd told him the truth about Janine, Gina went on to tell him about her conversations with Bernice since the woman had risked her life to spare Gina's. She was relieved when Radcliffe agreed with her decision to have Bernice promoted to a position of helping care for Janine, and he also agreed that they had every reason to trust Bernice, and that it was a good decision. He very much liked Gina's declaration that from this time forward they would no longer speak of the matter. It would now officially be put to rest, and Janine would be considered her daughter in every way. Those who knew the truth would never talk about it even in whispers, which would prevent any possibility of their secret ever being overheard.

When there was suddenly nothing more to say, an abrupt silence claimed the room. Gina realized that neither of them had eaten anything, and they'd barely taken a few sips of tea. But their conversation had been necessary and productive, and she was grateful.

Radcliffe chuckled tensely and said, "I suppose we should eat a little something or we'll be very hungry by the time dinner is served."

"I suppose we should," she said, although she still felt as if there were things between them that hadn't been clarified. She was grateful for the lack of tension, and to know that the trust between them was as it should be. But she had no idea if the love they shared was still intact in any form, and she didn't know how to ask.

Gina was relieved when Radcliffe said, "I wonder if you would take a walk in the gardens with me tomorrow morning. Say ten o'clock? I know it's cold outside, but we don't need to stay out very long. And hopefully the sky will be as blue tomorrow as it is today."

"I would like that very much," Gina said. "I believe I've been spending far too much time indoors. Some fresh air would do me good, even if it *is* cold."

"Excellent," he said, seeming relaxed and relieved. He then turned his attention to the food and they each enjoyed the fare that had come from the kitchen, just as they'd done countless times before. In fact, the mood between them was so relaxed and calm that Gina could hardly believe the confessions they had been sharing not so many minutes ago. She prayed that this was evidence of the healing beginning to take place between them, and that with time all would be well.

❧

That night, Gina had trouble falling asleep as she recounted the secrets that Radcliffe had shared with her about Dwight. She still didn't feel as upset as she believed she should have. But as she analyzed her feelings, searching through the past to examine the entirety of their relationship, she could now see ample evidence of Dwight's infidelity. And now that he had been dead for nearly a year, learning such deplorable things about him only gave her a strange sense of validation. In her marriage she had often believed that her feelings were not valid, that her opinions were meaningless, and that any suspicions she might have had would have been completely disregarded as absurd. Sometimes she had felt downright insane. But now she could put all the pieces together and see very clearly that Dwight's cruelty toward her may have often been difficult to understand, but it had nevertheless been deep and cutting. Now she knew that he had been dishonorable in such horrible ways, and he had likely been treating her badly in order to draw the attention away from his own hideous misdeeds.

Gina finally came to a calm resolution and sense of closure regarding Dwight. Now that she knew the whole truth, she felt as if she could truly put her past with him away and have peace in knowing that while she was certainly not perfect by any means, the greatest source of the problems in her marriage had been due to Dwight's selfishness and bad behavior. Now she could look to the future, and she felt hopeful that the challenges between herself and Radcliffe would continue to mend, and perhaps he might eventually be a part of her future after all.

Gina woke later than usual since it had taken her so long to fall asleep. She rushed to eat some breakfast, help bathe and dress Janine, and make herself presentable for a winter stroll with Radcliffe. Wearing a heavy cloak and soft leather gloves, Gina arrived only a few minutes late at the place where they usually met for walks and found him waiting, looking very dashing in a long coat. The smile he offered in response to seeing her prompted a quickening of her heartbeat, and she couldn't help hoping that this would be the beginning of a new relationship with Radcliffe, one based in absolute trust and honesty.

"Shall we, m'lady?" he asked, holding out his arm.

Gina returned his smile and took his arm. They strolled slowly along familiar paths, and Gina instinctively kept lifting her face toward the sun, whose warmth helped compensate for the distinct chill in the air. Gina wasn't surprised when Radcliffe guided her to the bridge where they stood together in the center to look over the rail at the water flowing beneath them. But she was taken off guard with the way he turned and took both of her hands into his, looking into her eyes with a gaze that had not so long ago been delightfully familiar. The love and adoration she had so desperately missed in the days since she'd told him her deepest secrets had now returned, and if anything, the evidence of his love for her was even more brilliant.

"Regina," he said, and her heart quickened both from the especially tender tone of his voice, and the fact that he'd used the full version of her name— something he did very rarely. "I daresay we still have a great deal to talk about regarding all that's happened, and we will certainly talk about it as much as we need to, nevertheless . . ." he hesitated and drew in a deep breath, ". . . I can't think of a single reason to wait one more day before I make certain you have no reason to doubt my love for you. Despite all that has happened, I only love you more, Gina. And . . . well I . . ." He seemed mildly nervous, which caused

Gina's heart to beat even more quickly, and she felt a little breathless. "It's been nearly a year since you became a widow, G. And I don't want to wait any longer than absolutely necessary." Gina gasped as he dropped to one knee, still holding both of her hands tightly in his. "Marry me, Gina, and I will devote my life to your happiness. I will do everything in my power to protect you and Janine, and I will do it joyfully. Nothing could make *me* happier. Please tell me you'll marry me."

Gina had to swallow carefully and force herself to breathe before she could manage to utter, "Yes, of course, yes. Nothing could make me happier."

Radcliffe laughed with perfect delight as he stood and wrapped her in his arms, spinning her around twice before setting her on her feet while they held to each other in order to let the dizziness subside. He then drew her closer, looking into her eyes with such adoration that she couldn't keep tears from rising in her own eyes. "I love you, Gina," he whispered. "I love you with my whole soul."

"And I love you," she whispered in reply before he lowered his lips to hers and kissed her. Never had she imagined that a kiss could be so perfectly blissful. She might have been a widow, but Radcliffe had a way of making her realize more and more that she'd never experienced real love, and she knew beyond any doubt that they could share a good life and make each other happy. He drew back and slowly opened his eyes to look at her, smiling as if she'd made him the happiest person in the world. Gina felt certain it was the other way around as he held her more tightly and kissed her again.

EPILOGUE

RADCLIFFE AND GINA WERE MARRIED one year and one day following Dwight's death. In the weeks and months that followed, Gina continually marveled that she could be so thoroughly happy. She wasn't at all surprised at how well Radcliffe treated her, yet the contrast of his attitudes and behaviors to those of her late husband was astonishing.

Gina awoke later than usual to find sunlight filling the room and her husband absent. He'd clearly awakened earlier and had chosen not to disturb her. Gina was glad for the extra sleep, given that her recent discovery of being pregnant had left her feeling more tired than she had ever felt in her life. But the joyful prospect of having another child come into their family more than compensated for any discomfort or inconvenience.

Gina instinctively reached her hand across the bed and set it upon Radcliffe's empty pillow. Just knowing he had recently been there filled her with a warm fluttering of happiness that she hoped would never dissipate, no matter how many years of marriage they had shared.

"There you are," she heard her husband say and turned to see him climb onto the bed, stretching out beside her as he greeted her with a kiss.

"And there *you* are," she said, kissing him again.

"How are you feeling, my love?"

"Fine, except . . . I do believe I will need something to eat very soon."

"And Ruby has left a tray for you," he said, motioning toward the table near the windows.

"Ah," Gina said with some relief, knowing how eating would ease the mild nausea smoldering inside her, "they think of everything."

"Yes, I believe they do," Radcliffe said, "and I do believe you should get up and eat and get dressed. The seaside is waiting for us."

Gina gasped as she recalled their plans for today. "Oh, my! I'd honestly forgotten. I was thinking about it when I fell asleep, but . . ."

"But you forgot that today is our daughter's birthday?" He laughed and kissed her brow. "One year ago today was an eventful—and difficult—day, for certain. But now we have so much to celebrate."

"Indeed, we do," Gina said and felt suddenly motivated to get out of bed.

Gina had discovered in a conversation with her husband a couple of weeks earlier that they lived less than an hour's carriage ride from the sea. In all the time she'd lived here, she'd had no idea; Dwight had never once mentioned it, likely because he'd had no desire to take her there, and she surely would have wanted to go if she had known. And now that she *did* know, she had insisted that they needed to make excursions to the seaside a tradition during the warm months of the year; she wanted her children to grow up with such lovely experiences. And Janine's first birthday seemed the perfect day to make their first outing to the sea.

An hour later—with Ruby and Emerald's help—Gina was ready to go, and thanks to Elaine and Bernice, Janine and Tommy were ready to go as well. The women and children went down the stairs together where they found Radcliffe and Milton chatting while they waited.

"What a lovely sight," Milton said with a grin as he looked up to see the little group descending the last few steps.

"Indeed!" Radcliffe said with exaggerated enthusiasm.

They all went outside to where two carriages were waiting, and Garn was there to drive one of them. Hampers of food, and blankets to spread out on the sand had already been loaded. Ruby and Emerald got into one of the carriages with Elaine and Tommy, and Gina and Radcliffe got into the other with Milton, Bernice, and Janine. The ride was pleasant and enjoyable, and Gina couldn't help but take notice of the miracle that had made it possible for Janine to be in their lives, and for Bernice to also be a part of their household. She had proven to be even more kind and generous than Gina might have expected, and she was always perfectly polite and respectful in her assistance with Janine, always acknowledging Gina as the child's mother in a way that was completely natural. Gina had grown to love Bernice just as she loved Elaine and the three siblings who had come with her to Stonebridge years earlier.

"We're getting closer," Radcliffe announced, and Gina was surprised at how quickly the ride had passed. "Listen," he said, "and smell the air."

Gina closed her eyes and followed his instructions. It was difficult to hear anything over the sound of the carriage wheels on the road, but by listening carefully she could hear the rush of ocean waves, which made her giggle. And she could also smell the salty sea air. She'd only been to the sea a couple of times, and that had been in her childhood. Her memories of the waves lapping over her feet, and of playing in the wet sand, were tender and fond, but she'd often wondered if her childlike perspective might have distorted the experience.

The carriages halted in a place that was as close as they could get to the beach, but they all had to walk down a sandy path that wound between tall grasses that waved in the breeze. The sound of the waves was loud now, and Gina felt fluttery inside as she anticipated sharing such an experience with her husband. Rad held her hand while he capably carried Janine with his other arm. She looked adorable in her pink bonnet that matched the dress Elaine had made for her birthday. Gina knew that Janine would never be able to remember her first birthday, but all the people who loved her would remember, and Radcliffe had been right earlier when he'd said they had much to celebrate.

When they all came around a bend in the path, the ocean came into view and they stopped for a moment to just look at its enormous majesty. Then it seemed they couldn't get to the water's edge fast enough. Tommy giggled and managed to jump up and down with excitement as he ran, but it seemed that the adults were every bit as excited. They quickly spread blankets on the sand where everyone could sit to remove their shoes and stockings. Breeches were rolled up and skirts were gathered into the ladies' hands as they all stepped tentatively into the water, laughing from the sensation of the cold water rushing over their feet. Rad dangled Janine above the water and slowly lowered her bare feet into it, which at first shocked her and she let out a little cry, but he did it again and again, carefully and slowly, until Janine became accustomed to the strange sensation, and she began to kick her feet and giggle, which in turn made everyone else laugh in response to her delight.

After playing in the water a long while, they all gathered on the blankets to share the lovely lunch that had been prepared for Janine's birthday celebration. There was a variety of sandwiches, fresh strawberries, savory biscuits, and plenty of cool water to drink. And best of all, there was a beautiful and delicious cake to honor the little lady's first year of life; that was how Mrs. Chester had said it when she'd turned the hampers of food over to Ruby and Emerald.

While Janine was crawling in the sand and getting delightfully filthy—since she hadn't yet taken more than a few steps on her own—Gina was surprised when Bernice came and sat directly beside her. No one else was nearby, since they were all once again enjoying the waves and the beach.

"Forgive me, m'lady," Bernice said in a whisper, "I know we promised to never speak of it again, and after this moment I never will, but . . ." Her voice cracked with emotion and Gina turned to look at her more fully. "It would be amiss for me not to thank you for . . . for everything. Of course, I'm grateful to know that she'll always have the finest of everything, but far more than that, I'm grateful to see how loved and cherished she is. Few women who find themselves in trouble are ever so blessed as I am . . . to know that my daughter has such a good life, and for me to be given the privilege of being a part of it. So . . . thank you. That is all. I just had to say it."

"It's no sacrifice on my part, Bernice," Gina said, taking the young woman's hand. "Janine is one of the greatest blessings in my life. I am certain that God led her from your arms into mine—that it was meant to be. And I too am grateful that you can be a part of her life. Together we will make certain that she is always safe and happy."

Bernice smiled but seemed too emotional to speak. Gina just squeezed her hand and shifted her attention to the comical display of Janine playing in the sand, looking as if she were covered in cinnamon and sugar.

Bernice slipped away to enjoy the ocean waves with Elaine and Tommy, and Gina looked around at the beautiful scenery, enhanced by the sound of the crashing waves and the smell of the sea air. She marveled at the beauty of God's creations, but even more so, she marveled at how truly blessed she was to be surrounded by the people who were here. Garn and the other driver who was Garn's friend were diving in and out of the waves, soaking themselves completely, but laughing in a way that was contagious. Emerald and Ruby were holding their skirts high and walking in the water, talking softly except when they giggled loudly as the result of a wave rushing over their lower legs. Gina's father was stretched out on one of the blankets, relaxing with his eyes closed; but the smile on his face revealed that he was thoroughly enjoying himself.

Gina's gaze shifted to her husband who was following Janine everywhere she wandered, making certain that she remained safe. Gina loved him so deeply that his presence in her life filled her entire being with joy. Even when they disagreed over a matter, he never spoke to her with any lack of respect, and he always went to great lengths to make certain that she knew he loved her, and that she was a treasure to him; Gina believed it was the other way around.

As if Radcliffe had sensed her watching him, he turned to look at her and they exchanged a tender gaze and a warm smile. But it was short-lived since he had to hurry and try to stop Janine from putting a handful of sand into her mouth, which made Gina laugh.

ABOUT THE AUTHOR

ANITA STANSFIELD HAS MORE THAN seventy published books and is the recipient of many awards, including two Lifetime Achievement Awards. Her books go far beyond being enjoyable, memorable stories. Anita resonates particularly well with a broad range of devoted readers because of her sensitive and insightful examination of contemporary issues that are faced by many of those readers, even when her venue is a historical romance. Readers come away from her compelling stories equipped with new ideas about how to enrich their own lives, regardless of their circumstances.

Anita was born and raised in Provo, Utah. She is the mother of five and has a growing number of grandchildren. She also writes for the general trade market under the name Elizabeth D. Michaels.

For more information and a complete list of her publications, go to anitastansfield. blogspot.com or anitastansfield.com, where you can sign up to receive email updates. You can also follow her on Facebook and Twitter.